What Reviewers Say Abou

KIM BAL▌

"'A riveting novel of suspense' seems to be a very overworked phrase. However, it is extremely apt when discussing Kim Baldwin's [*Hunter's Pursuit*]. An exciting page turner [features] Katarzyna Demetrious, a bounty hunter…with a million dollar price on her head. Look for this excellent novel of suspense…" – **R. Lynne Watson**, *MegaScene*

"*Force of Nature* is an exciting and substantial reading experience which will long remain with the reader. Likeable characters with plausible problems and concerns, imaginative settings, engrossing events, and a well-tailored writing style all contribute to an exceptional novel. Baldwin's characterization is acutely and meticulously circumscribed and expansive." – **Arlene Germain**, reviewer for the *Lambda Book Report* and the *Midwest Book Review*

RONICA BLACK

"Black juggles the assorted elements of her first book, [*In Too Deep*], with assured pacing and estimable panache…[including]…the relative depth—for genre fiction—of the central characters: Erin, the married-but-separated detective who comes to her lesbian senses; loner Patricia, the policewoman-mentor who finds herself falling for Erin; and sultry club owner Elizabeth, the sexually predatory suspect who discards women like Kleenex…until she meets Erin." – **Richard Labonte**, *Book Marks, Q Syndicate, 2005*

"Black's characterization is skillful, and the sexual chemistry surrounding the three major characters is palpable and definitely hot-hot-hot. If you're looking for a more traditional murder mystery, *In Too Deep* might not be entirely your cup of Earl. On the other hand, if you're looking for a solid read with ample amounts of eroticism and a red herring or two, you're sure to find *In Too Deep* a satisfying read." – **Lynne Jamneck**, *L-Word.com Literature*

ROSE BEECHAM

"…her characters seem fully capable of walking away from the particulars of whodunit and engaging the reader in other aspects of their lives." – *Lambda Book Report*

ROSE BEECHAM (CONT)

"When Jennifer Fulton writes mysteries, she writes them as Rose Beecham. And since Jennifer Fulton is a very fine writer, you might expect that Rose Beecham is a fine writer too. You're right… On the way to a remarkable, and thoroughly convincing climax, Beecham creates believable characters in compelling situations, with enough humor to provide effective counterpoint to the work of detecting." – *Bay Area Reporter*

GUN BROOKE

"*Course of Action* is a romance…populated with a host of captivating and amiable characters. The glimpses into the lifestyles of the rich and beautiful people are rather like guilty pleasures… a most satisfying and entertaining reading experience." – **Arlene Germain**, reviewer for the *Lambda Book Report* and the *Midwest Book Review*

"*Protector of the Realm* has it all; sabotage, corruption, erotic love and exhilarating space fights. Gun Brooke's second novel is forceful with a winning combination of solid characters and a brilliant plot." – **Kathi Isserman**, *JustAboutWrite*

JANE FLETCHER

"*The Walls of Westernfort* is not only a highly engaging and fast-paced adventure novel, it provides the reader with an interesting framework for examining the same questions of loyalty, faith, family and love that [the characters] must face." – **M. J. Lowe**, *Midwest Book Review*

LEE LYNCH

"There's a heady sense of '60s back-to-the-land communal idealism and '70s woman-power feminism (with hints of lesbian separatism) to this spirited novel—even though it's set in contemporary rural Oregon. Partners Donny (she's black and blue-collar) and Chick (she's plus-sized and motherly) are both in their 50s, owners of the dyke-centric Natural Woman Foods store, a homey nexus for *Sweet Creek*'s expansive cast of characters.…Lynch, with a dozen novels to her credit dating back to the early days of Naiad Press, has earned her stripes as a writerly elder. She was contributing stories to the lesbian magazine *The Ladder* four decades ago. But this latest is sublimely in tune with the times." – **Richard Labonte**, *Book Marks, Q Syndicate, 2005*

Visit us at www.boldstrokesbooks.com

UNEXPECTED
TIES

by

Gina L. Dartt

2006

UNEXPECTED TIES

ISBN 1-933110-56-2
THIS TRADE PAPERBACK IS PUBLISHED BY
BOLD STROKES BOOKS, INC.,
NEW YORK, USA

FIRST EDITION, OCTOBER 2006

CREDITS
EDITORS: SHELLEY THRASHER AND J. BARRE GREYSTONE
PRODUCTION DESIGN: J. BARRE GREYSTONE
COVER DESIGN: SHERI (graphicartist2020@hotmail.com)I

By the Author

UNEXPECTED SPARKS

Acknowledgments

To Susan & Dru who did more than just believe. They are sorely missed. To Jay, who is my good friend and always supportive. To the editors of Bold Strokes Books, who teach me so much. And to my friends and family here in the Maritimes who keep me properly humble. To Sherri and Darlene, for being there when I needed you most. Thank you all so very much.

DEDICATION

To Corine, who makes my heart beat faster.

CHAPTER ONE

The air was damp and cold when they exited the taxi, the last of winter stubbornly holding on, while spring had yet to firmly grip the Canadian Maritimes. Overhead, dark clouds hid the stars and threatened rain, granting a fuzzy halo to the lights of the Glengarry Hotel. The group quickened their steps to the front entrance, and as they entered the lobby, a pall of impending doom engulfed Nikki Harris.

"I don't think this is a good idea at all."

"It'll be fine," Kate Shannon, her lover of a few months, assured her. Her steady manner granted Nikki enough courage to steel herself for their actual entrance into the lavish conference room.

"What are they going to do? Lynch you?" Susan Carlson asked as she tucked her arm neatly into the crook of her husband Ted's elbow.

His dark, even eyes danced at the comment. Tall, slender, and very quiet, he tended to let his shorter, stouter, and very outgoing wife do most of the talking.

Nikki glanced at Kate's best friends and wished she were somewhere else. The Historical Society Dinner was formal, and she didn't do well with formal affairs, not that she had ever actually been to one. Furthermore, she didn't know these people, and would probably never know them under normal circumstances, but they probably had preconceived notions about her. A rope was exactly what Nikki was afraid would happen, and perhaps even a nice little bonfire added into the mix just for good measure.

She still didn't understand why Kate, who normally kept a low profile, would choose this dinner as her unofficial coming-out party. Although Nikki was far from closeted, she was much more cautious than Kate, who, after years of married life and public approval, had now embraced her sexuality with all the fervor of the born-again. She acted as if she *wanted* to challenge the people of their small town with her recent change.

"Don't worry." Kate squeezed her hand tightly. "I'll take care of you."

Nikki had to be content with that reassurance, though the keen sense of not belonging, of being in unfamiliar, uncomfortable territory, remained. She suspected that she was safe only because Kate was one of the society's most generous contributors. The others wouldn't dare offend her.

Nikki, on the other hand, was just a poor country girl born outside the town limits. They might vent their displeasure on her rather than Kate for this blatant challenge to their cherished attitudes and perceptions.

As they walked toward the registration table, Nikki noted the head table, where the society president and other notables would sit. Covered with a snowy tablecloth, silverware and china gleaming, it stood in the exact center of the room, a place of decided prominence in clear view of everyone present. Nikki, her hand slippery in Kate's gentle grasp, was acutely aware of the stares and subtle whispers that followed her and Kate. Nikki steeled herself from pitching forward on her face in a spectacular display that would delight the interested observers surrounding them.

Nor did it help that the high heels she was wearing added two inches to her already generous five-foot-eight frame. Earlier in the week, Nikki had traveled all the way to Halifax, Nova Scotia's capital city located forty-five minutes south of Truro. There, she had willingly accepted advice from Kate's best friend Susan about what to wear at a formal dinner, though it had cost her most of a week's salary.

The cream-colored jacket and skirt tailored to her lanky body set off her crimson silk blouse nicely, while her hair and makeup were perfect after she passed most of the afternoon in a beauty salon under Susan's direct supervision. A diamond heart-shaped pendant, a Valentine's Day gift from Kate, rested softly against the hollow of Nikki's throat, matched by small diamond studs that adorned freshly pierced ears. Even contacts replaced the granny glasses she normally wore. The glow of Kate's gaze when she first saw Nikki confirmed that the whole ordeal had somehow been worth it, but privately, Nikki felt like a little girl playing dress-up. She had to force herself not to run screaming from the room.

To calm her nerves, she focused on Kate, whose sapphire dress complemented her compact form and highlighted her bluish-gray eyes and the auburn hair that fell softly about her classic cheekbones and rounded jaw. Hints of gold at her neck and ears glinted elegantly in the soft light, and Nikki could detect Kate's delicate perfume. She was stunning, and Nikki felt inexplicably proud. Despite her trepidations, she was here as Kate's date, and no one could take that from her.

Lillian Salter, whom Nikki recognized from Kate's earlier description of the woman, stood at the reception table, regarding them with barely concealed dismay. Fortunately, as the society's treasurer and secretary, Lillian respected and feared Kate's position in town, so she didn't indulge in any open hostility.

"Mrs. Shannon," she said, subtly emphasizing Kate's previous marital state. She scanned Nikki briefly with watery blue eyes and glanced away, frowning. "And guest. You're at the head table."

"Thank you, Lillian." Kate's smile was a display of bared teeth that offered challenge rather than any warmth, making the rake-thin Salter twitch uncertainly.

Susan and Ted were also located at the head table. When Susan raised an inquiring eyebrow, Salter informed them, "Apparently, a few of the board members decided not to come tonight, or," she almost, but not quite, squinted significantly at Kate, "requested seating at other tables."

Kate didn't react beyond a tiny smile that touched the corners of her mouth, but Nikki wasn't at all confused. She felt sick.

"Nikki."

Turning in reaction to the unexpected hail, Nikki faced Rick Johnson, one of the town's constables and her co-worker at the police station. Tall and broad-shouldered, he wore a dark suit that struggled to cover his broad, powerful body and tugged uncomfortably at his necktie. His cologne almost overpowered her, and Nikki tried not to inhale deeply as they drifted away from the group at the reception area.

"You clean up real good, Nikki." He gazed at her with dark, dispassionate eyes that called attention to the high cheekbones typical of his First Nation heritage.

"Thanks." She was relieved to finally receive an objective opinion. "Where's Betty?"

"Are you kidding?" He snorted. "It's bad enough I have to come to these things as part of my job. She wouldn't show up for this on a dare. It's not her idea of the ideal date."

Nikki sighed. "I know how she feels, but I wish she was here. Then I'd have someone to talk to."

"You have me and Susan and Ted," Kate interjected, joining them. She reached out to her old friend, clasping his fingers briefly. "Rick, I'm glad you could make it."

"Oh, I'd much rather be on a stakeout in a snowstorm, or having my fingernails removed. I'm only here because the chief couldn't find another sucker to represent the station."

"You mean you couldn't find a good excuse at the ready when he asked?" Ted laughed and shook Rick's hand. "I know the feeling. How do we let ourselves get talked into these things?"

The two men quickly fell into a conversation about hunting while Kate and Susan gleefully discussed the various people who were and weren't present, not always in the most complimentary terms. Left to her own devices, Nikki scanned the room restlessly and noticed a small group observing her.

Two of the three men boasted similar features, as if they were related in some way—stocky, though relatively handsome, with blond or silver hair and light-colored eyes. The other was darker and thinner. Two young, well-dressed women, one blond and the other brunette, flanked an older woman who glared at Nikki as if she were something a dog had done and no one had picked up. Shivering, Nikki turned away from their scrutiny just in time to see a man embrace Kate with undue familiarity. Nikki was unprepared when the newcomer immediately reached out to her.

"You must be Nikki." Of average appearance, with thinning brown hair and dark eyes, he was completely unremarkable, except when he smiled. Then warmth and kindness radiated from him like heat from a hearth and made him handsome in an unusual way. "I'm David Shannon."

Nikki was taken aback. *Kate's ex-husband?*

"This is my wife, Ellen."

"Nice to meet you." Nikki uncertainly accepted the woman's hand. Appraising the couple covertly, she decided that the man had not exactly traded down after Kate. Ellen was willowy and brunette, an elegant woman with a gentle smile who spoke readily to Kate.

Nikki remembered Kate telling her that the issue of children had caused her divorce, not any sense of personal rancor toward her husband. For the first time, Nikki vaguely understood how the marriage could have happened. David was affable in the same way Kate was, and possessed a ready charm and wit. Nikki experienced a mild twinge of jealousy when Kate put her hand briefly on David's forearm as they laughed and talked, in what seemed an unconscious habit. But since Ellen didn't appear concerned, Nikki decided that she shouldn't be either.

"I have to tell you, Kate," David was saying, "You really shook them up tonight. A lot of people didn't believe that you'd show. Or they thought if you did, you'd leave your significant other at home."

Kate lifted a thin brow. "I don't know why they would think that. I've *never* missed a dinner."

He laughed. "You're not taking any prisoners tonight, are you?"

Kate gave a thin-lipped smile. "Not on your life." She glanced toward the front of the room and grasped Nikki's hand firmly. "I think it's time to be seated."

As she accompanied Kate to the head table, Nikki leaned over to her lover. "No prisoners?"

Kate glanced at her, an amused glint in her blue-gray eyes. "He was joking."

Nikki suspected the warrior description was more accurate than Kate was willing to admit. A steely resolve ran through the core of that refined and gentle exterior, and while it didn't show itself often, very few people dared defy it.

So why was Nikki afraid that someone would do just that tonight?

CHAPTER TWO

As Kate picked at her catered meal, she glanced affectionately at her lover. She knew how uncomfortable Nikki felt and how big a sacrifice all this was for her. Still, Nikki didn't truly understand why attending this function was so important. Kate was determined to show the rest of her social circle in Truro that she was as comfortable in her relationship with Nikki as she had ever been with David. This public appearance would stifle the speculation, rumors, and flat-out gossip about them much quicker than if she attempted to hide, or act as if being romantically linked to a woman was somehow shameful or sinful.

Of course she could indulge herself in such brash behavior because she had literally nothing to lose. No one could touch her financially, and she contributed to social causes not because she desired to be part of any certain circle, but because she wanted to. While she understood why so many chose to remain in the closet, such secrecy wasn't an option for her. She didn't care if a few bigots were offended, but she did not want Nikki made to feel uncomfortable.

My darling definitely deserves a gift. Perhaps some new heart-shaped earrings to match the necklace now that she has her ears pierced.

"So, Kate, what do you think about the society's new project?"

Reluctantly, Kate tore her eyes away from Nikki and turned to the dinner partner at her other side, granting him her full attention. Matthew Turner, president of the Historical Society, had avoided any mention of her new romantic relationship all evening. In fact, he successfully hid any distaste, which contrasted markedly to his wife. Celia Elliot-Turner was ignoring both Kate and Nikki as she concentrated sullenly on her meal. Obviously she would rather be sitting with her family across the room. If Kate liked her at all, she might have pitied her.

"I think restoring the old post office is a wonderful idea," Kate said, as if she had been paying attention to the conversation the entire time.

As she continued to speak with Matthew about the proposition, she slowly became aware of eyes boring into her, and glanced over to meet the frozen gaze of Hannah Elliot, Celia's mother. A stout woman, with snowy hair and mud dark eyes, Hannah was a formidable figure in both appearance and wealth, and a friend of Kate's grandmother. Though Kate respected the Elliot matriarch's position in town, she didn't care for her personally, finding her overbearing and occasionally harsh. Hannah had reacted to Kate's coming out by demanding a change in seating. Kate did not miss her presence at the head table and her decision had afforded Susan, Ted, Rick, David, and Ellen the unusual privilege of joining Kate at the center of things rather than being scattered throughout the room as they had been in previous years.

Kate shrugged mentally, avoiding the offended glare. She certainly hadn't insisted anyone move from the head table, and she wasn't going to let Hannah's limited and ignorant worldview affect her enjoyment.

After coffee and dessert had been served, the crowd loosened up, people visiting other tables, milling and mingling for the social part of the evening. Kate, who had been talking to David and Ellen about the bookstore, was not pleased when she saw Hannah Elliot bearing down on the head table like the bow of a massive ship parting the waves. Next to her, Matthew rose to his feet at the same time Kate did, and they both forced smiles, though he couldn't hide his alarm at his mother-in-law's approach. Obviously he was no more ready to face her than Kate was.

"Mother Elliot," he said, manfully ignoring the fact that she was glaring past him at Kate.

"I can't believe your behavior, Kathryn." Hannah lifted her cane slightly to gesture in the general direction of Nikki. "Parading your disgusting lifestyle about as if it were normal."

Her jaw firming, Kate glared back, absolutely incensed. "Hannah, considering your family's reputation in this town, I wouldn't be so hasty to cast stones."

Hannah's head jerked back, and her eyes tightened. Kate supposed that it had been so long since anyone had challenged Hannah, she wasn't sure how to respond.

"Your grandmother would be absolutely appalled," she finally sputtered.

Kate stared her down scornfully. "My grandmother never backed down from anyone in her life. I'm no different."

"You can't believe Irene would ever approve this aberrant alliance. I warn you, Kathryn, you lie down with dogs, you're apt to get up with fleas." Hannah's face grew dangerously red.

Kate actually took a step toward the stout woman, unable to remember being this furious. She was vaguely aware of Susan hurrying around the table to grasp her shoulder, preventing her from going any farther.

"I think it would be a good idea to return to your table, Mother Elliot." Matthew positioned himself between them. Kate knew that being married to Celia had bound him to the Elliot family, but he would never go up against her, the granddaughter of Irene Taylor. He raised a hand weakly, obviously attempting to placate both her and Hannah and doing a poor job of it.

"I'm going to inform Irene of this situation as soon as possible," Hannah spat at Kate as the rest of the family tried to unobtrusively move her away from the conflict. "She'll know what to do with you."

"You do that," Kate responded hotly to the woman's retreating back. Literally shaking in fury, she turned around to see Susan regarding her with a sarcastic expression. "What?"

"Hey, don't snap at me." Susan raised her hands defensively, but the grin on her face indicated she was more amused than embarrassed. "Unlike you, I'm not spoiling for a fight."

Kate finally looked around, conscious of all eyes glancing in her direction, and she composed herself instantly, shoving her anger down where it wouldn't control her. Though neither woman had raised her voice, it was apparent that she and Hannah were exchanging unpleasant words, and the entire room had been watching and eavesdropping breathlessly, no doubt greatly entertained by the whole situation.

"Where's Nikki?"

"She went to the ladies' room not long after the catfight started." Rick's tone was unnaturally even. "I guess she wasn't as amused as the rest of us."

Stung by the casual comment, Kate gave him a dark look and

immediately headed for the powder room. Inside, she encountered some women from her golf club who took in her stormy expression, immediately cut off their conversation, and hastily vacated the premises. Leaning against the sink counter, Kate was astonished to discover she was still shaking. As she tried to compose herself, one of the stall doors opened and Nikki emerged, walking over to the nearest sink to wash her hands. She glanced at Kate, not appearing particularly upset, but definitely not happy, either.

"I'm sorry," Kate said after a moment, when Nikki didn't speak to her. "What occurred out there should never have happened."

Nikki shrugged. "It's what I expected. I'm just surprised it took so long for one of your friends to make a fuss."

Kate was stung once more. "Hannah is no friend of mine."

"One of your enemies, then." Nikki pulled some paper towels from the dispenser and dried her hands. "This is what happens. I tried to explain when you first came up with this idea. You just didn't want to listen."

"I don't believe the ranting of one old woman—"

"She just had the guts to say what all the rest are thinking." Nikki tossed her used towel into the trash bin. "Ultimately, this is how it works in a small town. Keep this life quiet, don't flaunt it, and people tolerate it to a certain extent. Make a show of it, try to rub people's faces in it, and you're just asking for someone to take offense. You thought no one would dare, but you were wrong."

"I'm not the one that's wrong, Nikki." Despite Kate's best effort, some of her anger spilled over. "Hannah's the one who's out of line."

"Probably, but does it really matter? We've made others restrain themselves around us slightly, Kate, but their fear and hatred of what's different is still going to be the same."

Kate started to respond and then took a deep breath, forcing herself to consider her words carefully. "Nikki, you can't keep turning the other cheek. That's letting them win—"

"Kate, you've been gay for all of a few months." A spark flared in Nikki's eyes. "You don't exactly have the experience to know what you're fighting here. There are far easier and more useful methods to make strides than to march directly into the heart of enemy territory waving your rainbow flag."

"But that's the point, Nikki, this isn't enemy territory. It's as much my world as theirs, and I'll be damned if I'll let these small-minded idiots tell me how I should behave at an event that I've attended since I was fourteen."

Nikki's jaw firmed visibly. Her eyes were still bright with anger. "You're right, this is *your* world. The trouble is, you keep forgetting that it's not mine. They don't want me invading their territory whether I'm sleeping with you or not."

Brushing past her, Nikki strode out of the room, and, jolted by Nikki's final comment, Kate followed, intending to continue their discussion. But she forgot their argument as she reentered the dining room and found herself transfixed by what had occurred in her absence.

Stephen Elliot III had collapsed across the table, a situation suddenly far more interesting to the crowd than Kate Shannon's date for the Historical Society dinner.

❖

"What the hell happened?" Nikki nudged Susan as Rick lifted the stricken man from his dessert. Another man loosened Stephen Elliot's collar and checked for a pulse. Stephen was lolling in the chair, mouth gaping open as chocolate mousse covered a face that appeared blue through the brown smears.

"I'm not sure. He must have had a heart attack."

Nikki gazed around. "Why isn't anyone doing anything?"

"They are. Rick called for an ambulance. And Dr. Lynch is staying out of the way because he's a podiatrist and wouldn't know what to do about a heart attack if he had instructions from God."

"Oh, dear." Kate looked horrified.

"Who are all those people around the old woman?" Nikki eyed the group warily.

"You mean Hannah Elliot?" Susan didn't exactly smile—Nikki supposed under the circumstances, that would have been inappropriate—but she did lift a significant eyebrow.

"Yes, the woman who likened me to a canine."

As Kate gave Nikki a stricken look, Nikki's heart twinged at her lover's obvious distress. With an effort, she relinquished her anger at Kate, deciding it wasn't worth allowing other people's attitude problems to come between them.

"Stephen is her grandson and runs the family business." Susan inclined her head slightly toward the brunette woman hovering nearby, extremely upset. "That's his wife Denise, standing beside Stephen's brother, Andrew, who's the oldest." Her voice became slightly mocking. "The bored-looking woman is Andrew's wife, Tiffany."

"Tiffany?" said Nikki. "You can't be serious."

"Hey, some people will name their kids anything. A few tried to shorten it to 'Tiff,' but she got so pissed about it, no one dares try it now."

Nikki studied Tiffany and Andrew, who stood off to the side. Tiffany was the type of blonde that came from a bottle—big, brassy, and bold, rather similar to Rick's absent Betty, though she didn't seem nearly as genuine or kind as Betty. She seemed out of place with the rest of the family. Nikki wondered what Andrew saw in her. Probably the hair and boobs, she mused. He looked like the stereotypical hockey player—all brawn and not too many brains.

Perhaps that's why his grandmother had passed over him in favor of his younger brother Stephen, who at least looked a little more intelligent. More like a soccer player, thought Nikki. And Stephen's wife Denise looked a bit more socially acceptable than the rebellious Tiffany. With natural-looking dark hair instead of bleached blond, she appeared docile, as if she would be the perfect corporate wife and obey both Stephen and her grandmother-in-law Hannah without question.

Nikki glanced at another man, who had a slight expression of disdain on his face as he patted the voluptuous Tiffany's arm. He was less stocky than the other men, slighter in build, with darker hair. *Definitely a tennis player*. "Who's he?"

"Martin. He's a cousin with no real money of his own but still manages to live a life of leisure. Don't ask me how, or why the family lets him stick around because I don't know."

Nikki mentally filed that comment away as she and the rest moved out of the path of the paramedics who had finally arrived. The medical personnel applied various techniques on Stephen before lifting him onto the stretcher and wheeling him out as the rest of the family followed in their wake. Then there was a general exodus, the implication being that this dinner, as entertaining as it had turned out, was finally over for another year. Nikki retrieved her coat from the cloakroom and followed

Kate and the rest out to the curb, where they hailed a taxi.

"That was sort of a bust," Susan remarked as they sped down Willow Street, interrupting the awkward silence that had fallen over them.

"I'm sure the society made their target amount." Kate's tone was distant, almost inaudible from where she sat in front with the driver. Next to Susan in the back, Nikki miserably glanced out the window at the darkness of the passing streets, not surprised when Kate directed the taxi to her apartment first.

After the car stopped on Queen Street, Nikki mumbled a brief good-bye to Susan and Ted, though she didn't dare say anything further to Kate, not in front of her friends at least. It hurt when Kate didn't even look in her direction as the taxi departed.

Blinking back tears, Nikki trudged up the stairs leading to the second floor where her cat greeted her. Powder was quite vocal about being left alone for the evening, though she paid him little mind as she walked into the bedroom. There she removed the expensive clothes and placed them carefully in the closet, aware of how different they were compared to everything else hanging there. After scrubbing the makeup from her face, she removed the contacts and replaced her wire-rimmed glasses, glancing in the mirror. She looked like herself now, not like some stranger she barely recognized. She could change a little for Kate, she thought sadly, make every attempt to try to fit into her world, but in the end, she didn't really belong there and never would.

Despondently, she pulled on a robe and padded barefoot out to the small kitchen where she made herself a hot chocolate. Carrying the mug to her threadbare sofa, she curled up with Powder, drying her tear-stained cheek against his snowy fur.

The knock that sounded at her door only twenty minutes later startled her. Besides the landlord and the other tenants of the building, the only people who had keys to the lower security door were her mother, her friend Kim, and, of course, her lover.

Wiping her eyes, she went to answer the door. Kate stood outside on the landing, looking greatly forlorn.

"May I come in?" Her voice was soft, barely audible.

Wordlessly, Nikki stepped back, raising her arm to indicate Kate was welcome to enter, but not quite ready to go further than that.

Kate bent her head and walked past her into the living room, where Powder glared at her with dislike and pointedly leapt from the sofa. Sauntering past her with his tail in the air, he displayed his utter disinterest in the whole situation in every line of his sinuous body. He had yet to warm up to Kate, and she returned his antipathy, though both maintained a sort of polite regard toward each other for Nikki's sake.

"I owe you an apology." Kate turned to face Nikki, her eyes dark and unhappy.

"For what?"

"For making you go to that dinner. For forcing you to play a role you weren't comfortable with. I didn't listen to what you needed, and I'm sorry."

Nikki felt her chest fill with love and tenderness for this woman in front of her, and she inhaled deeply, trying to loosen her throat so that she could speak without bursting into tears. "You didn't force me to do anything. It was my decision to go to the dinner." She stepped closer, within arm's length. "I'm really sorry it didn't turn out the way you hoped it would."

Kate looked defeated, and Nikki felt her heart ache. She gently pulled Kate close, wrapping her up in a warm embrace. "It's all right. I know it's not easy to face things like that. You were so brave to try. I should have been more understanding, more supportive—"

"But you were right." Kate's voice was muffled as she buried her face into Nikki's neck, surrendering to her embrace. "I shouldn't have tried."

"That's not what I meant," Nikki corrected immediately, resting her cheek on the auburn hair. "I know it may have sounded like that when we were at the hotel, and I'm sorry. I know you have to try, Kate. We both do. I just hate that you're so hurt when it doesn't work out."

"Damn that Hannah, anyway." Nikki could hear the anger bubbling to the surface again.

She made a small sound and nudged Kate over to the sofa, where they sat down. "If it's any consolation, she has more important things to worry about now." Curling a leg under her other thigh, she gazed at her lover.

Kate managed a wan smile and rested her chin on one hand. "I'm sorry about everything that happened tonight." With her other hand she brushed a strand of Nikki's hair back from her face. "I'm sorry for dropping you off without saying good night. I'm sorry for using you to rub the town's faces in it. I'm sorry for being...well, for being such a damned fool."

"You're not a fool." Nikki captured Kate's fingers and brushed her lips over the knuckles. "I'm sorry I ran out on you while you were talking to the old woman. I should have stood by you instead of trying to avoid the confrontation. That was cowardly of me."

"It's not your job to put up with the fools in this town."

"It's not yours either."

Kate stared at her before grinning ruefully. "I guess it isn't. You know, I didn't even tell you how spectacular you looked tonight."

Nikki dipped her head, suddenly bashful. "Thank you. I wanted... I hoped that I looked good enough for your dinner."

"Good enough? My god, darling, you put everyone there to shame."

Nikki shrugged, pleased but aware of being a trifle uncomfortable. "Kate, you know that isn't really me. I mean it's fun to dress up once in a while, especially for you, but—"

"I know." Kate tilted her head, trying to catch Nikki's gaze. "I don't ever want you to be someone you're not, darling. That's not what tonight was about. I'm just saying that you were absolutely exquisite, and I'm flattered you'd make such an effort for me."

Nikki stared at her, then nodded. "All right." She squeezed Kate's fingers gently. "I'm really glad you came back."

"I couldn't imagine going back to my apartment without telling you how much I love you." Kate slid closer. "Once the taxi dropped Susan and Ted off at their hotel and took me home, I just sat there outside my building. Finally, I asked the driver to bring me right back here. He must have thought I was crazy."

Nikki leaned over, touching her lips to Kate's. "I love your craziness," she murmured.

"As long as you do." Kate returned the kiss, her mouth soft as it lingered on Nikki's. "I promise to make tonight up to you, darling. What can I do?"

"You don't have to make up anything."

"Oh, but I want to." Kate nuzzled her. "Please, let me do something for you."

Nikki wrapped her arms around Kate, suspecting she would have to come up with something because Kate simply wouldn't let this go.

"What are you doing during the last weekend in May?" She nibbled a tender path along her lover's jaw.

"I'm all yours," Kate promised without hesitation, her respiration increasing measurably. "Why?"

"It's the annual canoe trip down the Stewiacke River." Nikki slipped her hands over the silk of Kate's dress, finding the zipper at the back and slowly drawing it down. "It's with Nova Pride, the gay group."

Kate chuckled, half in amusement, half in sensuality as Nikki's fingertips traced back up her spine. "I suppose that's fair. You came to one of my functions, so I suppose I should go to one of yours. But I have to warn you. I've never been canoeing in my life."

"That's okay." Nikki put her hand on the outside of Kate's leg and slipped along the warm, nyloned smoothness of it, sliding beneath the hem of the dress. "There's a first time for everything. Besides, I'd never let anything happen to you."

"Promise?" Kate caught her breath as Nikki trailed over to the inside of her thigh, stroking lightly.

"Promise." Nikki paused for another kiss, one that left them both shaking. "Stay the night?"

"Do you really think I could leave at this point?"

"I would hope not." Nikki rose to her feet, stretching out her hand in invitation that Kate readily accepted, then leading her to the bedroom.

CHAPTER THREE

H e's really dead!?"
Kate opened her eyes and blinked sleepily in the morning light, rolling over in a bed still warm from her lover's body. Through the door, she could hear Nikki in the living room, undoubtedly talking on the phone. Sunshine spilled across the bed, and the clamor from the birds on the wires outside made it difficult to hear the rest of the conversation clearly. Though she wondered what had inspired Nikki's outburst that woke her, Kate didn't get up. She would find out all the details once Nikki rejoined her.

In the meantime, she wiggled happily against the warm flannel sheets and glanced around the room. On the far wall was a bookcase full of Nikki's hardcover books, a wicker hamper for dirty clothes, and a huge cedar chest that was the only quality piece in the room. A cheap pressboard dresser completed the circle, standing beside a door that led into an extra room too large to be a closet, yet wasn't a second bedroom either. Nikki stored all her camping gear there, along with old computer parts and other absolutely useless items she seemed unable to throw out. It also contained her weight bench and assorted free weights.

Although the room had no sense of style or planned decor, Kate adored her surroundings. Here she had first understood what being with a woman really meant, where she had found the precious intimacy missing for so much of her life. This bed, though not the most comfortable, was a small haven where Kate first realized that she could sleep in another's arms, safe and at peace, snuggled close against the soft, smooth body that welcomed her without reservation.

She started slightly as Powder entered the bedroom and jumped up onto the cedar chest where he settled on his belly, tucking his snowy paws beneath him. His green eyes became slits as he finally surveyed the bed, not so much looking *at* Kate as looking through her.

Kate knew that she and Nikki were still in that initial, insane time when all they could think of was being with each other every second of every day. Only now, they were considering their future with their heads as much as their hearts, acknowledging what exactly each might bring to such an advancement in their relationship. For Kate, one of the issues to be faced before their eventual cohabitation was a feline that didn't necessarily like her. How she and Nikki would ever work that problem out was something she couldn't imagine at this point.

She glanced up as Nikki finally returned to the bedroom and slipped out of her robe to reveal pert breasts, a flat stomach, and slim hips. Her body was toned from a work-out regime that included exercises Kate had never before encountered, but certainly enjoyed watching, particularly when Nikki performed them in clinging shorts and a skimpy top.

Smiling as Nikki slid between the sheets next to her, Kate acquired a rather passionate good-morning kiss before finally settling down, her head nestled on Nikki's shoulder. Nikki's warmth was wonderful, and Kate uttered a soft sigh of contentment.

"Is everything all right? I thought you sounded a bit upset out there."

"Not upset, just a little surprised. That was Kim."

"What did she say?" Kim was Nikki's best friend, but she was not in the habit of calling so early in the morning, nor very often on a weekend.

"That guy who became sick last night?" Nikki wrapped her arm around Kate. "He died before they got him to the hospital."

"Stephen's dead? I mean, I knew he didn't look good when the ambulance left, but I thought they had it under control."

"Apparently it was on the news this morning. Kim wanted to know if I had seen anything." Nikki glanced down at Kate, her blue eyes quizzical. "Did you know him well?"

Kate shook her head. "Not very. Susan knew him better. She actually dated him briefly in high school. Hannah, on the other hand, lives next door to my grandmother in Bible Hill, and they're friends. I know her far better than I'd like."

"Is that why the old woman considers it her right to tell you how to live? Because she's a friend of your grandmother?"

"Actually, Hannah thinks it's her right to tell everyone how to live.

Her family gets it the worst, though, especially Stephen and Denise. They live…" Kate paused, the situation suddenly becoming real to her. "*Lived*…just down the street from her. It's understood in the Elliot family that Hannah's way is always the right way, and anyone who disagrees is in trouble…as you witnessed last night."

Nikki made a face at the reminder, and Kate decided it was time to change the subject. Placing her hand flat over Nikki's stomach, she began to rub it in slow circles. "So tell me more about this canoe trip I've committed myself to."

The corner of Nikki's mouth lifted. "A group of us get together for a weekend every spring and meet at one of the bridges in Upper Stewiacke, canoe down to the park, and camp overnight before heading home. It's really fun."

"If you say so." Kate kissed Nikki's neck. "I really don't know how to paddle a canoe or put up a tent or sleep on the ground—"

"Will you trust me to show you how? I'll make sure we take along everything you need to be comfortable."

Kate hesitated, but smiled when Nikki glanced at her sideways. "All right, I'll trust you."

She slipped her leg across Nikki's groin, pressing down slightly as she lifted her hand to Nikki's breast. Idly, she toyed with a rosy nipple, feeling it harden immediately.

"I bet you'll enjoy making love in a sleeping bag," Nikki said lazily, watching her through lidded eyes that were remarkably similar to Powder's all of a sudden.

"I'd enjoy making love with you anywhere," Kate murmured, brushing her lips along the line of Nikki's collarbone. "Though that's something I never thought I would say about anyone."

Nikki ran her hand along Kate's side, stroking her flank lazily as she half turned toward her. "Why?"

"Because I never thought of sex as particularly important." Kate paid closer attention to what she was doing with her fingertips, circling Nikki's soft nipple with more insistence. "Now, I find I need to be with you in a way I've never needed anything before. It's almost a craving at times."

"You should indulge your cravings." Nikki reached up and took off her glasses, placing them on the nightstand by the bed before reaching over and pulling Kate close, nuzzling her ear.

After further shifting, Kate slipped on top of Nikki fully, pressing down on her as they kissed until she was breathless. Those soft curves and warm flesh cushioning her body intoxicated her, and she settled onto them with rising desire. Nikki's mouth was sweet and tender, a connection Kate thought she would never get enough of as Nikki traced lazy patterns of sensation over her back, sides, and buttocks. Finally, Nikki slipped her hand between their bodies, and Kate lifted slightly, granting her lover room to touch her more intimately.

Kate shivered as she felt the fingertips brush over her, Nikki manipulating gently in a circular motion. Covering Nikki's breasts with her hands, she felt the nipples prod her palms as she moved her hips against the maddening caress. Uttering a small cry when she felt Nikki's fingers slip into her, she clenched around them as they flexed deep within her, the pleasure building with steady power. The ball of Nikki's thumb took up where the previous caress had left off, rubbing firmly back and forth, and Kate could feel the first tremors of her approaching orgasm. Forcing herself to keep her eyes open, she surrendered to Nikki's intent gaze, moaning softly as the caress intensified.

"Nikki…" she whispered, her breathing quick and ragged.

"I'm here, baby." Nikki squeezed Kate's breast lightly. "Let it go."

The combination was all Kate needed, and with another helpless cry, she felt the pleasure seize her fiercely, shaking her before finally letting her go. Weak and vulnerable, she collapsed against the welcoming form beneath her, the shudders still reverberating through her.

"God," she murmured, kissing Nikki's neck. "You're incredible."

"You're very responsive. Maybe you've been saving up for awhile."

"Certainly until I met you." Kate laughed shakily. "Honestly, love, I didn't know it could be like this."

"Between women? Or just in general."

"In general," Kate undulated slightly on the fingers that remained where they were, cupping her possessively. "You do things that overwhelm me"

Nikki nibbled Kate's bottom lip. "Really?" She sounded very pleased with herself. "Maybe I should overwhelm you again."

"No, it's my turn."

Kate was delighted that Nikki was so very open about what she liked and wanted, granting Kate the same comfort and freedom to try different things, even when they didn't always work. Half the fun was in the attempt, so they rarely had any complete failures in their exploration. Primarily, the sense of absolute love and trust Kate shared with Nikki granted their physical interaction a depth that she had not believed possible.

Afterward, lying in Nikki's arms, feeling boneless and sated, Kate wondered how anyone could be this happy. She was certain that she had discovered some brand-new secret that all the words in all the books could never come close to conveying their love in its entirety.

"Hmm, what are you thinking?" Nikki stroked Kate's hair.

"You...me…" Kate sighed. "Us."

"Ah. Any conclusions?"

"Just that I love you…forever."

Nikki hugged her, making that her response.

"You think I'm overstating my case." Kate smiled.

"I just count my lucky stars that I found you, and that you love me."

"It's not something that could have been predicted, is it?"

"Certainly not by this town." Nikki chuckled. "Honestly, Kate, you really do like to shake people up at times. Is that why your ex figured out you were taking no prisoners last night?"

"I think we should talk about something else."

"You know I'll get it out of you sooner or later." Nikki's hands drifted and Kate squirmed.

"Stop that," she demanded.

Ignoring the insincere request, Nikki growled and nipped at her neck, causing a corresponding murmur from the cat on the cedar chest.

All of a sudden, Kate realized that Powder had been there the entire time. "My God!" Kate pushed Nikki away as she sat up, staring wide-eyed at the animal. "He watched us make love!"

"I doubt that he derived any sort of thrill from it." Nikki tried to pull Kate back down beside her.

"Doesn't that make you...inhibited?"

"Not in the slightest, and since he's been here for the last hour, it obviously didn't inhibit you all that much, either."

"I didn't remember he was here. Now I do."

"Fine." Slipping out of bed, she scooped up the snowy cat and, ignoring his meow of protest, shoved him out the door, shutting it behind him. "Happy now?"

"Only if you get back in bed."

"You're hopeless." Nikki laughed as she slipped back between the the sheets, pulling Kate into her arms. "But I love you anyway."

CHAPTER FOUR

Lunchtime at the Mayflower Diner was busy on Mondays, and Nikki wasn't surprised to find her best friend Kim at her favorite table in the corner, sitting with her lover, Lynn. The gay community in Truro was small but active, with the couple acting as its primary social directors. They were the motivating force behind the upcoming canoeing trip.

They greeted Nikki with a wink as she took the last empty chair in the diner and immediately asked how the dinner on Saturday night had gone, particularly curious about the mysterious death in one of the town's better-known families. Nikki couldn't tell them much more than what she had already discussed with Kim over the phone, though she did fill in the few details about the Elliot family that she had dug out of Kate during their weekend together.

"So who killed him?" Kim's blue eyes shone as she regarded Nikki.

Nikki shrugged. "It was probably a heart attack. He looked the type, soft and too much cholesterol."

"So you haven't heard?"

From the half grin on Kim's face, Nikki deduced that she knew something juicy. "Heard what?"

"Rumor has it, the man was poisoned." Kim laid that bomb with all the elated casualness of a card shark laying down a royal flush.

Nikki felt her jaw loosen and barely kept it from dropping open. "Really?" A combination of excitement and dismay swirled in her stomach, a sense of expectation that she was on the verge of some special adventure. But considering the last one had involved an arsonist and nearly left her dead, she wasn't sure she should be looking for another so soon. "How do you hear these things, anyway?"

"Actually, *I* heard about it," Lynn offered. More reserved than her outgoing and vivacious partner, she rarely volunteered information, but when she did, it was usually accurate and to the point. "I do some accounting work for the hospital, and when I was there this morning, I overheard some nurses talking about the dinner Saturday night. Apparently, something unusual was found in the toxicology report."

"It could just be food poisoning. Except…" Nikki shook her head, thinking quickly. "We all ate the same food. Besides, he became ill so quickly."

Lynn shrugged. "It could be something he ate earlier in the day."

"No, everyone said he just keeled over. One second he was fine, the next, he was facedown in his dessert."

"So someone may have had it in for him." Lynn looked thoughtful. "I wonder who."

Kim twirled a strand of strawberry blond hair around her finger. "Well, I wonder what's going to happen with the company. It's one of the few family-run businesses still around. Who'll take over for Stephen?"

Nikki thought about the Elliot manufacturing plant located in the center of town, next to the river dividing Truro from Bible Hill. The large brick building was blackened from more than a century of smoke and grime, despite the fact it had been updated with every pollution control dictated by government regulation. It had been one of the main employers in Truro for as long as it had existed, and while some of their business practices were still reputedly stuck in the 1800s rather than the twenty-first century, particularly when it came to pay and benefits, the plant hadn't pulled up stakes and moved to Mexico as so many other businesses had when the NAFTA deal came down. There was something to be said for them staying put, something honorable. The Maritimes were home to the Elliots, and in the Maritimes they would remain.

"Remember how long it took for Hannah to decide Stephen could run the place?" Lynn said. "She passed over Andrew even though he was the oldest, and the one everyone expected to take over after their father died."

"I didn't know that."

"It was big news at the time," Kim said. "From what I heard, Andrew was really mad about it, threatened to sell his stock to an outsider, but he didn't in the end." She grinned. "I guess Hannah got to him, and everyone knows, what she says, goes. Maybe he'll take over the position now."

"I never encountered any of them personally until Saturday night." Nikki thought about how the family had done their part to ruin her evening with Kate and ground her back teeth. Stephen keeling over into his mousse was only part of the contribution. "Frankly, I'd be just as glad to never have heard about them at all."

"So what do you think happened, Nik?" Lynn's question was almost challenging. "Who wanted Stephen dead? You're the crime expert."

"I don't care." Nikki didn't sound particularly convincing, not even to herself, and after a second, she forced a smile. "Probably, in the long run, it'll turn out to be a heart attack after all, and all this talk about poison is nothing but a lot of speculation and gossip."

"All right then," said Lynn, "if you don't want to talk about that, tell us the latest on you and Mrs. Kate."

Their latest appellation for Kate was a not-so-subtle reminder that not only was she much older than Nikki, fourteen years, but had once been married to a man. Nikki eyed them both, but decided not to challenge them this time.

"We're just fine. As a matter of fact, we're going down to the city next weekend to visit her friend Susan. While we're there, I want to show her Venus Envy, and maybe I can even get her to check out a bar."

The couple regarded Nikki in blatant amusement, obviously having a difficult time picturing Kate in a gay bar, or even Venus Envy, though it was just a shop.

"She's also coming on the canoe trip," Nikki added casually.

Kim gaped at her. "I thought she didn't like camping."

"She's willing to try it. Let's hope nothing goes wrong."

Lynn eyed her narrowly. "It's one of our canoe trips," she said in a tone that indicated Nikki should know better. "Something *always* goes wrong."

"Let's hope nothing goes wrong for me and Kate," Nikki amended, remembering past excursions with a bit of a sigh.

Kim started to speak, hesitated, and then as the others looked at her, grinned somewhat sheepishly. "The Summer Twins are coming."

Nikki closed her eyes as Lynn groaned.

"Hey, it's not my fault," Kim protested. "It's an open trip for whoever in the group wants to come."

Nikki felt her teeth grinding again. The Summer Twins were neither twins nor related in any way. They were actually a couple, a stout little brunette named May Hayward and a bleached blonde, June Allison. Though Nikki hadn't known of their reputation the first time she had met them, she had instinctively loathed them on sight and continued to avoid them ever since. The two lovers enjoyed an open relationship, which essentially meant they liked to play games with other lesbians, particularly couples, delighting in trying to lure one partner away from the other. Worse, they apparently didn't care what consequences their actions caused, either for themselves or other people. They drank to excess and could be counted on to provide at least one embarrassing or offensive display during any outing.

"Maybe Kate and I can go play golf or something that weekend," Nikki said, frowning. Golf was Kate's passion, and with the warm weather approaching, Nikki was keenly aware that she would have to learn a great deal more about it.

"There'll be plenty of other women there," Kim adopted a soothing tone. "You won't even have to talk to the twins."

"Oh, everyone gets to encounter them at least once. Plus, Kate's new, which means they'll be all over her."

Lynn grimaced. "You don't think Kate will go in for their games, do you?"

"Of course not!" Though a small part of Nikki wondered if that, indeed, was why she was so agitated, she realized she simply wanted this concentrated exposure to other lesbians to be a positive experience for Kate in a way that the Historical Society Dinner had not been for her. In other words, she wanted her friends and the rest of the women in the group to be perfect, which was a totally unrealistic expectation. "I guess Kate will have to take the bad with the good."

"That's the spirit," Kim encouraged. "Don't let the Twins keep you from participating in something you've always enjoyed. Especially don't let them keep you from bringing Kate along."

"Kate's just not into camping." Nikki sighed. "Not the real camping."

"Hey, her and a lot of these folks," Lynn reminded her. "Remember how long it took to pack up Cheryl and Gail last time? My god, they brought everything along but the kitchen sink. It took all seven of us an hour to get their stuff back into the car."

Nikki laughed, her good humor restored by the memory. "It was mostly because they set up in that hollow by the river. It was easy going down there, but they didn't think how hard it would be to lug all that stuff back up the hill."

Lynn shook her head in disagreement. "They had far too much stuff for an overnight trip."

"Well, I don't think anybody needs a battery-operated hair dryer while camping."

There was a brief silence. "I brought the hair dryer." Kim's tone was more than a little affronted.

The other two managed to hold their composure for few more seconds, hardly daring to look at each other, before they broke down completely at Kim's expression of wounded dignity.

"Yeah, well, so I think camping should be comfortable. Sue me." She glanced at Nikki. "Besides, don't you think Mrs. Kate will need more than her share of coddling if you ever expect to get her out there again?"

Nikki exhaled sharply. "Damn."

"I'm sure you'll both be fine," Kim declared with a confident chuckle. "It's only one night."

"I'm sure that's what Stephen Elliot thought," Nikki said. "Only one night. Who knew he wouldn't get to see the next morning?"

Kim and Lynn didn't say anything, but abruptly they looked apprehensive.

CHAPTER FIVE

Kate glanced up as she heard the bell over the door tinkle, pleased to see Linda Fennel, a teacher from the local high school, enter the store. Immediately, she stopped what she was doing and moved around the counter to hug her.

"How are you, sweetie?" She had known Linda since their university days in Wolfville. When Linda found a job in the town's educational system a few years later, they had become close friends, though not as close as Kate and Susan.

"I'm fine. How about you?" Linda smiled. "A lot's been going on, I hear."

"Too much," Kate agreed with a laugh. The last time they had encountered each other in the local grocery store, they had only time for a brief hello and good-bye.

Kate suddenly noticed that Linda had several strands of gray threading through her light brown hair, a stinging reminder that none of the sorority sisters were getting any younger. While she had probably inherited her grandmother's genes and wouldn't have to start concealing the gray in her hair until much later in life, Kate couldn't do anything about the wrinkles starting to appear around her eyes and mouth. She wondered glumly if Nikki had ever noticed them.

She dropped that depressing line of thought when Linda handed her a tan folder. "I'm sorry I haven't dropped these résumés by sooner."

Most high school students learned about preparing résumés and doing job searches in the eleventh grade, but Linda had gone out and arranged job interviews and work-terms for her students with local businesses. Kate found the extracurricular project invaluable when it came to hiring part-time help, though she had lost her last employee unexpectedly when the girl's parents insisted that she not work for a lesbian. She hoped that Linda had found someone from next year's class who could start right away rather than wait for summer break. Her long hours working in the store were starting to wear on her, and if she didn't find new help soon, she would have to put an ad in the paper and hire whomever she could.

Kate opened the file, somewhat dismayed to discover only two sheets of paper inside. "I usually have about twenty to choose from."

"I know. A lot of kids didn't want to apply. After all, it's still a little early in the year, plus, we have a new Wal-Mart by the highway, a new Sobey's downtown, other businesses are expanding—"

Kate pinned her with a look. "Are you telling me it didn't have anything to do with my being involved with a woman?"

"I'm sure that's part of it as well," Linda responded with the casual honesty so characteristic of her. "It's pretty well known by now that you're gay and out and proud of it. The Historical Society Dinner proved that, if nothing else".

Kate flinched and Linda's face abruptly clouded. She put her hand on Kate's forearm. "I'm sorry, Katie. Kids listen to their parents, even when they think they don't, and some parents are…well, still in the dark ages, but we have to be fair, too. The kids are just starting to get ready for exams and aren't looking beyond that to summer jobs yet. And you really do have a lot of competition this year. Most kids want to hook up with the large chain stores rather than take a part-time position that'll only last a year."

"I suppose I should be glad the town is growing." Kate glanced through the two résumés. "Do you have any particular recommendations?"

"Both Todd and Beth are good students." Linda offered Kate what could only be construed as an oddly significant look. "Both seem very interested in working for you."

"You think there's a particular reason for that?"

"I don't know." Linda took a seat on the stool by the counter and raked her fingers through her fine hair, leaving it slightly disarrayed. "Kids go through so much these days, and confusion about their sexual orientation is probably the least of it. In any event, it wouldn't hurt to have them exposed to a positive role model."

"Is that what I am now? A gay role model?"

"You were always a role model. A woman with her own business, a leader in the community..." Linda tilted her head. "Now you just have an added qualification to add to the list for certain kids."

Deciding to be pleased by the compliment, if not entirely sure how accurate it was, Kate smiled. "All right. I guess it's an ill wind, after all. I'll look these over, schedule the interviews, and make my decision."

"Thanks, Kate. I'll have them prepared."

"You always do." Kate motioned at the coffeemaker that sat in a concealed corner of the window ledge. "Can I get you a cup? It's pretty quiet at the moment."

"I'm on my lunch hour, so I guess I have time." Linda glanced at her watch. "We need to get together more often."

"Yes, it's been a while." Kate poured the coffee and handed her a mug. Once, she'd shared many outings with Linda and her husband, Roy, but that had been when she was still married to David. After the divorce, they had drifted apart, as couples did from friends who were suddenly single. These days their interactions were rare and revolved around Linda's project to find jobs for students and an occasional lunch or movie.

Linda looked regretful. She hesitated, then asked, "Kate, how are you? Honestly?"

"I'm fine." Kate took a seat on the other stool and sipped her own coffee. "Shouldn't I be?"

Linda looked mildly flustered. "I just...well, you know you surprised a lot of people."

"I know." Kate tried not to sound satisfied at the notion. "Were you one of them?"

Linda pursed her lips thoughtfully. "I'd have to say yes. Which is odd because, frankly, I was one of the few people who wasn't surprised when you divorced David."

"Really? Why not?"

"I'm not sure. I guess it seemed that whenever I saw you with him, you were...sad."

"You never said anything."

"What was there to say?" Linda's brown eyes were dark and concerned. "Besides, I'm not sure you could have said why you were unhappy, anyway."

"You're right, I didn't say anything. I only knew that I had every-thing any woman was supposed to want or need, and I still wasn't satisfied."

"I wonder how many others are like that. Living their lives as everyone thinks they should, not daring to consider other possibilities."

Kate studied her curiously. "Are you trying to tell me something, Linda?"

Linda looked briefly startled, then amused by the suggestion. "No. I mean, there was that time in college—"

"What?" Kate froze, mug halfway to her mouth.

"I was drunk. So was she. Things happen sometimes."

"Not to me." Kate stared at her in total amazement. "Who was it?"

"I don't think you need to know." Linda chuckled. "We were just having fun, and besides, I'm perfectly happy with Roy, as she is with her husband. It was just a youthful indiscretion. But I'd never have guessed it of you. Maybe that's why it surprised me, Kate. I thought I knew you as well as any friend could, but I discovered that I really didn't know you at all. It's made me question my assumptions about people and whether I can trust my judgment about what they might do."

She paused, her expression almost wistful. "I'm a teacher, and I try to look out for things in the kids. I try to see problems or the other influences in their life. How do you suppose it makes me feel to know one of my closest friends was going through this, and I didn't have a clue it was happening?"

"If it's any consolation, I didn't see it coming either, Linda. I didn't go looking for it. It just worked out the way it did, but it feels absolutely right. I can't explain any better than that."

"It must be right." Linda shook her head. "I don't sense that sadness in you anymore. I'm glad you're happy now."

"I am. Nikki's absolutely wonderful."

Linda looked suddenly uncomfortable, but soldiered on. "You should bring her over to dinner some night."

Kate didn't quite choke on her coffee, but it was close. "Are you serious?"

"Yes. I'd love to see her again."

"'Again'?" Kate stared at her. "I didn't realize you knew her."

"I had her, Kate."

"What?"

Linda lifted her brows at the astonished outrage in Kate's voice, apparently thought about it, and laughed as she raised her hand in a gesture to slow things down. "I meant I was her teacher in her final year of homeroom," she elaborated. "What did you think I meant?"

"Nothing," Kate lied, surprised by her immediate assumption. "I guess I wasn't thinking of that. She told me she attended high school in town. Of course you would have taught her."

"There does seem to be a bit of an age difference involved here." Linda's tone was suddenly careful.

"I know. It's been pointed out to me before. Susan was worried about it."

"She's not anymore?"

"She doesn't bring it up."

"Meaning I shouldn't, either." Linda smiled crookedly.

"Meaning that the age difference is there. I recognize that it exists, and I won't say it doesn't matter at all because sometimes it does, but it doesn't matter enough to be a major problem. At least, it hasn't yet."

"I'm glad to hear it." Linda stood. "I have to go. I have a class in ten minutes." She hugged Kate. "Don't be such a stranger."

"You either." Kate returned the hug, intrigued at how much she was learning about her friends and herself since becoming involved with Nikki. "I'm glad you came by. I'll call you with the interviews."

As Linda left the store, the phone rang stridently and Kate picked it up. "Novel Companions. How may I help you?"

Her knees became weak as she listened to the unexpected, but very familiar, voice at the other end of the line.

CHAPTER SIX

Nikki yawned as she opened her eyes, half-blinded by the afternoon sunlight. Working twelve-hour shifts at the police station as a dispatcher from six at night to six in the morning left her with little energy to do anything more than to come home and fall directly into bed. But now her workweek was over, and she could look forward to the four-day weekend that made up for the long hours and occasional stressful calls she received while on duty.

Glancing at the clock with blurred vision, she managed to make out that it was almost three o'clock, and she wondered how she should spend the rest of her Friday afternoon. Sighing, she rolled over and stretched her arm across the sheet, wishing for a warm body to fill it. Novel Companions, along with the rest of the retail stores in the downtown core, tended to stay open until nine on Thursday and Friday nights. Ever since she lost her part-time help, Kate had been forced to work all those hours so Nikki really couldn't expect any quality time with her until late Saturday afternoon, when they were to make their scheduled trip into the city.

She considered going back to sleep, but Powder abruptly appeared on the bed, rubbing his head forcefully against the parts of her showing above the blankets and purring loudly. She contemplated him from beneath heavy-lidded eyes.

"What do you want? I know it's not food because that dispenser I bought gives it to you whenever you want. And I filled the reservoir in your water fountain when I came home this morning."

He sat down on his haunches and regarded her with unblinking expectancy. When she showed no signs of getting up, his jaws parted in a particularly piercing meow, reverberating in her ears. Honestly, there had to be a touch of Siamese in him somewhere. She had never heard such a penetrating sound from any other cat she had owned. She shoved him off the bed and covered her head with the pillow. Within seconds, he was back, sliding a paw beneath the pillow to pat her cheek as his cries became more demanding. He was merely being difficult, but she groaned and slipped from the bed anyway, wondering if other people were as well trained by their pet, or if she were the only one so cowed.

She felt better once she was in the shower, more alert as she started to sing lustily while scrubbing away the lather. The phone was ringing when she stepped out, and, wrapping a towel around her, she hurried to the bedroom where she picked up the receiver.

"Hello? Debbie? What's going on?"

"The nets are up."

"This early?" Nikki was surprised.

"We've been playing since last week. Listen, I have another player for four o'clock and need a fourth for doubles. Can you play?"

"I'm on my way."

Nikki tossed the towel on the bed and turned on the small television sitting on the dresser to check out the temperature. As she flipped open the lid of the cedar chest, retrieving the shorts she had put away six months earlier, she wondered why it had taken Debbie a week to call her. Probably her friend's competitive edge in action. They did play doubles together, but also competed on the singles court every so often. Nikki held a long-time, decidedly one-sided advantage that aggravated Debbie to no end. Getting in a week's worth of practice before Nikki started playing was probably Debbie's attempt to get a jump on her.

She pulled on a light jacket and sweatpants over a pair of green shorts and a large T-shirt, before retrieving her tennis bag from the closet. It felt good to be repeating this ritual of spring, preparing to go out to the courts and hit the ball once more. Invigorating, even.

Powder's outraged meows floated down the stairs after Nikki as she slipped out of her apartment building. The fresh air hit her like a heady draught of spring water, and she hummed as she walked down the sidewalk, her bag slung over her shoulder. Cutting across two parking lots, she strode easily down the sidewalk on Prince Street, the main thoroughfare of the town, enjoying the bright sunshine and the light green misting over the trees. A passenger train was pulling away from the railway station on the Esplanade, and she had to wait at the crossing until it had chugged past on its way toward Halifax.

The delay made her late, and she began to jog until she reached Brunswick Street, her tennis bag thumping against her side. Entering Victoria Park, she crossed the common toward the tennis club, lifting her hand in greeting at the players already out on the courts. All four nets were up and the door to the clubhouse was wide open. It was a little early in the season, but obviously she wasn't the only one anxious to get started.

Debbie was waiting by the front deck of the clubhouse, leaning against the stairs as she stretched out her hamstrings. Also stretching were her partner, Audrey, and Elaine, a girl Nikki knew only in passing from the previous year.

"Hey, Nik." Debbie straightened up as Nikki approached. Small, boyish, with a blond buzz cut that ghosted over her skull, she was a good player. Nikki had first met her during Pride Weekend in Halifax several years earlier. She and Audrey were probably Nikki's closest and most dearest friends after Kim and Lynn.

Nikki nodded at her, then grinned at Elaine. "How was your winter?"

Elaine smiled shyly. "Too long."

"Not long enough," Audrey said as she rested her leg on the back of a nearby bench and stretched it out. Tall, dark, and lean, Audrey seemed to look out on the world with the easy benevolence of a basking lioness. She and Debbie were avid skiers and loved snow shoeing, enjoying the winter months as much as the summer ones. Naturally athletic, she moved well on the court, with good anticipation, particularly at the net.

Nikki shook out her shoulders and began her own stretches. Usually she did a more involved routine at home, but the phone call had left her little time. Now, she did her legs and shoulders. The rest would just have to warm up as she did.

As she pulled her racket from her bag and took off the cover, she glimpsed a figure on the far court and stopped to stare as she recognized Tiffany Elliot.

Debbie followed Nikki's gaze. "You know her?"

"I know who she is. Has she played here before?"

"She always buys a membership," Elaine said. She was more girlish than the other three, Nikki noted, wearing a skirt rather than shorts and moving with less athleticism, but more grace. "She usually plays at the Lake, though."

Nikki considered that information. The "Lake" was actually Shortt's Lake, a resort community located some twenty kilometers outside of town where certain wealthier citizens, such as Andrew and Tiffany Elliot, maintained permanent or summer homes. The residents enjoyed the use of several courts at the rather exclusive country club located on the shores of the large lake, and the only reason to purchase a membership in both clubs was to be able to play in the Truro club tournament, an indulgence resented by the town members, particularly when they were knocked out of the competition by one of the Lake players.

"Why is she here?"

"Slumming, maybe?" Debbie shrugged.

Elaine chimed in. "She's a real snob. But my mom knew her from high school. She says Tiffany is the last person who should be like that, considering where she grew up."

Nikki was intrigued. "Where was that?"

"Court Street Trailer Park."

There was a hint of condescension in Elaine's voice that Nikki couldn't help but relate to. She knew the area well simply from reputation and from her job with the police station. Hardly a weekend passed without a unit dispatched out there to look into a disturbance of some kind or another. Everything from domestic abuse to excessive public drunkenness to periodic raids on the resident drug dealers.

She narrowed her eyes as she turned back to scrutinize court three, identifying the man Tiffany was hitting with. *I knew he was a tennis player.* Martin Elliot, tall and tanned even this early in the year, and looking much less sullen than he had appeared at the Historical Society Dinner, yelled something indistinguishable to his opponent, who laughed.

Watching them, Nikki felt her inquisitive instincts stirring. *There's something there.*

As the four women went through the gate to set up on the first court, Nikki kept half an eye on what was happening on court three. Martin and Tiffany weren't playing a match; they were simply hitting the ball back and forth. No reason to think twice about that but it seemed odd for them to travel all the way to Truro to do it on a Friday afternoon. The Shortt's Lake club was closer and generally had more courts available than the Truro club, though it was possible that the Lake club didn't have their nets up yet. Perhaps Tiffany just had to be in town for some reason, and Martin asked to meet him here, but on the face of it, that didn't make sense. Nikki wondered if they didn't want to be seen hanging around together too often at Shortt's Lake, particularly by Tiffany's husband.

That thought made her miss an easy put-away, and when she saw the smirk on Debbie's face, she decided that she had wasted enough attention on the Elliots. Debbie and Audrey were already up three games to one, including two breaks of serve, and if Nikki didn't want to see this set gone, she was going to have to start playing better. Despite her winter rust and Elaine's limitations, they could certainly offer a better challenge to their opponents than they had so far.

"Sorry," Nikki said as she went back to receive serve. "I guess I'm still getting into it."

Elaine smiled and ducked her head, a slight blush staining her cheeks.

Nikki looked back across the net at Debbie, who was bouncing the ball, bent over in the classic serving position. Debbie had a pretty good serve. The technique wasn't by the book, but she managed to get both pace and spin whenever she wanted, which, at this level, made it fairly dangerous. Nikki drew her lips back over her teeth in a feral grin as she leaned forward.

Debbie took note of it and aborted her toss, taking a second to peer over the net at her nemesis. "Whoops. Look at who just woke up."

"I see," Audrey said, and glanced over her shoulder at Debbie. "Took a while, didn't it?"

Nikki knew they were trying to distract her and ignored them, ready to receive the ball. Debbie and Audrey exchanged glances again, and then, grinning, Debbie served.

Nikki took a full swing at the ball, the yellow, fuzzy sphere impacting solidly with the strings in the center of the racket and smashing back down the alley that Audrey had not quite been covering.

"Good shot," Debbie said, somewhat sourly as she changed to the other service court.

Nikki dipped her head modestly, but inwardly delighted in the shot as she took two steps up to the service court. That was why she played tennis, that sweet, wonderful elation when the ball did exactly what she wanted and did it in a way that finished the point. She didn't even particularly care if she won, just so long as she played well. That was the real difference between her and Debbie's game, and why she held the upper hand in all the matches between them in the club tournaments. Nikki derived a pure, simple pleasure from hitting the ball, whereas Debbie always wanted to win. Her desire tended to cost her on crucial points when she tightened up, preventing her from swinging freely, while Nikki continued to hit the same way as she always did, regardless of the situation. Elaine managed to return Debbie's next serve cross-court. Her shot was weak, but when Audrey returned it, hitting it back at Elaine, Nikki took two quick strides, intercepting it to volley back between her two opponents, out of reach of either. Fifteen-thirty, and suddenly the game and set were no longer out of reach. Nikki flashed a smile at Elaine, who blushed in return, and settled down to knock the rest of the rust off her game.

An hour and a half later, she hefted her bag over her shoulder, pleased with her play. She had seen Tiffany and Martin leave earlier, noticing them hop into a sporty Mustang convertible together. Pondering what she had seen, she strode briskly down Brunswick Street, cut across the railroad tracks behind the Truro Center, and used the alley to come out at the crosswalk. Novel Companions was just down the block from here, on the corner of Outram and Prince.

Nikki felt a smile edge her lips a few minutes later as she stepped into the familiar, warm surroundings of the bookstore. Kate was behind the counter, waiting on a few customers, and Nikki lingered in the store until they left, daring to lean across the counter and kiss Kate quickly on the lips once the door had closed behind them.

"Hi, there." Her voice was suddenly husky. Sometimes the emotion she felt for Kate welled up and made it difficult to talk.

"Hi, yourself. What were you up to?"

"First game of tennis," Nikki said happily. "Have you eaten?"

Kate suddenly looked weary. "First break in customers I've had today. Good for business, bad for my stomach."

"Let me use your shower, and then I'll bring you down a little something to tide you over until dinner."

A grateful look crossed Kate's classic features. "Would you do that for me?"

"Any time." Nikki would have kissed her again, but the door opened as more customers came in, so she contented herself with a smile and headed for the rear of the store and the staircase leading to Kate's apartment.

CHAPTER SEVEN

K ate sat cross-legged on the sofa and hungrily scooped up another bite of chicken fried rice and moo goo gai pan. Nikki had popped down to the China Rose, their favorite Chinese restaurant just down the block from Novel Companions, and picked up dinner. Now Kate was enjoying her meal after a long and profitable day. The lights were subdued, music played quietly on the stereo, and Kate thought she should feel completely content. She supposed she would, if the phone call she had received a few days earlier still didn't weigh so heavily.

"Feeling better?" Nikki asked as she sank back against the sofa cushions.

"Much."

"Are you sure? You looked pretty frazzled in the store earlier. Is not having any help getting to you?"

"Honestly, Nikki, I'm fine." Kate was startled by the snap in her tone. "I'm sorry," she apologized quickly. "It is becoming a little difficult to work all these hours, but Linda brought by some résumés so hopefully I'll hire someone soon."

"Good." Nikki studied her, blue eyes dark in the lowered illumination. "Is that all?"

"You *are* starting to know me well, aren't you?"

Nikki looked pleased at the comment, but her eyes didn't waver in their intensity. "Enough to know when something's bothering you."

"I had a call a couple of days ago from my grandmother." Kate poked a piece of chicken with her fork absently. "She's coming home in a couple of weeks and wants me to prepare for her arrival."

"Prepare?"

"Make sure her house is stocked with groceries, that her house-keeper is rehired, that she's picked up at the airport...that sort of thing."

"You don't like doing it?"

"I always do it," Kate explained. "Just not this time of year. She usually doesn't come back from Tampa until the middle of June. It's only the end of April. It couldn't have come at a worse time with me alone in the store."

"Did she say why she was coming back early?"

"She mentioned, quite pointedly, that she wants to discuss the changes going on in my life."

"Meaning?"

Kate inhaled slowly. "I think Hannah Elliot has been telling her all sorts of things regarding you and me. I have the impression Grandmother isn't pleased."

"Oh." Nikki's face went still, and a muscle jumped sporadically in her jaw.

Immediately, Kate put her plate onto the coffee table and reached out for her lover, pulling her into a warm embrace. "Regardless, nothing she can say would ever alter my feelings for you. I love you. That won't change."

Nikki put her hand over the arm holding her around her chest. "All right." She paused. "It's going to be hard for you."

Kate hugged her closer, lowering her head onto Nikki's shoulder. "It might be. My grandmother is all I really have left. Her opinion has always meant a great deal to me. I won't lie. It'll hurt a great deal if she disapproves of our relationship, but I can handle it."

"I'm sorry." Nikki nuzzled her hair gently.

"I am, too."

They sat for a moment, unsure of the future but trusting that they would face it together.

"When does she arrive?" Nikki asked.

"The twenty-fourth of May. She's coming in at two. I need to have someone hired by then and trained enough to leave them alone. That, or close the store for the rest of the day. It's not just picking Gram up from the airport. It's getting her settled at home and doing anything else that she needs that day." Her head ached at the thought of what had to be done before then.

"I could go pick her up." Nikki had an odd expression in her eyes, half-challenging, as if she wanted to confront Kate's grandmother immediately but also half-frightened Kate might take her up on the offer.

Kate smiled gently. "I don't know if that's such a good idea."

"Maybe not." Nikki's features firmed as she gathered her arguments. "But it's more convenient for me to pick her up. And I have to meet her sooner or later."

Kate considered the offer. "It certainly would make a statement about us being together from the very beginning." She hesitated. "Nikki, my grandmother can be quite unpleasant if she puts her mind to it. She never has with me, but I've seen her with others."

"Oh." Nikki frowned as that possibility sunk in, and Kate felt a wash of affection for her. "I can do this," she insisted after a moment's silence. "I love you, and I'm with you, and I don't want anything or anyone to get between us. I also don't want there to be any question about how I feel about you."

"There isn't." Kate kissed her softly. "The sooner Grandmother understands how much you're a part of my life, the better. But I don't think the airport is the proper time or place."

Nikki regarded her for a long moment and then grinned. "I wouldn't want to give her a stroke."

Kate chuckled. "She'd give you one, first. Believe me."

"Maybe she'll actually like me."

"Of course she will. She'll adore you as much as I do." Kate traced a path up Nikki's neck with her lips, finding the soft lobe of her ear and nipping at it lightly.

Nikki laughed—a low, sensual chuckle. "Well, I don't know if I want her to like me that much." She shifted, pressing Kate back against the sofa.

Kate reached up, removing Nikki's glasses and placing them carefully on the coffee table. Her breath caught as Nikki's mouth found hers and Nikki's gentle weight pushed her down into the yielding cushions. They kissed deeply, their embrace warm and sheltering. Kate felt so safe and secure in this position, Nikki's lips a benediction upon hers.

"We could take this into the bedroom," she murmured between the long, slow melting kisses.

"We could," Nikki agreed, but she showed little desire to change position.

Several moments passed as they continued to kiss, their hands lazily caressing, loosening and removing each other's garments. Kate hummed happily as Nikki finally managed to unhook her bra and toss it aside, lowering her head to cover a nipple, prodding it lightly with her tongue.

"Oh, my," she whispered. "That's…rather nice."

Nikki glanced up momentarily to grin at her before continuing her loving assault, the tip of her tongue circling relentlessly, provoking the most delightful chills. Kate closed her eyes as she surrendered to the sensation, hugging Nikki's head to her. She so adored when her lover paid attention to this area of her body. Nikki loved her with a superb delicacy, drawing out the wonderful sensation until Kate thought she would lose herself utterly.

"Oh, Nikki," she managed. "I think—"

"Shh, relax. Let me love you."

Kate had no defense to offer, nor did she seek one. She quivered as Nikki finally stopped, bestowing a gentle kiss to each exquisitely tender nipple before moving slowly downward. Strong hands tugged at Kate's pants, unfastening them and pulling them down her legs, drawing the lace panties with them. Suddenly exposed, Kate felt a warm breath rush over her, and she cried out again, helpless beneath the skillful touch of her lover. Nikki's mouth covered her, an intimate dance of lips and tongue over her sensitive flesh, pleasuring her until Kate could no longer hold back the tide of her rapture.

Trembling in the aftermath, her body still resonating with lingering delight, she tangled her hands in Nikki's hair, weaving the silky golden strands around her fingers. Nikki rested her head on Kate's abdomen, stroking her lightly with gentle fingertips, patiently waiting as Kate basked in the warm afterglow.

"I love you," Kate whispered, overwhelmed.

Nikki lifted her head, a white flash of teeth appearing in a warm smile. "I love you, too." She dipped her head, kissing a spot just below Kate's belly button, then again, just above it, making a slow trail up her body.

Finally, Nikki was in her arms, settling onto her once more with sheltering warmth, her mouth firm on Kate's. Kate could taste herself, piquant and lingering on her lips, and she kissed her deeply, openly, almost dizzy from the sheer intimacy of it.

Nikki groaned softly into her, and Kate tugged restlessly at the clothes that still obstructed her. "Let me…" she murmured.

Nikki drew away briefly, stripping away the last garments that separated her and Kate until warm flesh was on flesh, skin sliding sensually against skin, their hands no longer hindered as they roamed free over curve and plane. Kate sought out and found the wet heat awaiting her, and her moan echoed Nikki's as she stroked lavishly, knowing her partner needed firmness at this point and not any teasing caress.

Nikki's body was hot on hers, moving against her fingers insistently, her breath a sob in Kate's ear. There was a moment of hesitation, a cry of demand and anticipation, before Nikki shuddered helplessly, the sound at the back of her throat no longer coherent or intelligent, merely ragged with the intensity of the sensations rippling through her.

Kate hugged her lover, stroking the head that had fallen onto her chest, feeling protective and needful at the same time and aware that Nikki was feeling the same. Snuggling closer, requiring the sanctuary of her love, Nikki freely offered the haven of her own.

Finally, Kate smiled, wiggling beneath Nikki. "The bedroom."

"The bedroom."

Leaving their clothes where they had been discarded, though Nikki did retrieve her glasses, they linked hands and moved into the bedroom, slipping between the cool sheets to wrap themselves around each other. Sleep came quickly, and Kate didn't resist, knowing that the next day would arrive soon enough with its challenges, but feeling ready to face them so long as she had Nikki by her side.

CHAPTER EIGHT

Surrounded by warmth and the musky fragrance of her lover, Nikki woke in blissful satisfaction. Kate still slept, cradled in her arms, her face smoothed out and much younger than her forty years, vulnerable in the early morning light. Carefully, Nikki rose to an elbow and looked down at her. Contentment filled her chest. She had thought she would never find love again, that she would never be able to trust anyone with her heart. Then Kate had come into her life, and slowly Nikki had allowed herself to fall in love again. She knew the consequences of this leap of faith would be much harder on her if it didn't work out.

Forcing away the dark thought, she gently kissed Kate's forehead and slipped out of bed, refusing to be disappointed that her lover didn't stir. Donning an old robe of Kate's that was far too small for her, she padded out to the kitchen and set about fixing breakfast.

So involved was she with her preparations that when the arms slipped around her waist, she barely avoided dropping an egg on the floor.

"Good morning." She leaned back into Kate's warmth. "I was going to bring you breakfast in bed."

"Were you? That's so sweet. Thank you, love." Kate hugged her tightly. "You know, you look really good in that robe, making breakfast. Makes me feel all warm inside."

Nikki felt the heat in her cheeks as she cracked the egg, separating the shell with her fingers to allow the inside to slip into the bowl. "You must be in love. My hair's a mess, and this robe has a big hole in it."

Kate reached through the rip and patted Nikki on the hip. "That's why I like it," she said in a throaty voice.

Nikki laughed. "Go sit down. I'll finish making breakfast."

Kate hugged her once more, clearly reluctant to release her before finally moving around the counter to sit on one of the stools lining the breakfast bar. Propping her chin up with her hands, elbows on the polished surface, she regarded Nikki with a devoted expression.

"I really like having you here in the mornings."

Nikki felt a sudden flutter in her stomach as she mixed the egg with tiny bits of ham, green pepper, and mushroom, pouring the combination into a heated frying pan. "I like being here."

There was a pause. "Have you ever considered…being here all the time?" Every word sounded carefully considered before it was allowed to slip from Kate's lips.

It had been awhile since they had discussed moving in together, coming to a mutual understanding that the subject would come up again, hopefully at a more prudent time. Nikki placed four pieces of bread into the large toaster and pushed down the lever. "You know I have."

"Recently?"

"Sure," Nikki managed casually. "A lot, actually." She flipped the omelet and raised her eyes to meet Kate's. "I just don't think we're ready yet."

"What concerns you specifically?" Kate's bluish-gray eyes were bright and intense. "Powder?"

"Among other things." Nikki sliced the omelet in two and slid it onto two plates as the toast popped up. "Kate, moving in together is a big step. Not for some people, but for me, it's always been like marriage, especially since we weren't allowed that sort of legal union until recently. I want our living together to be a real commitment, the kind that lasts a lifetime." She lifted her head to meet Kate's gaze squarely. "Does that make sense?"

Kate nodded slowly. "Yes. I hadn't thought about it that way. I just want to be with you, but maybe I'm taking it more lightly than I should."

"I don't think you're taking it lightly." Nikki carried the plates and utensils over to the table, while Kate assembled glasses and a pitcher of juice. "It's still a big step for you, but for a lot of straight people…" She trailed off at the look on Kate's face and smiled. "I know, but seriously, you've been living straight for most of your life, and that affects how you think about things."

Kate frowned but finally nodded, apparently allowing the point. "Anyway, for a lot of people, living together is just that step between dating and getting married. It's not as…as serious as marriage. You might perceive it that way." She looked across at Kate as they sat down to eat. "I'm just saying for me, it's a lot more than that. I never ever imagined that I would be able to get married, so the idea of living with someone has always been like the wedding and the honeymoon and being a wife all rolled up into one. It should mean wills, and insurance, and shared banks accounts, and everything else. You know?"

Kate nodded, her features serious. "I suppose I understand. Is that why you didn't live with Anne when you moved to the city?"

The lack of reactive flash of hurt when her ex-lover was mentioned made Nikki realize she was truly over the first woman she had ever loved. "Probably. But Anne didn't ask me to move in, either. Maybe she understood what it meant to me, even if we never talked about it." She chewed her toast thoughtfully. "Did you live with David before you were married?"

"No." Kate colored faintly. "We were still a little old-fashioned back then, even in the eighties. Everyone else might have still been enjoying the sexual revolution, but not David and I."

Nikki, born much later and still very young when Kate married her husband, had no comment. To her, the eighties were the hazy memories of growing up, of looking at life through the eyes of a child, and she had to take her lover's word about what they were like to an adult. Kate might as well have been talking about the cultural mores of the fifties and sixties for what little context it offered her.

"Tell me, Kate," Nikki said softly. "Are you ready to marry me?"

Kate's face altered abruptly, and Nikki knew those words had penetrated, even if the others hadn't. A little sadness filled her chest, but she managed a smile. "When you are, ask me. Then I'll give you my answer."

Kate regarded her soberly. "All right. I will. I promise."

"So what are your plans today?"

"I have two people to interview for the part-time position." Kate seemed relieved at the change of subject. "If they can start Monday after school, I should have him or her trained well enough to stay on their own by the time I have to pick up Grandmother."

"You know, I can hang around here that day. I've spent enough Saturdays in the store with you to have some idea how things operate."

"That would be wonderful." Kate beamed. "I'd have a little extra peace of mind knowing you were just upstairs in case something goes awry."

"Glad to do it." Nikki's heart lightened at the pleasure in her lover's eyes, knowing that she had done something useful. She still wondered if perhaps she should pick up Kate's grandmother, but she was content to go with whatever Kate decided. After all, Irene Taylor was her relative. Nikki had her own problems when it came to family ties. "What about that weekend?"

Kate glanced up. "What about it?"

"The canoe trip?" Nikki prodded. "Do you think your help will be ready to handle the store by then? It's different being only a call away while you pick up your grandmother and being out of contact on the river all day."

Kate looked undecided, but finally nodded. "I'm sure they will." She took Nikki's hand and squeezed it gently. "Even if they're not, it doesn't matter. I made a promise to you. I'll close the store if I have to."

Touched, Nikki dipped her head. "Thank you." She couldn't remember anyone willing to give up so much for her before. "So tell me about these students you're interviewing."

Kate sipped her orange juice. "Not much to tell. There are two applicants, Beth Shaw and Todd Densmore. They both seem to be good students, and Linda seems to think they would benefit from working for me."

Nikki lifted an eyebrow. "Are they gay?"

"I don't know, but that's possible because Novel Companions was their specific first choice."

"Wow." Nikki thought briefly about having had a boss like Kate for her first part-time job and abruptly frowned. "Hire the boy," she said flatly.

Surprised, Kate glanced up at her. "Excuse me?"

"The last thing you need is an employee who develops a crush on you."

"Is that what you're worried about?" Kate looked amused.

"I'm not worried." Nikki felt a little defensive. "But if I were a teenager coming to work here, thinking I'm gay and having you as my boss, knowing you're gay, I'd be in seventh heaven. How could I *not* fall for you? In fact, I'd be all over you like white on rice."

"You're exaggerating. I'll hire the best candidate, regardless of gender."

"Don't say I didn't warn you." Nikki waved her toast for emphasis.

Kate laughed and shook her head. "So what are you up to today?"

"I'd like to help out in the store this morning, if you'll have me."

"Of course I'll have you." Kate's gaze grew suddenly predatory. "Even on the counter, if you'd like."

Startled, Nikki stared at her before her face relaxed into a grin. She was always taken by surprise when Kate made comments like that; they seemed so odd coming from someone she perceived as so refined. "Promises, promises. I thought I'd help out until this afternoon, then head back to my place and get ready for our trip to Halifax."

"Do you want me to pick you up?

"Sure, that'll save me coming back here. Are you still planning to leave at three?"

Kate drained her coffee. "Yes. Business is slow between three and five on Saturdays so it won't hurt to close early. If we get away at three, we'll be there by four. You said this Venus Envy doesn't close until five. We'll have an hour to browse before we meet Susan for dinner."

Nikki laughed, wondering if Kate understood what they would be browsing for, and decided to change the subject again. "Did you know that Martin Elliot and Tiffany play tennis at the club?"

Kate fixed her with a penetrating stare. "No, I didn't. Why?"

Nikki offered her a bland, innocence personified. "I just thought it was interesting, that's all."

"Nikki, are you getting involved in something?"

"Involved in what?"

"Listen, Stephen Elliot's death was unfortunate but it was—"

"A murder."

"What?" Kate was wide-eyed.

"The toxicology report Rick got Wednesday says Stephen was poisoned by some kind of chemical solution from the factory. There's no word on how he got it, but family members were the only ones close enough to slip something to him."

"That's horrible. But if it was a chemical solution from the factory, he could have ingested it accidentally."

"At the Historical Society Dinner?" Nikki asked scornfully, before holding up her hand in mute apology. "I just think it's really interesting that the cousin and the older brother's wife spend a lot of time flirting on the tennis court. Do you know anything about him?"

"Only that he's the son of Hannah's youngest sister, from the less affluent side of the family."

Nikki's ears pricked. "What does that mean? 'Less affluent.'"

Kate seemed suddenly embarrassed at letting that slip, but she answered with her customary honesty. "The Watson side of the family never had as much money as the Elliot side. They come from far less fortunate circumstances."

"Like a trailer park, for instance?"

Kate stared at her, obviously baffled. "What are you talking about?"

"Nothing." Nikki filed that information away and decided to do some follow-up research later. Was that where Martin and Tiffany had met, growing up together on Court Street? If so, it made their connection run deeper than first glance indicated. "So he and Tiffany have that much in common, coming into money after having none."

"Martin didn't come into money," Kate sounded certain of that.

"No? That's not what Susan says."

"What would she know?"

"She says he doesn't do much but he seems to live pretty well. Maybe Tiffany's footing the bill."

"Why would she do that?"

"That's the question, isn't it? They seemed awfully cozy at the club. Something's going on there that's been going on for awhile."

Kate sighed. "Nikki, we were unfortunate to witness Stephen's death, but that's no reason to snoop into things that don't concern us."

"All right." Nikki wasn't going to argue, nor was she going to go looking for trouble, but if certain things came to her attention, she wasn't going to ignore them either. Kate would understand. She did the last time. Conjuring a bright smile, Nikki decided it was time for yet another change of subject. "Don't you have to open soon?"

CHAPTER NINE

K ate glanced at the clock in the kitchen and bit off an oath at her lover's words. Nikki obviously thought she had been afforded a reprieve from their conversation. Though Kate didn't have time to pursue it, she did intend to bring it up again later because she didn't believe that she had convinced Nikki to stay away from the Elliot investigation.

After taking a quick shower, Kate dressed in a light blue blouse and navy trousers, then dashed downstairs where sunshine filtered through the large glass windows, glinting off the dust motes in the air. She quickly moved the float from the safe to the cash register before finally unlocking the door. It was a beautiful spring morning, the fresh green vibrant in the bright light, and she flipped over the closed sign to read open, glancing down the street before returning to the interior.

On a notepad, she listed things she wanted done by closing, even as the first customers started to trickle in. A half hour or so later, Nikki wandered downstairs to check out the latest batch of lesbian mysteries, dressed in a T-shirt and a pair of shorts that showed off gloriously long legs. After wasting a few moments admiring her partner as she perused the new arrivals, Kate sent her out back to finish packing several boxes of returns. As she waited on the first wave of customers, she was reminded once more that morning was the busiest time on Saturdays, and if Nikki hadn't been there to lend a hand, she wouldn't be able to accomplish half of what she wanted. She really needed more help as soon as possible.

At precisely eleven o'clock, a young man entered the store, glancing around in interest. He boasted short, spiky hair, dyed a particularly unnatural white-blond, while several metal circles and studs pierced his face from his ears to his eyebrows to his bottom lip. His jeans were neat and his jacket very conservative, but his black T-shirt sported a psychedelic logo of some rock band. His dark brown eyes lit up when he saw Kate.

"Mrs. Shannon? I'm Todd Densmore." He shook her hand eagerly.

Over his shoulder, Kate saw Nikki doing her best not to laugh out loud and shot her a quelling look before turning her attention back to the young man. "I'm happy to meet you, Todd. Please, come with me."

Leaving Nikki to cover the counter, she led the teenager to the small office that doubled as her storage room. It was cramped, but since she did most of her paperwork upstairs, it usually wasn't a problem, except for moments like these. A small table struggled for space amid stacks of collapsed boxes and countless loose books that filled the narrow shelves.

Todd sat in one of the folding chairs while she sat in the other, and for a brief moment, they regarded each other much as two separate species would. Kate simply couldn't believe the fashion sense of today's youth, but she supposed it wasn't so different from the platform shoes and hip-hugging, wide-legged bell-bottoms of her teen years. Of course, those had apparently made a comeback as well, and she shook her head.

You know you're old when the fashions of your youth come back to haunt you, she thought wistfully. "So, Todd, tell me about your long-term goals. What do you see yourself doing in ten years?"

Todd hesitated, then bashfully looked down. "Can I be honest, Mrs. Shannon?"

Kate wondered if it was such a good idea, but she nodded. "Please."

"I haven't a clue. A lot of kids my age know exactly what university they want to go to, what profession they want to pursue, and how much money will make them happy, but I don't even know what I want to do next weekend. But I'm a hard worker, and if you give me a chance, you won't be sorry."

Kate was aghast. Linda did her best to prepare her students for the interviews, but they were still kids, and they had a habit of coming out with the most amazing stuff, things that an older person, experienced with job interviews, wouldn't think of saying.

"I'm sure I wouldn't." Kate glanced down at the resume and the list of questions she had prepared beside it. "What can you offer me that another applicant can't?"

Todd took his time to respond, his brow furrowed. Kate waited patiently and smiled again when his face brightened, indicating he had an answer. He really was a charming sort.

"My appearance."

Kate took another look at his mismatched outfit and facial adornment. "Your appearance?" Despite her best effort to moderate it, her tone was very skeptical.

"I'm no suit, despite what Mom made me wear today. I look like a kid, and that'll make other kids want to buy their books here rather than from the boring store at the mall. A gay bookstore is cool, and I'll make it cooler."

Well, I certainly hadn't considered that angle.

"This isn't a gay bookstore."

He frowned. "You carry gay books, right?"

"Of course."

"Then it's a gay bookstore." He shrugged.

Kate wasn't sure she could argue with that logic. Labels had a way of sticking despite one's best effort to prevent it.

"Is that important to you? That this bookstore carries alternative literature?"

He dropped his eyes. "Uh, maybe."

Kate suspected that was as far as she dared go in that direction at the moment. "You realize that this is a place of business and that it will never become a 'hangout.'"

"Absolutely."

Kate peered at him with a touch of doubt, but it wasn't an important point to pursue unless she hired him.

"I know you don't have any work experience since this is your first job application, but have you done anything that required a lot of organization and concentration, outside of your school work?"

Kate realized some people would consider his hesitation a lack of confidence, and it probably did indicate that to a certain extent, but she liked that he took his time to consider his answer rather than blurting out the first thing that popped into his head.

"I have my own Web site." He reached into his pocket and handed her a card with his name, the name of the site, and the URL listed underneath. "I'm really into Tolkien. I do a lot of research to make sure the information is accurate, which is very important to me." He stopped and blushed. "I know a lot of people would find it a waste of time, but I enjoy it."

"Doing what you enjoy is never a waste of time," Kate said honestly, studying the card. "I'll check this out. Seeing how you've set it up will tell me a lot about your skills in tackling tasks and organizing information."

She asked him a few more questions and then said good-bye, after assuring him that she would call Linda with her final decision later that night. Normally, she would fax an individual report on each job applicant to Linda so that she could help the students understand what went into the process and how they could improve for the next job interview. In this case, with only two applicants, Kate could make her report over the phone.

She glanced at her watch, seeing that she still had a few minutes before her second appointment. Out front, Nikki was leaning over the counter, talking animatedly to a couple, one of whom held several newly purchased books. Curious, Kate drifted over to the counter.

"Hi." Nikki immediately put her arm around Kate's waist, indicating that either the two women were lesbians or they were lesbian-friendly, since Nikki tended not to be publicly affectionate unless she felt completely safe. "This is Audrey and Debbie. I've told you about them."

"Yes." Kate reached out to shake hands. "Nikki's told me a lot about you."

"Uh-oh." Audrey grinned crookedly. "We should be worried."

Nikki laughed. "They're going on the canoe trip. You'll get to know them a little better there. You'll get to know a lot of people better." She suddenly looked worried, and the other two women exchanged a glance that Kate didn't completely understand. She let it go for the moment.

"Nikki tells me that you're both avid campers and hikers. I'm glad to hear that because I'll probably need all the help I can get."

"Aw, you'll be okay," Debbie told her. "It's an easy campground."

Nikki squeezed Kate lightly. "It's not like what they do when they go camping. These guys just grab their packs and go into the woods. We'll be in a park."

"It's a midrange area," Audrey said. "There aren't any electrical hookups or registration office, but there are fire pits, picnic tables, and refuse cans, plus it's free. No site fee."

Kate wasn't really assured by this pronouncement, but she didn't pursue it because the door opened and a teenager entered the store. The girl was wearing a somewhat shapeless dress, looking very uncomfortable in it, and Kate suspected that this was her next appointment. The teen drifted over to the magazine stand, glancing over to the counter now and again, and Kate was struck by the look in her pale eyes. It was almost hungry, as if she saw something there she wanted, yet was desperately afraid of it at the same time.

Nikki had apparently recognized the arrival as the probable applicant and dipped her head in unspoken agreement that she would continue to cover the counter. Kate excused herself to Audrey and Debbie before moving over to where the girl stood pretending to study the covers of the magazines.

"Beth? I'm Kate Shannon." The girl's handshake wasn't particularly firm, but it was clear to Kate that she was very shy. Obviously, this was someone who would benefit greatly from working with the public.

"Hello." Beth's voice was very soft. She was a little overweight, with brown hair that fell to her shoulders. Kate suspected her hairdresser could do wonders with it. Even though she hadn't hired the girl, she was already planning what she would do to bring out the best in her.

"My office is in the back." As they walked to the storage room, Kate glanced sideways at her prospective employee. She could do something about those clothes as well, she thought with all the zeal of a missionary. *Just give me a few weeks.*

Chapter Ten

Nikki finished filling Powder's bowl with fresh water and glanced around the apartment to make sure she wasn't forgetting anything. She looked forward to introducing Kate to the community down in the city, including elements such as gay bars that Kate had only read about. Nikki laughed at herself, suspecting that whatever she had read about was bound to be more exciting than the reality. As cosmopolitan as Halifax was to the Maritimes, it was still a far cry from cities like Toronto and Montreal, not that Nikki had ever sampled the nightlife there either.

Still, even if Kate didn't enjoy the bar scene, she would like Venus Envy, known as much for its books and candles as for its other merchandise. The only person in Truro who sold similar merchandise was an entrepreneur in Bible Hill who peddled fireworks out of his back yard. In addition to the roman candles and firecrackers, an entire wall of adult toys was hidden behind a large flag in the garage that doubled as his store. Nikki much preferred the quiet elegance of Venus Envy. It didn't leave her feeling as if she needed a shower.

She heard a sharp toot outside, from a black and silver SUV idling in the parking lot. She waved, though she wasn't sure Kate could see her, and snatched up her small overnight bag, making sure the door was locked behind her. After she climbed into the passenger seat of the "dykemobile," she leaned over and kissed Kate on the cheek.

Kate flashed her a quick smile and shifted into drive, pulling out onto Queen Street and coasting to the intersection where she waited for the light. She wore a pair of jeans, a black T-shirt and a gray blazer, and Nikki found her incredibly sexy.

"How did the interviews go? I didn't have a chance to ask before I left."

"Very well." Kate's hair blew lightly about her face from the breeze coming in through her window. She was a careful driver, both hands always on the wheel, paying close attention to the traffic around her as her gaze shifted often to check her rearview and side mirrors. Nikki always felt completely safe with her.

"Have you decided which student you're going to hire?"

Kate sighed. "It's tough. Todd is the better choice, I think. He seems well organized, he knows how to apply himself if his Web site is any indication, and he seems more self-possessed."

"Web site?"

"He has this extensive Web site devoted to *Lord of the Rings*. I know that sounds somewhat frivolous, but honestly, the amount of work that would have gone into creating it is incredible. He has reams of information organized into easily navigable paths. I was impressed. Plus he has a great deal of natural charm. The customers would take to him, despite all those rings hanging from his face."

"But?"

"But Beth would benefit far more from being hired." They turned down the street leading to the 102. "She's quite shy and withdrawn, and she doesn't have any fashion sense whatsoever. But she seems very intelligent."

Nikki made a small sound in the back of her throat, one of rueful amusement. "Sounds like someone I used to know."

Kate glanced at her as they accelerated down the swooping ramp onto the TransCanada. "Were you like that?"

"Not far from it." Nikki grinned. "I'm still not far from it."

"So you see my dilemma." A moment passed as they considered the problem.

"Hire them both."

Obviously surprised, Kate turned her head to look at her. "What?"

"I mean, can you afford to hire them both?"

"*I* can. The store…well, it would be tight, but yes, I could fit both salaries into the budget, particularly with the government incentives for hiring students." She tilted her head. "But besides not having to choose between them, what reason would I have?"

"Kate, for as long as I've known you, you've worked Friday night and Saturdays, even when you had help. I bet you'd work Thursday evenings too, except you reserve it and Tuesday night for all your social clubs and charities."

"So?"

"So who says you always have to work six days a week? Why not hire both students so you can take Friday night and Saturday off? Give yourself a break."

"I want and need to work, Nikki."

"I know that, and I'm not saying that you should give up working altogether." Nikki took her time. "I don't know if you noticed, but between my job and yours, we don't get to spend as much time together as I would like."

"I've noticed."

"I have a vacation coming up at the end of September. I want to spend that time with you, maybe even take a trip somewhere, but that can't happen if you're working." She lifted an eyebrow. "When *was* the last time you took a vacation?"

"I don't know. It's been quite a while."

Nikki put her hand lightly on Kate's thigh, feeling the muscles in it flex as Kate pressed on the accelerator. "Sweetie, you may need and want to work, but there *is* such a thing as working too much."

Kate made a face. "Maybe you're right. Maybe I *should* hire them both."

Nikki slid her hand higher on Kate's leg so that her fingers were perilously close to the heat radiating through the blue jeans. "It would be to your advantage. I want to spend plenty of private time with you."

Kate shifted away from the caress. "Not while I'm driving." She sounded chiding but amused.

Nikki chuckled but obediently withdrew her hand and focused on fishing some CDs out of the console. She selected a Dixie Chicks CD and put it in the player. Leaning back in her seat, she studied the profile of her lover, feeling amazingly happy and content.

"Do you know how much I love you?"

Kate smiled, a flash of white teeth between her wine-shaded lips. "As much as I love you?"

"More."

Kate glanced at her. "Perhaps. Perhaps not."

Nikki grinned, then looked at the highway. There wasn't much traffic at this time of day; it should take less time to reach the city than they anticipated.

"Where exactly is this store?"

"On Barrington Street, across from the Discovery Center. Do you know where that is?"

"I can find it. Eastside Mario's isn't far from it. Maybe we could meet Susan there for dinner."

"Great." Nikki didn't add that Introspections was also close by. She wondered if Susan would mind dropping into a gay bar for a few hours. Somehow, she didn't think so. Susan was remarkably open and liberal, more so than Kate in some ways.

As they approached Halifax, Nikki fell silent. They were coming in from the Dartmouth side, crossing one of the two major bridges that spanned the harbor between the twin cities. She enjoyed looking down at the dramatic sweep of the city skyline, the deep blue waters of the harbor, and the varied ships docked along the shore. Her friend Audrey was the captain of a tugboat and had undoubtedly helped bring in some of the massive vessels, including the American ships and submarines that were much larger than anything the Canadian navy boasted.

Before long, they had crossed the bridge and made the turn onto Barrington Street, running parallel to the waterfront. Kate decided to park in the lot across from Sackville Landing, which meant they would have to walk a few blocks up a fairly steep hill, but neither of them minded the exertion. People who lived in downtown Halifax usually had great calf muscles, the hilly streets surrounding the harbor providing plenty of exercise.

Nikki watched Kate's expression as they entered Venus Envy. The store was brightly lit, with tall wooden bookshelves and tables displaying an array of candles and knickknacks. Kate seemed lost right away, avidly perusing the various sections. Despite owning her own bookstore, she enjoyed shopping for books as much as Nikki did, and they delighted in finding out-of-the-way shops that offered an unusual selection. Even though Kate handled offerings from a host of independent publishers, she found several books here that she didn't have, and from the furrow in her brow, Nikki knew she was making notes about buying a few for her own store.

The other merchandise was located along the back wall and not readily apparent. As Kate walked around the last shelf, she was confronted with an impressive collection of adult toys and the store's most infamous display: a large rack of dildos in a dizzying selection of colors, shapes, and sizes. A sign helpfully encouraged the customers, "Please, play with the toys."

"Oh, my God."

Nikki resisted the urge to snicker.

"I, uh, thought this was a gay bookstore." Kate said in bemusement.

"It is, but mostly it's a store for women, and for those that love them. That's their slogan, as a matter of fact."

Kate swallowed, the muscles of her throat moving visibly. "Is this why you wanted to come here?"

"Well, you can find some of this stuff in Truro—"

"You can?" Kate stared at her in pure disbelief.

Nikki chuckled. "Sure, but it's a lot nicer to shop for it here." She tilted her head curiously. "Does it bother you?"

Kate shook her head. "I just…I, ah…didn't know you were into… uh, this sort of thing."

"I'm not, necessarily. I mean, I certainly don't *need* any of this stuff. I just thought it would be fun for us to check it out." Nikki slipped her arm around Kate's waist and whispered next to her ear, "Be honest, Kate, wouldn't you like to give a few of these things a try? We don't have to, but wouldn't it be interesting to experiment a little?"

Nikki heard Kate's breath catch and felt her tremble. Her color was rather high, her cheeks wore a rosy glow.

"I didn't expect this."

Nikki picked up a rabbit-shaped vibrator that had a variety of functions.

"Imagine this in action." She turned it on. The demos all were ready to operate. "See how the ears vibrate. If you were using it, the tips of the ears would be right against your—"

"I get the picture," Kate interrupted, glancing over her shoulder.

Nikki tried not to laugh. "It's a little too hard and plastic for my liking." She put it carefully back on the shelf and inclined her head at the silicone and gel dildos. "Perhaps one of those would be better?"

She shut her mouth and let Kate make up her own mind. But if she could judge the glint in those bluish-gray eyes, and she suspected that she could quite well by now, Kate was intrigued. Definitely intrigued.

❖

Kate found it difficult to breathe, knowing her face was flaming as certain images danced in her mind, inspired by all the adult accessories.

"Well," she managed in what she hoped was a diffident air, "I suppose we could pick up a few items, just to have them on hand."

Nikki's soft chuckle near her ear was positively lascivious, and a thrill shot up Kate's spine, zapping her groin like an electrical charge. It was from either the possibilities opening up to her, the taste of the forbidden, or just the proximity of the woman she loved so much. She had never considered utilizing aids to enhance the sexual experience, though she and Nikki constantly explored new sensations and experiences. To Kate's surprise, as well as expressing their deeper emotions, making love with Nikki was pure and simple fun. Sometimes they laughed so hard in bed that they could barely catch their breaths, enjoying each other not just as lovers, but also as playmates. Were "toys" such an odd addition to that interaction?

Gathering her courage, she picked up a smaller black dildo, surprised at how pleasant it felt in her hand. Soft and smooth, it was filled with some gelatinous material that maintained its firmness, yet was yielding at the same time. Nikki had drifted away and was now browsing through the contraptions hanging on the wall, a varied collection of leather straps, belts, and buckles. Kate had never seen that type of harness, but she knew what it could be used for, and she considered the dildo in her hand with renewed deliberation.

As Nikki turned and suddenly smiled, Kate envisioned her actually utilizing the combination of merchandise to pleasure her as a man would.

She shivered. Sex with her husband had never been terrible, mostly because of her honest affection and caring for him, but it had never been particularly pleasant, either. Yet, imagining Nikki offering the same sort of physicality left Kate aching with desire and longing to explore such carnal delights as soon as possible.

"What do you think of this?" Nerves made her voice quiver, leaving her embarrassed.

Nikki took it from her and evaluated it carefully. "For you or me?" she teased, as she eyed her from beneath her lashes.

"Maybe both?" Kate moistened her lips, her mouth dry.

"Would you like to do me like that, Kate?" Nikki moved close to Kate, speaking in a low voice. "Spread me out on the bed and just *fuck* me?"

The sudden surge of passion that swept through Kate left her weak in the knees. She had never experienced such an erotic sensation, and Nikki wasn't even touching her. Heat radiated from Nikki, brushing over her like a palpable thing, and if they weren't in public, Kate would immediately leap on her and tear her clothes completely off.

Nikki drew back, smiling gently as if she knew her effect. "I think that could be arranged."

Kate thought she would faint.

"We'll need a belt," Nikki continued in a conversational tone. "Leather, I think…one with a vibrator attachment maybe? We'll need lubrication, too."

They spent the next few moments carefully choosing accessories. Kate was amazed to be actually shopping for things she had only heard about in dirty jokes and catalogues sent in plain brown wrappers.

If only the Historical Society could see me now. They'd probably drop dead of a collective heart attack. As it was, Kate wasn't entirely steady on her feet as Nikki added some massage oil, several candles, and a few books to the pile, and then carried everything over to the counter. The salesclerk treated the transaction as casually as if they had been buying a pack of gum, leaving Kate both relieved and wondering exactly what she had expected, that the girl behind the counter would leer and ask what they were going to do with all this equipment?

She was still shaky when they left, blinking in the bright sunshine.

"Are you all right?"

She felt suddenly as if their ages were reversed, she the callow youth exposed to an adult world that she had never imagined.

"I'm just…I guess I'm not used to this."

"Was it fun?"

"Oh, yes."

"Let's take this back to the car." Nikki lifted the bag. "Do you want to call Susan?"

"That's a good idea." Kate dug into her pocket for her cell phone. As they walked back to the car, she made arrangements for her to meet them at the nearby restaurant.

"It'll take her about an hour to get dressed and call a cab," Kate explained after she had cut the connection.

Nikki shut the trunk, their new acquisitions safely stored from sight. "Want to walk along the waterfront?"

"That sounds wonderful."

When Nikki took her hand, Kate decided that she must be more comfortable showing affection in the city than at home, perhaps because they were more anonymous here, far away from the small town mentality of Truro. They walked along the landing and noted the newly constructed sculptures and a museum, several shops, picturesque docks, and a graveled trail right next to the water.

It was colder here, the wind stiff as it came off the harbor, chilling Kate as she huddled in her light jacket. They sat on a bench, and Nikki put her arm around her, warming her with her body heat.

"I'm glad you suggested we come down this weekend." Kate murmured.

"I am, too." Kate felt her deposit a kiss on the top of her head. "I really enjoy spending time with you, Kate. Even if we weren't a couple, I'd want to spend every moment with you. I *like* you."

Kate was touched. She knew Nikki wasn't always comfortable speaking about her feelings, perhaps because of her previous heartbreaking affair. Nikki hesitated to share what was on her mind and was constantly on guard, never letting most people know what she felt. Kate understood. She didn't always know how to express her love and desire for Nikki either.

"I like being with you, too." Kate hugged her, then drew back. "Shall we head for the restaurant?"

"Good idea." Nikki shivered. "It's cold down here."

Chapter Eleven

Susan was already standing on the sidewalk when Nikki and Kate arrived at the Italian eatery.

She greeted them effusively, hugging Kate and staring intently at her face. "I swear, love must agree with you, Katie. You're looking better every time I see you." She also gave Nikki an affectionate hug. "How are you, Nikki?"

"I'm fine. It's really good to see you again."

"At least it's under better circumstances. Let's hope nobody drops dead over dinner tonight." Kate winced, but her reaction didn't slow Susan down one iota. Linking her arm in Nikki's, she said, "I want you to tell me everything you've found out so far."

In the restaurant, they settled in a booth, Kate and Nikki pressing their legs against each other beneath the table in hidden connection. After ordering, they brought each other up to date and were finished by the time their food arrived. The talk immediately turned to Stephen's death, despite Kate's desire not to go there.

"So Kate tells me that you used to date him." Nikki eyed Susan almost challengingly.

"A couple of times in high school, back in the Jurassic era." Susan lowered her tone suggestively. "He was the class 'bad boy.'"

"Really? How so?" Nikki's keen interest filled Kate with dread, and she nudged Susan's foot under the table. Susan offered a blank look, obviously missing the warning, and returned her attention to Nikki.

"Oh, you know, the usual. He drank, ran around on the weekends with his buddies, drove fast cars and wrecked half of them, which Mommy and Daddy replaced immediately. He was always on the verge of getting kicked out of school, not to mention his occasional brush with the law. He was a wild one, that's for sure, and, honestly, how could an impressionable young thing like me resist?"

"Easily, I would think," Kate said acidly.

Susan finally took note of her tone, at least, apparently realizing Kate didn't care to explore the topic.

"Anyway, my parents put a stop to the whole thing, and my whole rebellious stage ended with a whimper instead of a bang, much to my disappointment." Susan's emphasis on the word "bang" left little doubt what she meant, and Nikki laughed while Kate winced.

She still remembered how desperately she had tried to convince Susan that losing her virginity to Stephen Elliot was a very bad thing, not something to be proud of, a real bone of contention between the then teenage girls, when everything was so big and dramatic and "forever." Fortunately, the senior O'Briens made the whole point moot before anything happened and before Kate and Susan's friendship was damaged beyond repair.

"So, what would you like to do tonight?" Susan finally seemed to sense Kate's discomfort and changed the subject. "Catch a movie? Maybe check out the museum on the waterfront before it closes?"

"I was thinking we could drop by Introspections," Nikki said.

Susan immediately looked interested. "The gay bar up the street?"

Kate frowned, surprised at the suggestion. "But—"

"What a great idea! I'd love to go." Susan looked thoughtful. "I've never been in a gay bar. Do you think some woman will hit on me? Hey, maybe I'll get lucky!"

"Susan!" Kate stared at her friend, who looked completely unrepentant as Nikki grinned. "What would we do in a gay bar?"

"We could dance." Nikki gave her a soft look. "I don't get to dance with you very often. I could also show you off."

Though Kate wasn't sure how to take that remark, she decided it was a compliment of sorts. "Really? Show me off?"

Nikki blushed.

Outvoted, Kate stifled her protests and leaned back in her chair. If Nikki wanted to try it, and Susan was ready for anything she might encounter, then the least she could do was be open to the experience.

❖

Kate didn't know what she had been expecting, but she was rather disappointed. Introspections was pretty similar to every other bar she had ever been in. The décor was nothing special; the tables were made of the same heavy wood found in the taverns in Truro and the place was poorly lit. Perhaps the owners were trying to create a mood, but in reality, the dim lighting only prevented the patrons from seeing how dingy everything was. There were a couple of pool tables in a back room, and a fair-sized dance floor occupied one end of the bar.

Only the patrons were different. They were predominantly female, and the women were all in couples or groups, while the men kept to themselves. The scene reminded her of an adult version of a junior high dance, with the genders politely ignoring each other, except for a couple of women at the bar in evening dress. Several men were hovering around these women, and Kate wondered if they were hookers before she realized they weren't women at all. As she sat down at a table, she wondered how these drag queens managed to look better than most of the women she knew. Some of her straight friends could definitely benefit from their expertise with hair and makeup.

"You should see this place on Pride Day," Nikki said after they ordered a round of drinks. "It's absolutely packed."

"We should make an effort to get down here that weekend."

"I'd like that." Around them, the music throbbed with an insistent beat. "Would you like to dance?"

Uncertainly, Kate glanced at Susan, who smiled and waved her away. "Go on, I'll be fine. Maybe someone will ask me to dance, too."

Somewhat guilty about leaving her friend to her own devices, Kate allowed herself to be swept out onto the dance floor. She was nervous at first, not just because she was with a woman, but because everyone else seemed so young and she wasn't sure of the steps. They danced several fast numbers and then a slow one that she found particularly appealing, clinging to Nikki as they swayed amid the other couples, completely safe to show their feelings for each other. There was a heady sort of freedom in that, Kate realized, a sense of being a part of a community.

"I'm glad you suggested this," she murmured as they drifted back to their table. "I'm having a really good time."

"I hoped you would."

Nikki's expression appeared to be equal parts happiness and relief. She must have been somewhat apprehensive about sharing this part of her world, and Kate squeezed her hand affectionately.

Surprisingly, their table was occupied by a group of extremely handsome young men, many of whom were hanging on Susan's every word and regarding her with surprising devotion. As Kate and Nikki approached, Susan introduced her new acquaintances, offering not only their names, but also where they were from and what they all did for a living.

"Gay guys," Nikki told Kate. "Straight chicks love 'em, and they love anyone who will mother them."

Kate didn't know what to say. Some things never changed. Even in a gay bar, Susan managed to garner most of the male attention.

CHAPTER TWELVE

I ran into Audrey and Debbie Saturday morning," Nikki said as she sipped the milkshake made with frozen blueberries, yogurt, and skim milk. Lately, the Mayflower Diner had started serving low-fat alternatives to their regular menu. Nikki suspected it had to do with the cholesterol test of Eddie, the diner's cook and owner; the results had left him shaken and Addy tremendously scared.

Nikki had already decided to get into the best possible shape, so she was rather pleased with the new selections, though she seemed to be the only one who ordered any of them. Kim, meanwhile, was perfectly content with her triple cheeseburger and fries, served with a thick chocolate milkshake made with real ice cream and chocolate syrup.

"What have those two been up to?"

"They were down in the city that morning and popped by the bookstore on their way home." Nikki poked at her salad, wondering what the red and white bits were. A cautious bite identified them as radishes. "They're looking forward to the canoe trip."

"A lot of people are." Kim glanced at Nikki beneath her eyelashes. "The Summer Twins offered to provide the entertainment."

"Meaning what?" Nikki was perturbed. What would those two come up with as a form of entertainment?

"I don't know. I told them that after a day on the river, people probably wouldn't be in the mood for organized entertainment."

"Smooth."

"I thought so," Kim said smugly. She took a healthy bite of her burger and chewed only a couple of times before she swallowed.

Nikki wondered why her friend had never choked to death. Shaking her head at the thought, she leaned over and picked up her tennis bag. "I'd better get going. I'm hoping to pick up a match this afternoon."

"Want a lift? I'm heading home so I can drop you off at the club."

Nikki waited until Kim finished her meal before paying their respective bills and leaving. Kim's blue Honda was parked up the street, and Nikki slung her bag into the backseat before slipping into the front. The car's interior was hot, and Nikki rolled down her window as Kim drove to the tennis club, letting the slight breeze cool her off.

As they turned up the quiet side street that ran alongside the tennis club, a car pulled out of a parking spot and cruised past them. It was the Mustang convertible with the top down, revealing Martin Elliot in the passenger's seat with Tiffany laughing and tossing her blond hair behind the wheel like some model in a television commercial.

"Who's that?" Kim had noted Nikki's intense interest in the passing vehicle.

"Martin Elliot and his cousin's wife. I think they're having an affair."

"Yeah?" Kim didn't appear interested as she stopped by the gate leading to the tennis club.

Nikki looked over her shoulder, watching as the car turned left on Brunswick Street. "Let's follow them."

"What?" Kim looked over at her, her blue eyes wide.

"Turn around. I want to see where they go."

Kim stared at her as if she had suddenly lost her mind, but she took her foot off the brake and put it on the accelerator, doing a quick U-turn on the lightly traveled side street. "What if they spot us?"

"Truro's a small town." Nikki's eyes were intent on the vehicle ahead of them. "There's a limited number of ways to get to places, and everyone uses them, so they shouldn't notice someone's following them deliberately unless they go somewhere out of the way. Besides, their car is easy to spot while yours is, well—"

"Ugly?"

"I would have said nondescript." Nikki patted the dash of the little blue Honda affectionately. "Perfect for surveillance."

"I'll be sure to tell Lynn." Kim's voice was tinged with amusement. "She wants to sell it and buy a van. Maybe we can add that feature to the newspaper ad."

"You're selling the car?" Nikki was oddly stricken. She didn't often need a vehicle, but when she did, Kim readily lent her this one, and Nikki had become rather fond of it. She didn't think her friend would be as quick to lend her a brand-new car, nor would she enjoy driving it as much.

"Yeah, Lynn's business is doing well, and I just got a raise at the Sportsplex. Lynn replaced her truck with the Mazda last year, and we decided it was time for me to trade up as well. We want something that can haul stuff around."

"So you're going to trade it in?"

"Actually, no, we think we'll get more with a private sale." Kim glanced at her friend. "You interested?"

"I hadn't thought about buying a car."

"Well, you're making pretty good money at the police station now. Maybe it's time you considered it."

"Maybe." Nikki examined the idea, starting to like it more and more with every passing second. Her mind was alive with possibilities until she saw the black Mustang accelerate toward Robie Street.

Her heart sank. The route led out of town, and she was afraid Kim wouldn't be willing to follow their quarry all the way to Shortt's Lake, which was probably where the Elliots were headed. Disappointed, she was about to tell Kim to go back to the tennis club when the convertible cruised past the ramps leading to the 102, the customary route out to the lake.

"Just a few more minutes," she begged. "If they look like they're going way out of town, we'll turn around."

"No problem."

Nikki knew she was fortunate in her choice of friends. They let her be as weird as she wanted and didn't say a word about it. She was rewarded when the car turned again, this time onto the Lower Truro road.

"That's odd. They're heading back into town."

Kim smiled. "No, they're not. They're going to the Tideview Motel."

"There's a motel up here?" Even as she asked, she saw the motel's huge billboard a short distance ahead, the Mustang turned into the motel's parking lot.

Kim drove casually by and continued down the road a hundred meters or so until she reached the parking lot of a heavy equipment sales depot, positioning the car so that it faced the motel before she turned off the engine. "The binoculars are in the dash," she informed Nikki.

Thankful that Kim had replaced the binoculars lost during the unfortunate encounter with an arsonist in the woods, Nikki hauled them out and peered through them at the motel on the hill just in time to see Martin come out of the office and get back into the car. Tiffany backed out of the parking space and drove to the far end of the sprawling structure, stopping in front of the last unit. Martin took a bag from the backseat, then he and Tiffany entered the motel room hand-in-hand.

"Wow, I guess this proves it." Nikki felt the same tiny thrill she always did when she discovered information she wasn't supposed to have. "I just didn't expect them to be so open about it."

"What's so open?" Kim peered up the road cynically. "Seriously, if any questions come up, they'll just say they're playing tennis. Enough people see them playing at the club, and if they take a half hour or an hour detour on the way home, no one really notices. People gossip, but only if there's something unusual enough to gossip about."

Nikki lowered the binoculars, regarding Kim with renewed respect. "That's brilliant. How'd you come up with that?"

"If you're up to no good, then it's easier if whatever you're doing is hidden in plain sight." Kim looked back toward the motel. "But what does all this prove? I mean, if Stephen's wife was fooling around with the cousin, I could see some kind of motive, but this is Andrew's wife."

"Maybe Stephen found out about them and was going to tell Andrew," Nikki speculated. "Or maybe Stephen was also having an affair with Tiffany, and Martin decided to remove his rival."

"Or maybe it has nothing to do with anything at all."

"Maybe not." Nikki peered through the glasses once more, refusing to allow Kim's skepticism to dampen her investigative fervor. "Martin lives in an apartment on Marshwood Drive. He lost his license last year for driving under the influence. The Mustang belongs to her."

"Nice to see that you've been putting your position at the police station to good use." Kim sounded faintly sarcastic. "What does Kate think about it?"

"I haven't mentioned it to her." Nikki hesitated. "She doesn't like me messing around in police investigations."

"Who can blame her? The last time you snooped, you were almost barbequed."

Nikki flinched. "I know." She lifted the field glasses again. "That's odd."

"What?"

"Another car just pulled up beside the Mustang" Nikki narrowed her eyes. "Some guy is getting out and going into the room. He didn't knock either. He's carrying something in a grocery bag."

"Andrew?"

"No, it's a stranger." Nikki focused the glasses on the car. "Write this down." Kim sighed and found a piece of paper and pen in her handbag. "CDW 808."

"What are you going to do with that? Run the license plate?"

"Yes. Then I'll know who was visiting Martin and Tiffany. I wonder what he's doing there?"

"A threesome?" Kim suggested.

"Two guys and a girl? Poor girl."

"Are you kidding?" Kim laughed. "From what I hear, two is better. Don't forget that guys run out of steam after they get their rocks off. They don't have our advantages of being able to keep going and going and going—"

"Like the pink bunny."

"Why do you think he's pink? Besides, I'm convinced the bunny's a girl."

Nikki chuckled, but even as she did, her mind was on the motel and the people going into it. What were the Elliots up to?

CHAPTER THIRTEEN

"You seem pensive tonight."

Fresh from a Saturday evening at the movies and a late supper at the Wooden Hog, Kate and Nikki were pleasantly weary and looking forward to calling it a night at Kate's apartment. Putting her coat into the closet, Kate watched as Nikki went in and sat on the sofa. "Is something wrong?"

"Just thinking." Nikki shrugged. "I was talking to Kim this week about selling her car."

"The blue Honda?" Kate sat beside Nikki, pleased when her lover immediately draped a possessive arm around her shoulders.

"Yeah. She wants thirty-five hundred for it, but she offered it to me for three."

"You're thinking of buying it?"

"I wouldn't mind having my own car. That way I wouldn't have to borrow one when I wanted to go somewhere. Plus, it would be nice to drive to work sometimes, especially when it's raining."

Kate immediately thought about offering to buy her the car, but restrained herself. "You should have a car," she said instead. "Are you going to buy it?"

Nikki frowned. "I don't know where I'll come up with the money. I mean, give me a few months and I could save it up, but I can't expect Kim to wait that long."

Again Kate swallowed the words that jumped unbidden to her tongue. Money was a touchy subject with them, and three thousand dollars was enough to cause trouble if not handled correctly. "Have you considered taking out a loan at the bank?"

"I could try. I probably won't get it."

"Why not? You have a well-paying job."

"Yes, but I've only had it since the beginning of March." Nikki stared off at the room, her eyes dark. "After high school, when I was first working at the diner, I got a few credit cards. It was like having free money, and I got into a lot of trouble with them very quickly. I cut them up and managed to pay them all off, but I really can't be trusted with one. That's certain to be on my credit record."

"If it's any consolation, you're not the only young person who's gotten into trouble with them," Kate said. "Personally, I don't believe anyone should be issued a credit card unless they have a five-year work history and some awareness of how to handle things financially. Instead, they give them to kids in college."

"Plus I'm still paying on my student loan," Nikki sighed. "I doubt my bank would want to increase the debt load."

Kate pursed her lips, thinking about how she would present her idea. "You should try anyway. If they won't give you the money, I will." She held up her hand to forestall the protest she knew was coming. "I'm talking about a loan, Nikki, not a gift. I'll have my lawyer draw up a contract and even charge interest if you want." She gazed at her lover. "Please let me do this, darling. You should have a car if you want it. I know you'll pay the loan back."

Nikki's expression was a mix of hope and wariness, torn between pride and the need to accept help. Kate forced herself to be patient, remaining silent as she worked it out.

"Only if the bank won't give it to me," Nikki said finally.

"Of course." Kate felt a flicker of triumph curl one corner of her mouth up in a smile, and she shifted so that she could slip her arm around Nikki's waist in the hollow between her body and the back of the sofa. Wrapping the other across Nikki's stomach, she rested her head on Nikki's chest, feeling the throb of her heartbeat beneath her cheek. "Let me know when you need it, if you need it."

After a pause, Nikki kissed the top of Kate's head, hugging her. "Thank you. This means a lot to me."

"You're welcome." Kate spent a few moments delighting in the sensation of her lover's body, basking in her fragrance and warmth. "Anything else going on that I should know about?"

Another pause, significant in its weight, and Kate lifted her head to look into Nikki's eyes, suddenly tense. "Darling?"

Nikki appeared definitely sheepish. "I saw Martin and Tiffany Elliot at the tennis club again."

"Oh?" Kate prompted, suspecting there was more to it than that.

"I followed them."

"You what?" Kate was amazed at how even her voice sounded.

"Actually, Kim and I followed them. They went to the Tideview Motel in Lower Truro."

"I see."

"But get this, it wasn't what I thought." Excitement colored Nikki's tone. "Ten minutes after they went into the motel room, some other guy shows up and joins them. He doesn't knock, he just walks right in and there's no big blowup, so obviously they were expecting him."

"Who was it?" Kate was drawn into the story despite her best intentions.

"I don't know. It wasn't one of the Elliots, at least not one I've seen before. He was there for something, and it probably wasn't on the up-and-up. Otherwise why would they be meeting at a dive like the Tideview?"

"How do you know it's a dive?" Certain thoughts and ideas involving Nikki and a motel room suddenly spun through Kate's mind. She didn't much like the images they inspired.

"Kim told me." Nikki's unconcern immediately shut down Kate's sudden detour into the realm of a jealous suitor. "We wrote down the guy's car license number, and I'm going to have someone run it for me the next time I go in to work."

"Can you do that?"

"I don't know. Maybe Rick *might* run the plates for me. Depending on what he finds, I may or may not have to tell him why I'm asking."

Kate took a deep breath. "Nikki, I can't believe Rick would do such a thing and I don't like you getting involved in this."

"Yes, you mentioned that." Nikki's tone suddenly became very even, her face expressionless.

Kate started to speak, checked herself, and thought about what she wanted to say and how she wanted to say it. "I don't want to tell you what to do," she said finally. "That's not it at all, but this sort of thing can be dangerous. I'm afraid for you."

Nikki's eyes, which had started out a brilliant blue behind her glasses, hard and unyielding, abruptly softened, and she gathered Kate to her, brushing her lips over her temple. "I'm not going to do anything stupid, Kate. I promise. I also promise to tell you everything I'm doing. That's why I told you about following Martin and Tiffany. I don't want to hide anything or keep you out of my life." She held Kate's stare. "But it *is* my life."

Kate sighed. She always had to be careful when she objected to Nikki's behavior. Their age difference made it easy for her to come across as a parent or older sibling, and she didn't want to be perceived as either. Plus, she had to fight against her own propensity to treat her young lover like she treated her part-time employees, as an inexperienced and naïve person who always needed her guidance. She could offer her opinion and advice on occasion, yes, but she could never make Nikki think she believed her incapable of making her own decisions, not if she wanted this relationship to succeed.

"What if they had noticed you and Kim following them?"

"Then they probably would have tried to lose us."

"And then?"

"They would have." Nikki laughed. "Kim was driving. She managed to lose the group on the way to the South Shore for one of our outings, and that was when the person she was following was *deliberately* trying to lead her."

Kate frowned, not amused, and skewered Nikki with a stare. "Is this the real reason you want a car? So you can 'tail' people?"

Nikki looked thoughtful. "You know, I hadn't considered it, but what a great idea. I was really lucky that Kim was giving me a lift to the tennis club. If I had been walking, I wouldn't have been able to follow them, and I wouldn't have found out what I did." Kate closed her eyes and groaned, dropping her head to Nikki's chest. "What?"

"I give up," Kate said wearily. "You're going to meddle in this whether I like it or not. All I can do is be there to pick up the pieces when it's all over."

Nikki rested her cheek against Kate temple. They sat together for a while before Nikki nudged her gently. "You know I love you, Kate. I really don't want to worry you."

Kate didn't say what was on the tip of her tongue. It wouldn't accomplish anything, nor did she think Nikki would hear it. Instead, she contented herself with hugging Nikki tightly.

After another pause, Nikki kissed her hair, and murmured, "So, have you thought about trying out the toys we picked up at Venus Envy?"

Kate felt the same sudden spurt of illicit pleasure that she had experienced in the store, a delightful sense of the forbidden, of unexplored territory just waiting to be discovered. It was suddenly hard to breathe, and her heart began to pound in her chest, throbbing with the same beat that pulsed in her loins. If Nikki had been deliberately trying to take her mind off her detective work, she couldn't have chosen a better method.

"Seriously?"

"Well, it seems a shame to spend all that money and not try them out."

Kate debated the issue for all of two seconds. "Um, all right."

Whatever the night might hold, it would certainly keep her from worrying about Nikki and what she planned to be up to in the future.

CHAPTER FOURTEEN

I'm glad you find this funny," Kate said as she opened the wooden box she'd stored in her nightstand.

Nikki laughed at the sight of her lover gazing pink-faced at the contents. "I hate to break this to you, but no matter how sexy all this is, it's also a bit silly. I mean, no woman looks particularly gorgeous with a plastic pecker hanging off her."

"You're not making this easy."

"Sorry." Nikki slipped her arms around Kate's waist and sought out her lips, kissing her with lazy pleasure until she relaxed. "This is going to be fun, I promise."

"I know. It's just…I've never done anything like this before."

"It's just play, sweetie. We won't do anything you don't like. Just say the word and we'll toss everything back in the box. Then I'll make love to you all night long without any help."

"You say the sweetest things."

"It wasn't sweet. I just have the most beautiful woman in the world in my arms. Who needs toys?"

They kissed again, and then once more, tongues touching in a sweet duel of rising desire. Kate made a soft sound of happiness as Nikki started to loosen her clothes, peeling off her blouse before unfastening her trousers. Undergarments were tossed carelessly aside and then, between the kisses and brief caresses, Nikki quickly divested herself of her own clothes. She groaned as she felt Kate's compact body against hers, delighting in the silky smooth skin and the soft curves that pressed against her more angular form.

"So how should we do this?" Kate whispered as she stroked Nikki's sides and back lightly.

"Well, I know what you were imagining when you picked it out,"

Nikki teased her gently. "So you put it on first and we'll see how it goes."

Kate swallowed convulsively, the muscles moving visibly in her elegant neck. She released Nikki and turned back to the bed to open the box, revealing a black gel-filled dildo, a pink butt plug, a vibrator shaped like a penis, and a bottle of lubricant, all resting on a tangle of straps and buckles. She picked up the harness, eyeing it with a bemused smile.

"Uh, I don't suppose you know how this works."

"We'll figure it out."

After a few minutes of discussion and two abortive attempts to put it on, Kate finally managed to secure the contraption to her body. Nikki looked at the leather band covering her lover's auburn triangle, the strap disappearing between her legs, and felt her nipples harden in desire.

She quickly picked up the dildo and handed it to Kate. "This fits through the opening in the middle."

Kate slipped the artificial penis through the hole in the center of the leather triangle, adjusting it a few times until she was satisfied. "You're right," she said with a blush and a smirk. "It does look absurd."

Nikki leered at her. "Funny, I was thinking that you look pretty hot."

Kate blushed prettily again. "Have you…" she began, and then stopped as if unsure how to say it. "You told me once that you'd never been with a man."

"I haven't." Nikki studied Kate's expression, then realized what she might be curious about. "Um, well, I've been with other women who've wanted me to use toys on them, but I've never had one used on me. So I'm technically a virgin. It's up to you to pop my cherry, Kate." She knew she'd said the wrong thing as soon as the words left her lips, but she couldn't snatch them back.

"God, Nikki." Kate was suddenly very solemn, and Nikki wished she hadn't been so glib.

"Hey." She pulled Kate into her arms, ignoring the cool hardness of the dildo between their bodies. "It's okay. I'm only kidding about being a virgin. C'mon, we've made love before, and you've been inside me plenty of times."

Kate drew back, frowning slightly. "This is different, Nikki. This could hurt you."

"Kate, we've got plenty of lubrication, all the time in the world, and, seriously, you're not attached to the thing. You're not suddenly going to be swept up in the whole situation and forget what you're doing. Besides, it's not all that big, is it?"

Kate took a breath, glancing down at it again before meeting Nikki's eyes. "No, it's not particularly large, but darling—"

"Kate, I trust you completely," Nikki interrupted her before she could really start on the objections. "I've imagined what it might be like, but until you, I've never wanted anyone to do this to me. I *want* you to make love to me this way." She took Kate's hand and drew it down so that it was between her thighs. "Do you believe me now?"

Kate caught her breath, and Nikki knew she was assessing the wealth of moisture pooling at the juncture of her legs. Lowering her head as Kate fondled her slowly, Nikki drew her closer, sliding her hands down to her lover's buttocks, squeezing them lightly. "Are you saying you don't want me?"

"I'd never say that," Kate murmured, pressing against her. "But darling, I just…I need you to be sure."

"I am, Kate. I want you to be my first, my last, and my only one." She moistened her lips with her tongue as she felt Kate's fingers move over her gently. "I know you'll do absolutely right by me."

"We'll take things very slowly," Kate promised, her voice rather unsteady.

"Oh, I want you to be slow." Nikki swallowed against a mouth that seemed suddenly dry. "Until I want you to go fast."

Kate shivered. "Darling, if you only knew how much this means to me, your wanting me to do this…"

Nikki regretted that she had allowed this to become so serious, but if it meant that much to Kate, this perception of taking Nikki's supposed virginity, then she certainly wasn't going to argue about it. Besides, she couldn't ask for a better, more considerate lover for her first time, knowing with absolute certainty that Kate would focus completely on providing the most pleasure possible.

"I love you," Nikki told her quietly. "I want you in every way imaginable."

"I love you too, my darling." Kate continued to toy with Nikki, swirling gentle fingertips over her as Nikki spread her legs wider, offering more of herself to Kate. "Let's get on the bed."

Setting aside the wooden box, Nikki crawled onto the mattress, settling back onto the blue and ivory comforter. She carefully swallowed back her smile when she watched Kate crawl onto the bed with her, the dildo dangling from her groin. Reaching out, she pulled Kate down on top of her, seeking out her mouth in a searing kiss. Kate returned it hungrily, lips and tongue moving over Nikki's face and neck as if she couldn't get enough of her.

"Just lie back and relax," Kate told her in a throaty voice. "Let me do all the work."

Nikki smiled over the remark. The age difference between them showed up at some odd times, and this was one of them. It was obvious Kate considered herself the authority in this aspect of lovemaking and wanted to be completely in charge. Nikki had no problem with that.

Kate's body was a soft weight on top of her, pressing down with comforting familiarity. Her hands moved lightly over Nikki's skin, her mouth gentle where it kissed and licked her breasts. Nikki wasn't particularly well endowed; where Kate's breasts were fuller and more shapely, Nikki's were pert and sensitive, even more so when Kate made a special effort to accord them the proper attention.

Closing her eyes, Nikki let her head fall back onto the pillow, feeling the waves of pleasure steadily build as Kate caressed her. She almost cried out in disappointment when the tender touch stopped, and she half sat up, reaching out for her lover. "Where're you going?"

"Just getting ready," Kate retrieved the tall bottle of lube from her nightstand and squirted a blob of the clear, gelatinous fluid onto her palm." This feels like…well, a lot like you."

For some reason, that made Nikki feel oddly self-conscious, and she held her breath as she watched Kate slather the lubricant all over the dildo with sensual deliberation, making it gleam blackly in the low wattage of the bedroom lamp. Suddenly this whole scene was a lot less amusing, and very erotic, making the lower muscles in her abdomen clench in anticipation.

"Ready?" Kate leaned over her, bending down to kiss her with a deep, reverent tenderness.

"Sure." Nikki let out a slow, shuddering breath.

"You stop me if it becomes the slightest bit uncomfortable."

"I promise."

Reaching down and placing her hand gently on the inside of Nikki's thigh, Kate carefully spread her lover's legs apart, settling between them as she prepared to enter her for the first time.

❖

Kate felt somewhat nervous as she knelt over Nikki, but when she looked into the brilliant blue eyes, she saw only love and utter trust. Slowly, she rubbed the toy's rounded head against Nikki, dipping it briefly in the pool of wetness before swirling it lightly over the tiny ridge of her clit.

"Like that?"

"It feels good." Nikki had her knees bent to either side of Kate's hips, opening herself completely.

Kate stared down, stunned by the sight of the dildo rubbing against the delicate pink of Nikki's tender folds. "I want to be inside you. I'll go slow, so you can adjust."

"Okay." Nikki's smile was one of pure sensuality.

Kate couldn't imagine anything more arousing than the sight of her dildo slowly sinking into her lover's opening. Hindered somewhat by the tightness she encountered, Kate didn't try to force past it. Instead, she carefully eased the mushroom head deeper. The toy was both larger and thicker than Kate's fingers, and it had to be more intrusive than anything Nikki had ever experienced before.

Kate stopped when Nikki made a small sound, but her lover immediately urged, "Keep going. I want you all the way inside me."

Kate experienced a sharp thrill at the words and Nikki's rapid, unsteady breathing. Taking great care, she pushed steadily forward until she felt the warm, flesh of their bellies connect. Groaning, she lowered her body until she was resting on Nikki, breasts against breasts, stomach against stomach, Nikki's arms around her. She felt strangely connected to the toy buried in her lover. Its lack of sensation was meaningless; her own excitement was tied into the exchange of trust between her and Nikki, and an unfamiliar sense of power. She began to move her hips, tiny strokes knowing Nikki would feel every small movement inside her. "You have no idea how much this is turning me on," she murmured

breathlessly. "It's so incredible to be inside you like this, Nikki. I mean, I know it's not really me—"

"It *is* you," Nikki whispered. "It's you inside me that makes it feel so good to me. Does that make sense?"

Kate exhaled as she tumbled down into the warm gaze, feeling surrounded by her lover. "Yes, it makes perfect sense."

She continued her slow undulation, increasingly aware of a pressure against her center. "I think they designed this so that I could get something out of it, too. There's some kind of lump protruding inside." She caught her breath as she felt it bump over her.

"Sounds like you found the magic bullet." Nikki regarded her with a slight smile. "There's a small vibrator built into the harness where it meets your pussy."

Kate felt her cheeks grow hot. She always blushed whenever Nikki used that term because it sounded so wonderfully wanton. Nikki smiled and reached down between their bodies, seeking out the tiny switch attached to one of the straps. Kate jerked at the sudden buzzing sound and at the even more immediate sensation of vibration against her.

"Oh, my."

"Oh, *yeah*," Nikki hissed. "I feel that, too. We definitely made the right choice." She shifted beneath Kate. "It's just…I'm not sure this is enough. Can you play with me a bit?"

"Of course, darling." Kate eased over so that her weight was on her left elbow, creating some space so she could reach between them and touch Nikki, fingertips seeking out her clitoris.

Nikki arched against Kate. "Yes, I like that." She spread her legs wider. "Sweetie…I need…can you…" She seemed unable to articulate what she wanted. Perhaps she didn't know. Kate wasn't completely sure either, but she had a few ideas.

"Darling, I want you to touch yourself," she instructed softly, moving back on top of Nikki and lifting up slightly so that she supported herself on her elbows and knees. "I'm going to try something a little more active."

Nikki understood instantly what she was doing. "Oh, God, yes." Reaching down to replace Kate's fingers with her own, she hooked her legs around her lover's calves. "Fuck me, Kate."

Kate exhaled loudly, excited not only by the sensations she was experiencing, but the expletive that Nikki was not normally in the

habit of using. Driven by her obvious pleasure, as well as the rhythmic pulsation against her own clitoris, she began to thrust slowly. She felt powerful yet incredibly humbled, not understanding all the confusing emotions swirling in her mind, but readily accepting the predominant exhilaration.

With each thrust her clitoris bumped against the tiny vibrator, adding an extra jolt of pleasure through her. She began to wonder if she could hold on long enough to bring Nikki to her own peak.

"Kate…" Nikki's voice was almost a growl. "I'm close."

"Yes, darling." Kate moaned softly.

"Kate…oh, sweetie…faster…"

Kate obliged, shortening her strokes so that she could increase her own stimulation, bumping over the vibrator with increasing regularity. Then Nikki was abruptly shuddering, a cry ripped from her lips as Kate thrust a final time into her, feeling the orgasm rush through her, taking away the last of her strength and causing her to collapse into Nikki's welcoming arms and lips. She had barely enough energy left to find the switch and turn off the vibration that was now painful rather than pleasurable as her climax dissipated.

For long moments both of them tried to catch their breaths between long, deep kisses, connecting on an emotional rather than merely physical level. They were both covered with sweat, and Kate felt so close to her lover, yet strangely distanced as well. She wondered why.

Finally, Nikki let out her breath gustily and started to chuckle. "Well, *that* was fun."

"It certainly was." Kate withdrew slowly, taking care not to be too abrupt. Rolling over onto her back, she managed to unfasten the straps and put the entire contraption, still glistening with Nikki's moisture, onto the nightstand beside the box. She looked over at Nikki, who was sitting up. "How do you feel?"

"Like a beautiful woman has just thoroughly fucked me." Nikki seemed energized by the encounter, her eyes dancing with enjoyment. "I feel terrific! Maybe a little sore." She shifted slightly, looking rueful but completely unrepentant. "Not because of you, darling. You were fantastic. It's just because it was something new, you know?"

Kate smiled. "I know. You were wonderful, too." She was surprised when Nikki reached out and took the vibrator from the box. "Nikki?"

"You're not tired, are you?"

"Not at all," Kate did think she might be a little overwhelmed. "What exactly do you have in mind now?"

Nikki kissed her, parting Kate's lips with her tongue and deepening the kiss, until Kate felt a renewed surge of desire. When they finally parted, Nikki's expression was wanton.

"I was thinking that I'd just slip this inside you," she explained throatily as she held up the slim vibrator with the rounded base where a black button was located. "And while I do that, I'd be licking your clit."

Kate's eyes widened. "God, Nikki."

"Is that a yes?"

Kate swallowed hard. "What would I be doing?"

Nikki grinned evilly. "You'll just lie back and enjoy it," she said, echoing Kate's words from earlier. "Let me do all the work this time."

Kate felt a rush of moisture between her legs. "I think I could manage that."

Nikki lifted her brow as she pushed the button with no result. "Uh, I think the harness came with batteries. This didn't. Did you put any in?"

"Of course not. It didn't occur to me."

"Hmm." Nikki tilted her head as she opened the battery compartment. "I don't suppose you have a couple of double-A's lying around."

"I can take the ones out of the remote control." Kate scrambled from the bed.

Nikki's chuckles followed her as she went out into the living room. But instead of finding the remote, she went into the kitchen, switched on the overhead light and pulled out one of the drawers by the sink where she kept all her odds and ends. Nikki called it her "crap drawer," but it was actually fairly well organized. As she rummaged through it searching for the package of batteries she remembered picking up some weeks earlier, it suddenly occurred to her how much she'd changed in the past few years. While married to David, what they'd considered daring in the bedroom consisted of her occasionally getting on top of him. That was a far cry from standing naked in her kitchen as she scrounged up batteries for a vibrator to be utilized by her lesbian lover while performing oral sex on her.

The thought made her pause briefly, but only briefly, and with a mental shrug, she dived back into the drawer, seizing the black and copper package with a heady sense of triumph. Flipping off the light, she headed back to the bedroom, eager to return to Nikki as quickly as possible.

CHAPTER FIFTEEN

Nikki drove down Prince Street with the sort of cocky pleasure that came from owning a new car, even if it wasn't particularly new, in fact a six-year-old Honda Civic. The bank hadn't been eager to loan her the money, but Kate had co-signed. Nikki liked that. Watching her sign the papers, she felt as if they were buying the car together, as if they were truly and officially a couple now in the eyes of the authorities, whoever those might be.

The payments would take a chunk of her monthly salary, but not as much as she had feared. Being with Kate had taught her a little more about managing money, and she was starting to feel more like a grownup—a slow process, she admitted to herself ruefully, but an inescapable one.

She parked in the lot reserved for police station employees and carefully locked the car before she strode into the office. Sandy Wright, the dispatch supervisor, offered a nod and smile. A rawboned woman in her early thirties, she was rumored to really run the police station, and everyone else just worked for her, including the chief. Experience had taught Nikki just how accurate that rumor really was.

"New wheels?"

"Yeah," Nikki said proudly, unsurprised that her supervisor knew all about it. "I just registered it this afternoon."

"Nice."

Nikki grinned as she dropped by the staff room to put her lunch in the fridge and check the bulletin board for upcoming events. Rick Johnson, still in uniform, was leaning back on the battered couch, his feet up on the coffee table, flipping through a magazine. He glanced up as Nikki entered, giving her a lazy smile.

"Keeping busy, Nik?" He worked the day shift, and they usually only saw each other in passing. This was her first chance to ask her favor.

"You could say that." Nikki dug into her jeans for the slip of paper she had been carrying around with her. "Listen, could you run these numbers for me?"

"What's this about?" He eyed the writing on the paper suspiciously.

Nikki considered her answer. "It might be nothing, but if it turns out to be something, I'll tell you everything I've got so far. Otherwise, there's nothing to tell."

"I don't like this." Rick eyed her sternly. "You're playing detective again, aren't you?"

"Not exactly."

"What does that mean?"

"It means that I'm not doing anything too...intrusive," Nikki floundered. "I'm just researching what information I come across, purely by coincidence."

"Running a license plate is research?"

"Something like that."

Rick hesitated, then glowered at her. "For me to do this, you have to tell me why you want it, and what you're mixed up in."

"It might not fit with what I already have."

"That's the deal, take it or leave it." He crossed his arms over his chest.

"All right." Defeated, she told him everything she knew, including her tailing Martin and Tiffany to the Tideview Motel.

His jaw was clenched by the time she finished. "I can't believe you. You just don't know when to quit. Why can't you leave this to the professionals?"

"I'm more than willing to do that," Nikki protested, "but I can't help it if I come across information in the run of the day. I told you I'd let you know if it turns out to be important."

"You don't know what's important and what isn't."

"That's why I wanted to wait before telling you. I want to put it all together before I bring you the evidence."

"That's not your job."

She stared at him, her face set into stubborn lines. "Are you going to run the plates?"

"Yes," he said, tucking the paper into his chest pocket.

"Are you going to tell me what you find?"

"Probably not."

"Damn it, Rick—"

"No, Nikki." He held up a hand. "This is serious stuff. A man was murdered."

She raised her head. "So it *was* murder."

"Nikki—"

"Come on, Rick, what's the harm?"

"The harm is that you're not a professional, and if you blunder around, as you have a habit of doing, you're going to find yourself in a boatload of trouble, just like last time." He tilted his head. "Or don't you remember having to haul your ass out of a fire arranged just for you?"

"I remember," Nikki said sullenly. "That's why I'm being careful. Rick, we're just going around in circles. How many times do I have to tell you and Kate that I'm not doing anything dangerous?"

"I'm glad to hear that Kate doesn't like this behavior any more than I do. At least one of you is thinking clearly."

"Rick, I came to you in good faith," Nikki protested. "I'm not going to trust you with anything else if this is your attitude."

"That's the point I'm trying to get through your head." His tone was increasingly exasperated. "I don't want you to come to me for anything like this, nor will you if you just keep your damned nose out of things."

"That's your last word on the subject?" Nikki glared at him.

"It is."

"Then I guess there's nothing else to say."

Fuming, she turned and left the staff room, stomping down the stairs leading to the room in the basement where the dispatchers worked. Julia Watson, who covered days, and Dennis Langille, who was Nikki's partner at night, both looked up at her arrival.

"About time you got here," Julia grumbled good-naturedly.

Nikki glanced at the clock and saw that it was five minutes past. "Oh, Julia, I'm sorry," she said, honestly contrite. It was procedure to show up at five before the hour to replace the day shift, and a courtesy to show up ten minutes early to make sure the person being replaced could leave on time rather than spend ten minutes catching their relief up. "I started talking to Rick and lost track of time. It won't happen again."

"No problem." Julia logged off the computer and rose from her chair. Stocky, with salt and pepper hair, she had two kids and a husband who worked for the Department of Transportation. She handed over the headphone and tapped the clipboard on the counter. "Upstairs wants us to keep a close eye on Brunswick Street. If any calls come in, regardless of what they're for, we're to dispatch a squad car immediately, in addition to whatever else is required."

"Are they expecting some particular trouble from there?" Nikki sat down and logged in with her password.

"They always expect trouble from there. I think there's a dealer living in the area that they're keeping an eye on, just waiting for a chance to bust him for something big. Other than that, it's a typical Wednesday. Have a good night, Nik. I'll see you tomorrow morning."

"You, too."

Nikki scanned the calls that had come in over the dayshift and settled in for the night. Above her computer, a large, detailed map of Truro dominated the room, and behind her, on the other counter, stood a sparkling clean coffee pot. Since Julia knew Nikki didn't imbibe, she had washed it before her arrival. Nikki, on the other hand, knowing her counterpart would set up an IV with the stuff if it were feasible, usually made a pot around quarter to six in the morning so it would be ready for Julia. She was thankful that Kate's love of the bean was more reasonable.

Dennis looked over from his desk. "What did Rick want? To make you late, I mean."

"Nothing," Nikki grumbled. "Sometimes he just frosts me, though."

Dennis grinned, showing oversized teeth. Sandy hair fell boyishly over his forehead; he didn't look old enough to vote, let alone work as a dispatcher, but he was actually older than Nikki. "He has only the nicest things to say about you."

Nikki shot him a look before turning her attention back to her screen, feeling vaguely guilty both at Dennis's comment and because of her annoyance at the police constable. She knew Rick liked her. In fact, he treated her much as an older brother would, and with a great deal more compassion and kindness than her own blood relatives did. She knew that the police didn't like amateurs interfering with ongoing investigations, but she wasn't doing that. She just happened to find out useful bits of information now and again. Was she just supposed to ignore what she learned?

She had plenty of time to muse over the situation as the evening progressed. It turned out to be just as quiet as Julia predicted. It was raining, preventing the young people from hanging out around town, a source of many calls, and it was the third week of the month, which meant the trouble government cheques generated was at its lowest ebb. People didn't have the money to go out drinking, and the moon wasn't full, so the police didn't have that craziness to deal with either.

Nikki sometimes wondered what it would be like to cover the phones during a weekend. If things worked out and there were openings, she would eventually be promoted to weekdays and then to weekends. The most crucial shifts occurred on Friday and Saturday nights, which also paid the most. Nikki wasn't sure if she wanted to sign up for the stress, but she couldn't deny that working at the police station was a great deal more intriguing and challenging than her previous job at the hardware store. Even on quiet nights, something interesting usually happened, and she often felt like she was contributing something important to society, particularly after a 911 call where she was able to calm the caller as she dispatched the required emergency personnel. She had been involved in helping save more than one life during her short time on the job, and that provided a satisfaction that few other positions could offer.

She was in a much better mood by the time Julia arrived to relieve her the next morning, and she whistled quietly as she climbed the stairs to the main floor, stopping by the staff room to pick up her jacket and her thermal lunch bag. To her surprise, Rick was already there and handed her a piece of paper with a name on it.

Uncomprehending, Nikki looked at it. "Who's Monica Henderson?"

"I can tell you who she isn't. She isn't the guy who was supposedly driving her car, and she doesn't have anything to do with the Elliots. Are you sure you got the right license number?"

She stared at him. "Kim wrote it down."

"Then I guess she wrote it down wrong." He flashed her a slightly smug grin. "You need to leave this to the professionals, Nikki. You don't have the skills to conduct a proper investigation."

With an airy wave, he strolled out, leaving Nikki steaming. Kim surely hadn't written the license plate down wrong, so she was left with the burning question that she mumbled out loud to the empty room. "Who the hell is Monica Henderson?"

CHAPTER SIXTEEN

K ate sat in the Halifax International Airport and recalled the tragic day in September, 2001, when it earned its stripes along with every other airport in Atlantic Canada as all the planes, including several large-bodied transatlantic jets, were hastily diverted from the American East Coast airports. They landed them all safely, one after another, in the space of a few hours, managing to park them in every spare foot of pavement and offload tens of thousands of confused and frightened passengers even as they arranged the necessary facilities to house and care for them in the terrible days afterward.

Fortunately, Kate mused, there were only two gates to worry about here, one for domestic flights and another across the room for the international flights. The area wasn't conducive to waiting, having only a few hard, plastic seats and a couple of soda machines scattered around the large conveyor belts carrying luggage, but since Kate didn't expect to be waiting long, she didn't complain.

She leaned against the wall by the international gate where her grandmother would be coming through customs, her hands balled up into fists inside her jacket pockets. She had always been Irene's favorite grandchild, but she wondered if that was still the case. She had absolutely no idea how Irene regarded homosexuality. The subject had simply never come up before, but if Irene thought like Hannah Elliot, this was not a confrontation Kate was looking forward to.

Her breath caught as the passengers began filtering through the gate in ones or twos, and she expected to see Irene any moment. When she did, she had to smile. Where other passengers had lugged their own baggage through customs, Irene had coerced an airport handler to carry hers, the young man pushing a cart full of trunks and bags, his face red with exertion. Hopefully he would also carry it out to the car; Kate didn't think she could lift some of the bags.

"Kate," Irene presented a powdered cheek to be kissed. Taller than her granddaughter, she had immaculately styled snow-white hair, which looked a bit limp after her flight. Her light gray eyes missed little as they assessed Kate. "You're thin."

"Grandmother, you haven't been here three minutes and already you're criticizing?"

Irene colored faintly. "That wasn't my intention," she began, then frowned. "Stop looking at me that way."

"How was your flight?" Kate offered her arm, not because her grandmother had difficulty navigating, but because she was elderly, and Kate wanted to make sure she didn't stumble. Puffing, the airport attendant followed as they left the air-conditioned terminal and walked into the bright sunshine. Despite the relative warmth, Irene pulled her sweater tight around her, and Kate realized that after Florida, this was much cooler than she was used to.

"My car is just at the bottom of the stairs," she said as they crossed the lane in front of the terminal building and walked past the Hertz rental stand to the short-term parking lot down the hill.

"Do you still have that monstrosity?" Irene asked as they maneuvered down the handicap ramp.

"The SUV? It's only a year old, Grandmother."

Kate helped her up into the passenger seat of the black and silver vehicle parked in the last space next to the stairs, and then, went to the back of the vehicle where she opened the hatch. After helping the attendant load the luggage, she slipped him a ten dollar bill, for which he gave her a disgusted look and didn't linger.

Kate unlocked her door and slid behind the wheel, starting the engine. Irene was regarding her intently, and Kate resisted the urge to squirm, wondering how long it would be before Irene brought up the topic she was dreading.

"So you're a lesbian now."

Apparently not long at all, Kate thought, as she turned left out of the parking lot onto the road leading back to the 102. "Is that what you heard?"

"Are you saying it's not true?"

Kate waited until she was off the ramp and had merged with the traffic heading north. "I'm not saying anything. I'm just asking what you've heard."

"Hannah Elliot contacted me a few months ago to tell me you were involving yourself with an undesirable element." Irene's calm inflection matched Kate's. "Since then, she's spent her weekly phone calls informing me of your scandalous behavior."

All Taylor women became calmer as the situation became more emotionally charged. Nikki didn't always understand that approach to personal confrontations between them, but then she always burst into incoherent tears, which Kate found equally trying. Somewhere in between was a happy medium, but Kate wasn't sure how long it would take before they found it.

"I see."

"Of course, I thought she was exaggerating, but then I heard what happened at the Historical Society Dinner from other, more reliable sources."

"I'll just bet you did."

A silence. "It's true then. You're involved with a woman."

Kate took a deep breath. "I'm in love."

"With this very *young* woman?"

"Is that why you're upset? Not that she's a woman, but that she's significantly younger than me?"

"Don't try to change the subject."

"I wasn't." Kate gripped the steering wheel tighter. "Gram, I know this is probably upsetting, but I love Nikki with all my heart. I'm sorry if that's difficult for you to accept. I'm happy now in a way I wasn't before. Hopefully you can be happy for me, but if you can't…well, you can't."

Another silence, one stretching on as the pavement slipped beneath the wheels of the SUV. Kate felt frozen inside as she waited for her grandmother's response. Despite her brave words, she dreaded Irene's condemnation or even the disappointment in her eyes. She loved her a great deal and wouldn't recover easily from the shattering of that bond.

"Are you sure about this?" Irene's voice was very cold.

A lump formed in Kate's throat. "Yes." She risked a glance over and saw Irene purse her lips, her jaw moving as if she tasted something not very pleasant.

"Very well," Irene said finally after a moment that stretched to eternity. "When do I meet her?"

Kate blinked. "Who?"

"The love of your life." Irene lifted an eyebrow. "Bring her over to dinner Saturday night. I should be settled by then."

"Ah, um..." Kate managed to bring herself under control. "Just like that?"

"Honestly, Kate, what did you expect? Excommunication from the family?"

"I expected you'd be more upset than this."

Irene sighed, a trifle theatrically. "That's the trouble with you young people. You think that anyone older than your generation simply hasn't arrived in the current century. Furthermore, whenever you have a crisis you're always certain that you've come up with something entirely new. Did you really believe I haven't encountered anything like this before?"

Kate was flabbergasted. "Are you saying you have?"

Irene smiled faintly, as if thoroughly enjoying Kate's shock. "You do know that Aunt Sarah and Aunt Vera aren't sisters?" She was referring to a couple of elderly relatives living in Toronto who had shared a house for decades. Kate saw her great-aunts only rarely, but did exchange Christmas cards with them every year.

"I...uh, never thought about it." Kate inhaled slowly, getting over one jolt only to experience another. "You mean they're not?"

"Your grandfather only had three sisters." Irene sounded impatient with Kate's denseness. "The oldest was Maureen, the youngest was Karen, and Sarah is the middle. You never noticed Sarah and Vera had different last names?"

"Uh—"

"Honestly."

"So you're all right with this?" Kate dared.

"I'm not pleased to know I'm not going to have any great-grandchildren in your line, but when you reached thirty-five, I realized you weren't the maternal type anyway. I know you'll face aggravation in pursuing this path and I'm sorry that's the case. I love you, Kate, and I don't want to see you hurt. But I've been alive long enough to know that a person has to make their own way in life regardless of what other people think. It's up to you to decide if this decision is worth the consequences."

Kate exhaled, feeling warmth spread through her, thawing her frozen fear. "Thank you," she whispered. "I guess…I was afraid you would be ashamed of me."

"Are you ashamed?" Irene asked sharply.

"Not at all."

Irene's voice gentled a great deal. "Kathryn, if you were, then yes, I would be very much against this. I taught your mother to live proud, and I expect that she taught you that in turn."

"It's not always that easy."

"Of course it isn't." Irene snorted. "Nothing worth having ever is. Is this girl worth it?"

"Yes, she is."

"Then that's all that matters. Now, about Saturday night, I'm thinking of serving a clam chowder. This girl isn't allergic to seafood, is she?"

Because Kate's mind was still a bit clouded she didn't quite understand what her grandmother was saying, but when she did, she shook her head. "We can't."

"Excuse me?" Irene's tone became icy and Kate swallowed a smile. Her grandmother might be willing to take the lesbian thing in stride, but disrupt her dinner plans and there would be hell to pay.

"Nikki and I are going to be busy this weekend," Kate explained. "I'm sorry, Grandmother, but we made the arrangements weeks ago. I can't change them now."

"I see." Irene looked dissatisfied. "What are these plans?"

"We're going canoeing and then camping overnight by the Stewiacke River. We won't be back until Sunday afternoon."

Irene stared as if Kate had lost her mind. "You're doing *what*?"

❖

"Your grandmother sounds pretty cool," Nikki said enviously, glancing over at her lover.

"I guess she is," Kate agreed as she watched the passing scenery out the car window. "Frankly, she surprised me. The more you think you know someone, the less you really do."

"I still can't believe you have gay aunts that you knew nothing about."

"I know them. I just didn't know they were lovers. I thought they were just spinster aunts. Actually, I'd rather not think of them as lovers. It's…well, somewhat disconcerting after all this time."

Nikki swallowed a laugh and refocused on the road. Driving out to her parents' home to pick up her canoe, Nikki was grateful that Kate had taken time away from the store to help her. It was a two-person job to secure the boat on top of her Honda, and she doubted she could find any help at the farm on a Friday morning. Not that she wanted to run in to any of her family. Kate might have been pleasantly surprised by her grandmother's reaction, but Nikki had no illusions about what her family thought about lesbians and their relationships.

"I guess your new employees are doing okay if you're able to come today."

"I'm very pleased with Todd. He caught on quickly enough that I have no problem trusting him with the store. It's fortunate they had today off for exams next week. Besides, we'll be back before the afternoon rush today, right?"

"It shouldn't take very long to tie the canoe down."

"You know, I'm looking forward to meeting your parents."

Nikki took a breath. "They probably won't be home. Friday morning is when they do the weekly shopping, and then they visit Julie and her kids. They usually don't get back until later in the afternoon."

"I see." There was a somewhat significant pause. "Did you plan it that way?"

"Doing it today is more convenient than tomorrow morning," Nikki said, feeling defensive. "But I'm not disappointed that my parents aren't going to be there, if that's what you're asking."

"Are you ashamed of me?" Kate asked, her voice suddenly tight.

Nikki whipped her head around toward her, astonished. "Of course not. Truth be told, I'm ashamed of them…at least, I am of my sister and brother. My parents aren't too bad, but it would be awkward as hell. You don't need that. *I* don't need that."

"All right," Kate said in that eerily calm tone that Nikki was learning meant more than its superficial appearance of composure. "It's your call."

"Do you really want to meet them?"

"They're your family, Nikki. Of course I do."

"All right, one of these days I'll bring you out to meet them. It just won't be today."

"Fair enough."

Nikki clenched her jaw, believing she had ducked a bullet of sorts, even if it was one she couldn't duck forever. Turning down the dirt road, she felt her heart twitch as she saw the farm. It was home to her in a way no other place could be, yet at the same time, she knew she would never be able to return to it. That hurt profoundly. She swallowed her pain back as she turned into the driveway and parked before the main doors of the barn.

The house was a two-story, with large windows and a rambling front porch, painted white with red trim. A large red barn dominated the property, its silvery, metal roof streaked with rust. Undulating fields stretched out behind the buildings, while a corral by the side of the barn held two large horses. The animals' coats were a dark brown in contrast to their cream-colored manes.

"I didn't know your family had horses."

"Bob and Tom are older than I am." Nikki moved over to the fence and patted the closest, Tom, on his aged white muzzle. "Dad used to haul wood with them a long time ago. They don't really do anything now. They're just retired."

Kate reached over and lightly stroked a muscular neck, her eyes bright as she looked up at the large draft horse. "I've always loved horses. We lived in town so I was never able to have one, but I always thought that one day I would like to have a home with stables." She smiled wistfully. "It just never seemed to work out that way."

"Horses are a lot of work," Nikki said pragmatically. "Unless you really love them and are willing to devote a considerable portion of your time, energy, and money to them, then you probably shouldn't own one."

Kate glanced at her. "I guess you're not crazy about them."

"Oh, I like them okay. I had a pony when I was a kid and a horse when I was a teenager, but, no, I don't love them the way Mom and Julie do." She gestured to the field stretching out behind the farm buildings, rising until it met the trees on the ridge. Brown specks dotted the verdant green. "Mom still has a couple of riding horses, and Julie keeps her gelding here, too. A few neighbors also board their ponies."

Kate looked at the field, her eyes squinting in the bright sunlight. "Only a few cattle, though. Are the rest somewhere else? This is a very large barn."

Nikki shook her head. "Jeffrey was never interested in farming and neither is Julia's husband, so Mom and Dad sold most of the herd. They only keep a few now, mostly for the beef. I think Dad rents out some of the fields to the other farmers around here."

"You weren't interested in taking over the farm?"

Nikki turned and headed for the barn door. "I wasn't consulted in the matter." She didn't look back to see if Kate's expression altered at this admission or the tone in which it was uttered.

The barn was dark and musty with the scent of straw and animals. If Nikki flinched as she entered the structure, she was sure the dimness hid it from Kate, for which she was grateful. Moving past the large bales of hay, Nikki found the small tack room at the rear where a large, tarp-covered shape rested on two sawhorses. She flipped off the dusty cloth to reveal a fifteen-foot canoe painted a dark forest green. Kate, who had followed her lover without saying anything further about what she had learned in the barnyard, lifted an eyebrow.

"Can we carry that?"

"It's not that heavy, just a little awkward. The easiest way to carry it is on our shoulders."

"Like the pictures of portages I saw in school."

"Something like that. Ready?"

Kate nodded, though her expression was slightly skeptical as she moved to the rear of the canoe, following Nikki's lead.

Taking a firm hold of the front, Nikki glanced back at Kate. "On three. One, two, three." They hefted the canoe over their shoulders, and Nikki led the way out of the barn, directing Kate to lower it to the ground by the car once they were outside. "Are you okay?"

Kate grinned and dusted off her hands. "You were right. It wasn't as heavy as I thought it would be. But I can see where it's a two-person job."

"No kidding. I'm really glad you're here." She leaned over to kiss her lover quickly. "Not just because of your strong back, either."

Kate grinned and colored faintly. "What next?"

"I'll get the supports out of the back."

Her car was already loaded with the camping gear they needed for the next day, and she rummaged around in it until she found the lightweight canoe carrier she had purchased at Canadian Tire not long after buying her car. Eventually, she would buy a more permanent roof attachment, but for the moment, the Styrofoam supports were sufficient. With Nikki instructing Kate what to do, it wasn't long before they had the canoe resting on top of the car and secured with ropes at the sides, front, and back.

"It may be difficult to drive with that on the roof," Kate said, regarding the finished product as she stood with her hands on her hips. "Are you sure you won't have any trouble?"

Nikki glanced at her and, not for the first time, she felt a surge of tenderness and desire for Kate. Dressed in a dark blue T-shirt and jeans, a dusty smudge on her nose, Kate looked adorable as she stood in the farmyard.

"I've driven with one before." She put her hand on the door handle. "Shall we go?"

"Do we have to? I mean, would you mind showing me around a bit? I'd like to see where you grew up." Kate tilted her head appealingly. "Please?"

Nikki doubted that she would ever be able to refuse Kate anything, particularly when she wore that little puppy expression. "I don't mind," she said, not entirely truthfully. "What would you like to see?"

Kate shrugged unhelpfully. "Just around. Maybe we could go for a walk. It's a gorgeous morning. I hate to be out in such beautiful surroundings and waste the opportunity, particularly when I'm already playing hooky from work."

Nikki glanced unobtrusively at her watch, checking the time, before she nodded. "All right. I guess I can take you to my special place."

Kate's face lit up. "You have a special place?"

Nikki tried not to squirm as she began to walk down the driveway toward the road. "Once in awhile, I just wanted to get away from everyone. Sometimes I still come out here even if I don't stop at the farm, just to, I don't know, be by myself." She glanced sideways at Kate. "Being out here is different than being alone in town. I don't know if that makes sense."

"It does." Kate took Nikki's hand. "It's so peaceful here. No cars or noise in the background, only the wind in the trees."

"And the water." Warmed by Kate's understanding, Nikki turned down a lane that opened into a small gravel pit. "There's a trail through here. It's not far."

Nikki led the way through the gravel pit, then up the rutted road to the rise. A small path led into the woods, and, letting go of Kate's hand for the moment, Nikki ducked into the trees, winding her way through the ferns and underbrush, always moving upward until she stopped at a small clearing. A cliff dropped about twenty feet, and before them spread a panoramic view of the Shubenacadie River, making its way through the green hills of Colchester County. A tidal river, it was currently at its lowest point, a thin stream cutting through expansive mudflats, and Nikki grinned as she realized her timing had been good for a change. She was aware of Kate stopping beside her, her face expressive as she looked out over the expanse of the river.

"Wow."

Nikki took her hand. "No, that has yet to come. You know that pathetic excuse for a tidal bore that the Salmon River gets in Truro?"

"I've seen it."

"This is the *real* tidal bore. It shouldn't be long now."

"How wonderful." Kate sounded really delighted.

Nikki looked into the distance where the river turned a bend, knowing the tidal bore would first appear there. The Bay of Fundy produced the highest tides in the world, rushing up the ever-narrowing stretch between Nova Scotia and New Brunswick, through the Minas Channel to the Minas Basin, then into Cobequid Bay with its rivers. So strong was this tidal action that it crested in a wave that flowed up the river, a mass of seawater surging in its wake. It was like seeing a dam break twice a day, and what took six hours to reach low tide took a relatively short time to refill.

Nikki and Kate watched in awe as the mass of water finally turned the bend in the distance and began to spread out over the river before them, rapidly covering the sandbars and filling the wide expanse between the riverbanks where only a thin, muddy channel had trickled such a short time before.

"It doesn't matter how many times I see that, I still think it's cool." The rush of water in Nikki's ears was like a soothing melody, filling her with peace and contentment.

"It's very impressive. Now I understand why the tidal bore is considered such a tourist attraction."

"Too bad some of them go away thinking that the Salmon River version is the best there is. It's even better earlier in the early part of the year, when the ice has just thawed and there's a full moon."

Kate squeezed her hand and pulled her around. Nikki looked down into her face, soft and vulnerable. "Thank you for showing me this spot. It means a lot that you would share this with me."

"I wanted to share it with you."

The gentle blue-gray eyes mesmerized Nikki, and as she kissed Kate, she knew that this was their place now, not just hers, that the memory they were making this day would stay with them forever. Of course, if their relationship didn't work out, this special place would be forever lost to Nikki, but she pushed the unhappy thought aside and concentrated only on kissing her lover.

CHAPTER SEVENTEEN

K ate leaned back into Nikki's arms, watching as the river filled quickly, amazed by the surging water. Where it flowed around rippled sandbars and met on the other end, there was roiling confrontation, violent and fierce. She could easily imagine how so many people had died by ignoring the changing of the tide along the Bay of Fundy. It came up so quickly and could circle around, cutting off any retreat to the shore. Once it reached a person, they would have little chance of escaping the strong current that would sweep them away. Kate shivered as she shoved the disconcerting thought away.

They were sitting on the side of the cliff, Kate draping her legs over the edge and supporting her feet on a tiny ledge beneath. Nikki was behind her, her arms circling her in a warm embrace, her chin resting on Kate's shoulder as they stared out at the water.

Gradually, Kate became aware of a humming noise, and she lifted her head and tried to pinpoint it.

Nikki must have felt her confusion because her arms tightened, and she put her mouth next to Kate's ear." There, near the bend. Rafters. They ride the white water that occurs when the tide comes in over the sandbars."

"I've heard of them." Kate saw the three yellow inflatable rafts appear, filled with life-jacketed customers who had paid almost a hundred dollars each for the thrill of being on the river amid the rollicking tide. "I always thought it would be interesting to try."

Nikki shrugged. "I prefer to look from here. In fact, I've always resented them suddenly showing up while I'm trying to enjoy the view. I can't blame the operators for wanting to make a buck, but it takes away from the peacefulness."

"It's still beautiful scenery."

"Hmm, I'd still rather look at the bald eagles." Nikki nudged Kate, pointing across the river. "There's one now."

Kate followed Nikki's outstretched arm, watching as the stately bird sailed over the river, its large wingspan astonishing, for she had rarely seen the creatures outside of television documentaries or the local wildlife park.

"They nest along here, though the better place to see them is at the Cadel Rapids on the Fort Ellis Road."

"Will you take me there?"

"Soon," Nikki promised.

Kate breathed deeply, enchanted by the surroundings. The cliffs that edged the river were a unique red-brown color, streaked with lighter granite formations. She could see a few houses far off in the distance and, to her left, the Goss Bridge that stretched across the river to Hants County on the other side. The rafters were below them now, bouncing over the waves caused by the tidal action, getting as much from each rough patch as possible before moving up the river. Eventually, the persistent buzzing noise of their motors faded away as they passed beyond the bridge and moved out of sight, following the tide.

Kate snuggled closer to her lover, feeling Nikki's arms tighten around her protectively, and she smiled. "I can see why you love it here."

"I'm glad you're here with me," Nikki responded huskily and kissed Kate's neck, nuzzling her hair as she slipped her hands beneath Kate's T-shirt.

A tingle radiated through Kate, and she closed her eyes as Nikki began to trace sensual trails over her skin, moving over her stomach, then up to her breasts. "Nikki?"

"Hmm?"

Kate turned her head, allowing Nikki to kiss her, a long, slow melting kiss that left no confusion about what her lover had in mind.

"Oh, my," she murmured when they finally parted for breath. "Outside?"

"It can be more romantic in theory than reality, but I just want you so much right now."

"Oh" was all Kate managed before Nikki covered her mouth once more, kissing her deeply. "Are you sure it's safe?"

"No one will see us."

Kate hesitated for another second before surrendering completely, her head falling back onto her lover's shoulder, her eyes closing as Nikki unfastened her bra and began to explore the soft swells of her breasts without encumbrance. Her fingertips were inquisitive on Kate's nipples, playing with them tenderly, making them harden until the touch was almost painful. Nikki's thighs were aligned beside Kate's, and Kate could feel the muscles in them flex as she grasped them tightly, holding on desperately as she responded to her lover's hands.

"You like this, don't you?" Nikki whispered hotly into her ear, and Kate moaned her agreement, finding it difficult to reply any more coherently. "I love touching you like this. You're so soft...so smooth..."

Kate swallowed against a mouth gone dry and jerked again as Nikki reached down and unfastened her jeans, sliding her hand beneath the fabric to her panties and the heat radiating through them. Kate spread her legs wider, unable to resist undulating against the maddening sensation as Nikki rubbed her through the lace material before finally slipping her fingers beneath the elastic band and touching the tender flesh beneath.

"God, you're so ready for me," Nikki told her huskily, moving her hand rhythmically against the sensitive ridge as she cupped Kate's right breast tightly with her other hand, her thumb chafing the nipple in a corresponding motion. The combination was delightful, and Kate felt the pleasure build steadily, rising within her as strongly as the tide on the river below. She moaned, trembling as the sensation increased, until, abruptly, it peaked. She felt the contractions ripple through her loins, hard spasms that forced Nikki to hold her tight in a grip of steel to keep her from pitching forward off the cliff and into the river below.

Slowly, slowly, Kate felt the tremors ease, coming back to herself and Nikki's sheltering embrace. The sound of the breeze in the trees above her and the strong rush of water surrounded her with their power, making her feel both primal and infinitely peaceful.

"My God," she whispered.

Nikki nipped at her earlobe, hugging her lovingly. "You liked that?"

"Very much," Kate said, slowing her respiration with an effort. "That was wonderful. Thank you so much."

Nikki chuckled lightly as she drew her hand away and refastened

Kate's jeans, then used both hands to secure her bra and tug her shirt back down. "You're so very welcome."

Kate tried to turn. "What about you?" Nikki tightened her embrace, forestalling the attempt.

"I'm fine. I just love being here with you. This will be a more special place to me in the future."

Kate glanced back at her doubtfully. "Are you sure?"

Nikki pulled her back against her and kissed her neck tenderly. "I'm sure. I love you, Kate."

"I love you, too, my darling. You introduce me to such wonderful experiences."

They sat for a few more moments, enjoying the view and each other's company. The breeze had picked up when, finally, Nikki released her embrace, rising to her feet and reaching down to help Kate to hers. She hugged her one last time, kissing her tenderly. "We should be getting back."

"I guess so," Kate agreed, not all that anxious to end this special time.

As if reading her thoughts, Nikki took her hand in a warm grip, urging her gently to follow. Kate allowed herself to be tugged along, still pleasantly dazed from the afterglow, a smile curving her lips as Nikki led her back through the trees. As they descended to the gravel pit and began to walk along the road, she took a moment to make sure she didn't look as mussed as she felt, tucking her shirt into her jeans and raking her fingers through her hair, neatening it. She was doubly glad she had straightened herself up when they came in sight of the farmhouse and discovered a car parked beside Nikki's. Nikki stiffened abruptly when she saw it.

"Damn, they must have come back from town early. That or we took a lot longer than I thought."

Kate glanced at her and squeezed her fingers when Nikki tried to pull them away. "It will be all right, darling. I'm right here with you."

Nikki's steps faltered, but Kate didn't pause, and Nikki was forced to keep up as they approached the barnyard. The couple standing next to the car looked familiar to Kate, though she suspected it was more the family resemblance than anything else. The man was tall and sparse, with a white fringe of hair around his smooth head, his features strong, if too rugged to be really handsome. His pale blue eyes assessed Kate keenly as she walked toward him. Beside him, a thin woman in a cotton dress, her light hair streaked with gray, was equally as blatant in her regard of Kate.

Kate put a bright smile on her face and extended her hand, not waiting for anyone else to make the first move. "Mr. and Mrs. Harris, I'm Kate Shannon. Nikki's told me a great deal about you." She was aware of Nikki glancing at her with a combination of bemusement and uncertainty, but she didn't say anything, apparently content to allow Kate to take the initiative.

"Nikki has mentioned you," Adele Harris said quietly, taking Kate's hand and squeezing it briefly. Kate could see that Nikki had inherited her looks from her mother, particularly around the eyes and mouth. But the nose came directly from her father, as did her chin.

"Mrs. Shannon." Lorne's voice was cool, not necessarily unfriendly but with a certain amount of reserve. He shook her hand firmly when offered, and Kate decided that the couple was basically a "show-me" type. They simply weren't going to accept her at face value. She supposed that was fair, since her family was much the same way.

"You're picking up your canoe?" That was addressed to Nikki, and Kate thought it a rather obvious question since the boat was strapped down to the car. It was the sort of thing offered when one didn't know what else to say.

"The annual canoe trip is tomorrow," Nikki told her mother woodenly.

"I'm looking forward to it," Kate interjected cheerfully, maintaining her presence in the conversation. Nikki's parents glanced at her, and she deliberately put her arm around Nikki's waist. "I've never really been camping before so I'll have to rely on Nikki to look out for me."

A certain amount of silence greeted this statement before Lorne glanced at his youngest daughter. "She'll take good care of you. Nikki knows her way around the woods. Always has since she was little. You'll have a good time."

Nikki looked somewhat stunned at this comment, as well as by Kate's affectionate gesture. Kate's heart went out to Nikki. Obviously, this was a very difficult moment for her, though Kate suspected that her lover was actually making more of it than she really had to.

"I understand you own a bookstore?" Adele was gamely trying to keep the conversation going.

Perhaps Nikki was too close to the situation, Kate decided. It was easy to see that Nikki's parents wanted to connect with their daughter; they just didn't quite understand how to handle the whole situation. Kate decided then and there that she would make a concentrated effort to build a relationship among all of them. She would start by acting naturally, and she was sure that they would respond in kind.

"That's how Nikki and I met, actually." Kate offered Adele a warm smile. "She was one of my best customers. Still is, of course, though now she gets the family discount."

Nikki stared at Kate as if she had never seen her before while Kate wondered if the sense of distance from her family was all in Nikki's mind, generated by assumption, speculation, and a lack of communication.

"Nikki has always enjoyed reading." Adele glanced at her husband before extending her hand tentatively toward Kate. "Would you like to come in for a cup of tea?"

Kate opened her mouth to accept when Nikki finally managed to find her voice. "We need to get back." She quickly moved away from Kate's arm and over to her car, where she opened the driver's door. "It gets busy in the store in the afternoons, and Kate needs to be there."

"Of course." Lorne sounded regretful. "We'll have to get together another time."

"I would love that." Kate grasped Adele's hand. "It was very nice to meet you both."

"Our number is in the book." Adele looked earnestly at Kate as she squeezed her fingers. "Give us a call sometime."

Kate offered them a wave through the car window as Nikki pulled out of the driveway and drove down the road. She noticed that the couple stood and watched them leave, rather than going immediately into the house.

"I'm sorry," Nikki said softly after they were back on the pavement and speeding back to town. "I meant to be gone before they got back."

Kate put her hand reassuringly on the back of Nikki's neck. "It really wasn't that bad, darling. I think they rather liked me, in fact, or do your parents usually invite all your girlfriends in for tea?"

Nikki's face froze, and she looked stunned. "Uh, no. They've never invited anyone in. Do you think we should have accepted?" It was obvious the thought hadn't occurred to her until that moment.

"Don't worry about it. We will next time." Quite satisfied with how the morning had gone, Kate leaned back in her seat in quiet contemplation, watching the scenery on the way back to town.

CHAPTER EIGHTEEN

Out on the water, Nikki found herself truly enjoying the day. The stops were frequent, the scenery spectacular, and the conversation lively. She honestly believed that Kate was having a good time. Her lover took the opportunity to speak with many of the women, particularly those who were the most shy, drawing them out with her charm and wit. Nikki kept an eye on the Summer Twins and their crowd so they wouldn't get too close to her lover. Also, Nikki's friends regaled Kate with their past adventures on the river, some of which were at Nikki's expense, though that didn't keep her from laughing just as hard as everyone else.

As they paddled lazily around a bend, they all but careened into ten or twelve cows cooling their bellies in the water. Nikki was hard pressed to tell which was the most surprised, the cattle or the women. In either event, the cattle spooked, most splashing their way back to the bank where it sloped up to the pasture. But one black-and-white individual, perhaps a little more aggressive, or confused, than the others, took a few steps toward the startled women, who promptly panicked.

Two canoes immediately tipped over, spilling their contents into the river, while two more grounded on the opposite bank with the women scrambling out and dashing into the woods as if the hounds of hell were snapping at their heels. Nikki stopped near the shore, floating calmly in the water as she kept a judicious eye on the cow and hoped that Kate wouldn't overreact as the others had.

Instead, to Nikki's amazement, the cow paused only a few feet away from their canoe, regarding them with placid brown eyes. Kate looked back at the animal for a second before lifting her hand. The cow raised its head and tentatively extended its muzzle, letting Kate pat it briefly. Then it snorted as if washing its hoofs of the whole matter and turned around, ambling after its departed companions and leaving the river ahead clear.

Nikki glanced at Kate in amazement and then stared at the results of the unexpected encounter, seeing the Summer Twins stumble from the river, both screaming about eels and leeches and other creatures that may or may not have inhabited the waters. June had a piece of grass tangled in her hair and almost turned herself inside out trying to remove it as May offered all sorts of incoherent and unhelpful advice.

That was too much for Nikki. She bent over her paddle and laughed until she cried.

Some time later, when she'd finally recovered, she gestured to the van where half the women were piling in to drive back to the bridge where they had left their vehicles. "I'm going with Jackie to pick up the car," she told Kate. "Will you be all right until I get back?"

"I think I can manage." Kate glanced toward the grassy shore where their canoes were lined in a row, keel up.

Nikki grinned crookedly. "Am I nagging?"

"No, darling. You're just assuming I'm completely helpless outdoors, and that's not the case."

"Fair enough." Nikki kissed her before heading over to the van.

Once the van drove out of sight, Kate surveyed her surroundings. The park was little more than a large clearing next to the river, with a narrow dirt lane leading out to a paved secondary road. A couple of picnic tables stood near the graveled bank, next to a large fire pit where evidence of previous bonfires remained, including the fragments of scorched beer bottles. Kate supposed that the group would just set up their tents in a semicircle around this central area. She wondered where the washrooms were and then realized with a sort of creeping horror that there were none.

She sighed glumly. *The things I do for love.*

Drifting over to the nearest picnic table where others had already gathered to wait for their significant others, she sat on the hard, wooden bench opposite Kim and Lynn.

"Having a good time?" Kim asked.

Kate considered her answer. "It's been interesting. Nikki's really enjoying herself."

"It'll be better once we get set up." Lynn grasped Kate's hand, turning it over to examine the palms. "No blisters. I'm impressed."

"I was lucky." Kate moved her fingers a bit, feeling the tightness in her skin. "My arms and shoulders are a bit sore."

"Would you like me to rub them?" A slender, almost frail, blonde woman dropped onto the seat next to Kate. Her rounded features and high hairline put Kate uncomfortably in mind of a Komodo Dragon for some reason.

An expression of distaste briefly crossed Lynn's face at the newcomer's arrival. The woman had sat down far closer than necessary to Kate and was eyeing her breasts.

Startled, Kate edged away and quickly answered, "Uh, that's all right. That job belongs to someone else."

"Kate, this is June Allison," Lynn said in a flat tone. "I don't think you've met her yet."

Because Nikki had been carefully keeping her away from certain members of the group, Kate realized. She was beginning to suspect why. She had seen June's type countless times before at parties and gatherings, individuals who flirted outrageously beyond the bounds of good taste, all the while dropping sly comments designed to disrupt anyone else's enjoyment of the event. Some were particularly clever at sowing dissention between couples for no other reason than to prove that they could. This woman, Kate decided, was simply a gay version of people she'd learned to watch out for in her social set over the years.

"Hello, June." Kate didn't let her polite smile reach her eyes. She grasped June's hand firmly, assessing the woman with a cold, analytical dispassion. It was a look she had cultivated during countless dinner parties when someone was coming on to her or David, a gaze of pure ice that indicated she knew exactly what was going on, and how little it meant to her. Those capable of taking the hint would usually quit wasting her time, and it was seldom necessary to become less than polite.

Kate didn't know if June had ever encountered such a palpable aura of contemptuous amusement before. Certainly, it wouldn't have slowed other people Kate knew, such as Michelle Greenwald who prowled the Truro Golf Club as if it were her own personal feeding ground. But it definitely seemed to impact this young woman. June blinked and shifted away, managing a weak smile and an expression that revealed confusion and intimidation in equal measure.

"Uh, nice to meet you." She looked around, as if seeking an avenue of escape. "Oh, there's Jennifer. I'll talk to you later."

"Damn," Lynn said as June hastened off in the direction of another group of women. "How'd you do that?"

Kate feigned ignorance. "I'm not sure what you mean."

"I think we're a little out of our depth with you. June certainly is."

Kate felt a sudden qualm, not wanting to place herself apart from these people, particularly those closest to her lover. She had been amazed at how openly affectionate Nikki had been during their journey down the river, how she always had her arm around her shoulders or waist at the many stops they had made. Nikki clearly felt completely comfortable with these women, even with those she didn't like, and was able to act in a way that she couldn't in the greater part of society.

"I've just run into that type before," Kate said quietly. "They're a fixture at Christmas and office parties, particularly when a lot of alcohol is involved."

Lynn nodded, glancing over at the other group, her gaze speculative. "I suppose they are. It's harder for us to understand what people like that are up to because we're not looking for it, until it's too late."

Kate heard a certain tone in Lynn's voice, an indication that she may have personally fallen victim to game-playing.

"I suppose that's true. In any event, I'm not going to allow them to spoil my outing with Nikki. It's far too important to her."

Lynn tilted her head. "What about you?"

"If it's important to her, then it's important to me. I may not be particularly fond of this type of recreation, but I have to try it a few times before I can truly gauge my comfort level."

"You're a very fair person, Kate."

"I try to be." Kate glanced over at the others. "So what happens now?"

"After the rest get back, we'll start setting up the tents." Lynn nodded at a nearby group of trees. "See that little rise? Kim and I usually set up there, but there's plenty of room for two tents. You and Nikki can set up right next to us. The ground stays dry even when it rains because of the drainage, and it offers a good view of the river. It's also far enough away that you can get some sleep no matter how late everyone else stays up."

The low hum of engines permeated the air and, expectantly, Kate glanced down the lane as several cars, including Nikki's blue Honda, jounced into the campground. Kate watched her lover get out of the small hatchback with a sort of proprietary swagger that she had lacked until now. Nikki spotted her, and a bright smile lit up her face.

"Have you picked us out a spot?" Nikki had a bit of a condescending note in her voice.

Kate indicated the rise. "Right there," she said blandly. "It'll stay dry even if it rains, and it has a good view of the river."

Nikki seemed surprised. "Good call."

Kate grinned and helped Nikki unpack their gear from the back of the car. Under Nikki's direction, they soon had the tent up, the air mattress inflated, and their sleeping bags spread out. By the time they had finished, the sun was going down and all the women had gathered around the fire that crackled energetically in the pit. Kate sat down on a convenient log while Nikki took her place on the ground between her legs, leaning back into her embrace. Another woman had brought along a guitar and was strumming it lightly as the group chattered loudly while roasting hot dogs and marshmallows.

Kate brushed her lips over the top of Nikki's head, feeling warm and contented as she hugged her. She could almost understand the appeal of camping at times like this, with the roaring fire and the air around filled with companionship and laughter. She gradually became aware of being scrutinized and glanced up to meet June's burning gaze across the fire. Kate offered a cold smile, warning her away with an easy menace. It was June who dropped her eyes first, and Kate shook her head. These girls were so unskilled in this sort of thing. They might be capable of causing heartache in this group, but they wouldn't last a minute in the social set Kate normally ran with.

"What are you thinking?" Nikki's face was gentle as she looked up at her.

"How beautiful you are," Kate said, stroking her lover's hair languidly. "How much I love being here with you."

Nikki blushed. "You're dangerous. Don't show anyone else that charm or I'll be scraping them off with a spatula."

Kate chuckled as she leaned down to kiss her gently. The moment was interrupted when Kim plopped down beside them with an expression on her face that caused them to straighten alertly.

"What's up?"

"Apparently, Kate and Lynn are having this wild affair," Kim said dryly. "At least, according to May who just finished filling me in on the details on how chummy they got while we were picking up the cars. I guess they were actually holding hands."

"What?"

Kate could feel the surge of anger in her partner, the way Nikki abruptly tensed. "Gently," she advised. "Don't give them the satisfaction." She glanced at Kim. "You know that's not true."

Kim waved her hand dismissively, embarrassed. "Of course I know that. It's just the Summer Twins trying to cause trouble. I merely wanted to give you a head's up in case something gets back to you."

Nikki's body was a bowstring, actually quivering beneath Kate's palms as she glared across the fire. "I'm going to—" she began.

"No." Kate spoke softly but intently. "That's what they want. A reaction from you to let them know they're getting to you. That's where they derive their amusement, from the ability to cause dissention. Don't grant them that power over you, Nikki."

Slowly, Nikki relaxed, but her gaze was still troubled when she looked up at Kate. "We can't let them get away with it."

"They only 'get away with it' if they provoke us into retaliating. I'm sure if you went over there and made a scene, they'd have all sorts of ways to turn it back on you and make it appear to others who aren't as aware of what's going on that you're the one being unreasonable and out of control. Believe me, I've seen their type before. The only way to deal with them is to remain above the situation."

"Kate's right, Nik," Kim said. "You know better than to let them needle you."

Nikki was very still, breathing slowly and deeply for a few moments before finally dipping her head. "Fine," she said in a grating voice. "But I don't have to like it, or them. Why do people have to act like that?"

Kate shrugged. "People are unhappy, and they somehow translate that into trying to make others unhappy. Misery loves company, you know." She leaned down and nuzzled Nikki, slipping her arms across her chest to hug her warmly. "But happiness grows exponentially, my love. Concentrate on that rather than the small pettiness of a few malcontents."

Nikki's body relaxed further. "I'll try."

"That's all I can ask." But Kate frowned as she glanced across the fire, her keen mind evaluating her options.

CHAPTER NINETEEN

Strolling back to the fire after a brief trip into the woods, Nikki fumed over the perfidy of the Summer Twins. Kate was right about not letting them know they had gotten to her, but she still wished she could give them a taste of their own medicine. As she passed a group of canoeists huddled at a picnic table some distance from the fire, sharing another joint, she heard something that made her alter her path.

"Did I hear someone say Monica Henderson?" she asked as she squeezed into the circle.

"Yeah," one of the women said, looking over at her oddly. Nikki recognized her as one of a group from Pictou Road, a cheerful older woman named Victoria. Victoria was partnered with a dour individual named Jennifer, who was casual friends with one of Kim's acquaintances who used to date Debbie's best friend from high school.

Sometimes Nikki didn't think she knew these people as much as kept track of them by some eclectic chain of connections. It was somewhat like the six degrees of separation game, without involving Kevin Bacon.

"Do you know Monica?" Victoria asked.

"Uh, actually, no," Nikki temporized, trying to come up with a reasonable explanation for why she was asking. "I know…uh, her boyfriend."

Victoria's face cleared as if she knew what Nikki was talking about. Nikki was very glad that one of them did.

"You mean Pat."

A light went on in Nikki's head. Who else would have access to the woman's car? "Yeah, Pat," she said conversationally. "What's he doing now?"

"Still the shift foreman at Elliot Manufacturing." Nikki barely resisted the urge to thrust her fist into the air in triumph. Victoria frowned slightly, though she was too relaxed to really detect anything in Nikki. "I thought you knew him?"

"Only in passing." Nikki spoke glibly. "I just heard he was going out with Monica." She paused, trying to come up with something else to provoke further discussion without making it appear she was digging for information. "They're still getting along, aren't they?"

Victoria didn't seem to find this an unusual comment, which made Nikki suspect it was a volatile relationship. She just thanked the fates that gossip was such a prevalent pastime in this part of the Maritimes.

"Well, they had a pretty tough time when Stevie died." Victoria apparently thought that Nikki knew all about it, and Nicky wasn't about to disabuse her of that notion. "Pat was really torn up about it."

"Yeah?" This was far too easy. "He and Stephen were that close?"

"Best friends all through school. That's how Pat got the job."

At that moment, Victoria's partner came back from wherever she had been, and the conversation trickled away. Nikki hesitated, trying to figure out how to reopen it, but couldn't come up with a good angle. Momentarily defeated, she took a polite hit from the joint as it passed her way, handed it to the next person, then drifted away from the group and strolled back to the fire, worrying these new bits of information like a puppy with a bone.

So Pat was the man in cahoots with Martin and Tiffany. Of course, what exactly they were in cahoots about remained a mystery, and whether it had anything to do with Stephen's death had yet to be determined. As Nikki resumed her place next to Kate, she decided she would have to find out more about Pat. It was too bad that she hadn't gotten a last name, but he was the shift foreman at the Elliot plant. Tracking him down shouldn't be that difficult.

"What are you scheming about?"

Startled, Nikki looked up at her lover. "Who, me?"

Kate eyed Nikki through lowered lashes. "Yes, *you*. I know that furrow between your eyes. You're up to something."

Nikki flushed at the accusation, and at the accuracy of it. "Nothing much." She hesitated. "I found out whose car was at the motel. I think the man I saw was Pat, the shift foreman at Elliot Manufacturing."

"Pat Spencer?"

Nikki grinned. Sometimes the fact that her lover was at the center of Truro's business community was extremely useful. "You know him?"

"Not that well. He was a friend of Stephen's so I saw him on occasion at family gatherings."

Kate gave Nikki a stern glance, and Nikki decided it was time to change the subject. "Feel like going to bed?"

Kate continued to stare at her. "Are you trying to change the subject?"

"Do you have a problem with going to bed?"

Kate offered a smile that held a touch of sensuality. "No problem at all."

Nikki rose to her feet and pulled Kate up beside her. A chorus of "good nights" resounded from the circle around the campfire, along with a few knowing looks that made Nikki a little self-conscious. Taking Kate's hand in her own, she strolled over to the ridge and their tent.

Nikki switched on the small battery-operated lamp that gave them enough light to undress by, and undoubtedly offered anyone who was glancing in that direction an impromptu shadow striptease through the canvas. That thought, and the realization that it had grown considerably cooler in the late May evening, caused Nikki to suggest they retain a certain amount of clothing rather than strip down entirely. She waited until Kate was situated before she switched off the lamp and joined her.

Snuggling in their two sleeping bags zipped together, Nikki spooned against her lover and Kate made a small sound of amusement. "Listen," she said quietly.

Nikki paused, lifting her head. "What?"

"We can hear the conversations going on around the fire. Quite clearly."

"So?"

"So if we can hear them, they most certainly can hear us. I know you wanted to teach me the joys of two people in a sleeping bag, but considering the circumstances, I think we should just sleep."

"We could make love quietly, you know."

Kate exhaled audibly, almost a sigh. "You make that remarkably difficult, my darling." She reached back to stroke the outside of Nikki's thigh. "I tend to forget where I am or what else is going on when you do what you do to me, and I always express my appreciation." She paused. "Loudly."

"That you do." Nikki wrapped her arms tightly about her lover. "Fair enough." Despite her slight disappointment, she understood Kate's reservations perfectly. The thought of anyone from the group listening to them or, worse, making some sort of ribald or disparaging remark regarding their intimacy, was not anything Nikki was comfortable with either. Besides, it was very nice just lying there, wrapped around her partner in the cozy darkness of their tent.

"I do adore holding you," she murmured in Kate's ear.

Kate pushed back against her, turning her head so that her cheek was pressed against Nikki's lips. "I love your holding me. I want you to do it for the rest of my life."

"I will," Nikki said, her voice a bit ragged from the emotion suddenly filling her. "Forever." She inhaled deeply, basking in her lover's warmth, delighting in her lovely fragrance. "Did you enjoy yourself today?" she asked.

"I did."

Nikki was relieved and more than a little pleased. "Would you like to try it again? I can't promise cows every time."

Kate chuckled. "What, no cows? I don't know about that…"

Nikki started to laugh which set off Kate, and for the next few moments, the memory of the earlier bovine encounter kept them going until they were both weak, ribs aching from their mirth. Nikki didn't think she'd ever forget the sight of the Summer Twins thrashing their way frantically from the river. When their laugher finally trailed off, Nikki settled against her lover and closed her eyes, feeling happier than she had ever felt before.

"I love you, Kate."

"I love you too, darling," Kate told her quietly. "Sleep well."

"'Night," Nikki mumbled before drifting off with the infinitely pleasant sensation of her lover in her arms.

❖

She woke sometime in the night, uncertain where she was and feeling as if something was wrong. Fuzzily, she realized she was alone and that some sort of commotion was going on in the camp. She fumbled around for her glasses, slipping them on before she could find the lamp. Disturbed when she couldn't find Kate, she hastily pulled on some sweatpants and crawled out of the tent, wrapping her arms around herself and shivering in the cool night air.

"What's going on?" Kim demanded, looking equally confused and startled as she and Lynn spilled from their tent.

"I don't know." Nikki searched the darkness, trying to spot Kate. The fire had died out hours earlier and the moon had set, with dawn still several hours away. Other women were stirring, calling out uncertainly, and Nikki lifted her lamp high as she and her friends headed toward the area where most of the group had set up camp. As she moved closer, Nikki stared in astonishment at a convulsing mass near one of the picnic tables, muffled cries of outrage and curses issuing from within the collapsed tent.

"It's the Summer Twins," Kim identified dryly. "They must have put their tent up wrong. I can't imagine why. Do you suppose they were…uh, what, drinking a little?"

Others appeared to be drawing the same conclusion, and those who had gathered around the cause of the disturbance were showing less alarm and more disgust as May and June finally managed to crawl out of the entangling nylon. Mutters that were far from complimentary were directed at the Twins, the loudest coming from their own friends.

Nikki shook her head in aggravation at what seemed like another display of bad behavior from the duo, but she was far more worried about Kate's absence. She headed back to her tent, wanting to retrieve her shoes before she searched further. To her surprise and great relief, Kate was tucked into the sleeping bag, looking alert and curious as Nikki crawled into the tent.

"Where were you?" Nikki asked, zipping the entrance shut behind her.

"I had to go into the woods for a bit," Kate explained blandly. "What's going on?"

Nikki snorted in disgust as she peeled off her pants and slipped into the warmth of the sleeping bag. "May and June. Too drunk to put their tent up right, I guess. It collapsed on them." Nikki switched off the lamp, and they settled back against the mattress.

"Oh. That's too bad."

Nikki heard a tone in Kate's voice, a certain inflection that most would have missed. Feeling a thrill of suspicion, Nikki lifted her head. The thought that struck her seemed so outrageous, she could scarcely grant it credence. Yet, May and June were experienced campers regardless of their overindulgence, and on further reflection, Nikki found it difficult to believe they would put their tent up so incompetently that it would collapse on them.

Wishing she could see Kate's face, she asked, "Uh, while you were out walking around in the woods, you didn't happen to see anyone loosening some tent pegs?"

Kate did not respond immediately. She patted Nikki's hip then turned away from her and settled into the bedding. "Go to sleep, Nikki," she said, in case it wasn't clear enough that the conversation was over.

Unable to see a thing, Nikki stared into the night, lost in amazed admiration and the unmistakable sense that Kate had depths that she was only beginning to discover.

CHAPTER TWENTY

K ate lay awake in the misty light of predawn. Beside her, Nikki slumbered peacefully, her body rising and falling almost imperceptibly. The air mattress kept them off the ground, but every time Kate moved even a little, she feared that the plug at the end would give way and the whole contraption would collapse.

She had lain awake most of the night, with only the briefest spells of dozing, unable to toss and turn lest she disturb Nikki. She was sore and not a little out of sorts, longing for the luxury of her large, comfortable bed at home.

Feeling grimy and unkempt, she longed for a shower. She could always take a dip in the river, of course, but that held as much appeal as the rest of this camping exercise. The air was nippy, making the end of her nose cold, and she buried it in the warm hollow of Nikki's neck and shoulder.

She wondered how long Nikki was planning to extend this excursion into the great outdoors, and if she could come up with some way to hurry it along.

"Hmmm, Kate? You cold?"

"A little." Kate's answer was punctuated by a gust of wind that made the tent shudder. "You promised to keep me warm."

"So I did." Nikki's eyes narrowed lazily, and her hands started to wander beneath Kate's T-shirt.

"Nikki?"

"You didn't think I'd pass up the opportunity to make love to you in a sleeping bag, did you?"

"What about the noise?"

"Everyone else is still asleep. We'll just have to be quiet."

Kate quivered as Nikki found a particularly sensitive spot, her drowsiness forgotten, along with the grumpiness she'd felt earlier. "If you say so."

"I do." Nikki's voice was husky. "But first, there's something I want to ask you."

"I'm listening. Distracted, but…listening."

"Did you do something to June and May's tent last night?"

"What makes you think that?" Kate slipped her arms around Nikki's neck and kissed her deeply.

It felt so good to have Nikki's hands plying her with such skill, Nikki's lips tasting her hungrily as they moved together. She felt her T-shirt being pulled over her head, and she lifted her arms to help. Her panties were slid down her legs, and she kicked them off to disappear into the bottom recesses of the sleeping bag. Kate helped Nikki out of her clothes, no longer finding it cold in the morning air. Instead, it was warm and becoming warmer. Smooth skin slipped over hers as Nikki settled onto her, her weight a soft comfort in the gray dawn.

Though they tried to remain quiet, their breathing was harsh in the stillness, and Kate bit her lip as a whimper rose from her throat. She buried her face in Nikki's chest, gasping as her legs were lovingly forced apart and she was exposed to Nikki's gentle touch.

Kate reached out, finding her own path to the intimate delights that waited. Nikki felt silky smooth and wet on her fingers, and they shifted position to find a complementary rhythm, falling into a delicate dance of desire and wanton pleasure that rose within them in waves, each one stronger than the one before.

Kate felt the peak hover just beyond her, teasing, so close, yet so tantalizingly far away. She arched for it, needing it desperately as she felt her lover strive with her. They would reach that plateau together, she knew, and that knowledge made the pleasure even deeper, her response more potent, and the demand all the more powerful. She was almost there. Her heart rate accelerated and she found it hard to draw breath. Almost…there…

With a muted pop, the plug at the end of the mattress was forced out, and air hissed out like steam from a teakettle. They barely had time to recognize what was happening before the mattress collapsed beneath them, letting them drop to a hard ground studded liberally with stones. Kate let out a muffled oath as Nikki squashed her flat before regaining her balance and moving off her.

"Damn it." Nikki peered at her anxiously. "Are you all right?"

Kate wiggled her fingers and flexed her wrist carefully, deciding it wasn't broken or even sprained. Just tweaked a little. She wondered if she would have to strap it up with an Ace bandage. "I'm okay. I guess some things just don't work in a sleeping bag. That, or your other partners were much better at this sort of thing."

Nikki flushed. "Actually, I've never tried to make love in a sleeping bag before. None of my other lovers liked camping."

"That's not the impression you gave me."

Nikki looked embarrassed and her face grew even redder when Kim called from the next tent, "Hey, are you guys all right?"

"We're fine," Kate replied.

"What happened?"

Nikki scrambled to pull on her clothes. "The mattress collapsed. Nothing serious."

"Why'd it collapse?"

"Never mind."

Kim's snort of understanding was very audible as Lynn, apparently also awake, started to laugh. Kate covered her face with her hands. This camping trip just got better and better.

"I guess we should get up." She drew fresh clothes from her pack. "I don't suppose anyone brought a spare shower."

"Actually, Kate, we have one." Kim poked her head through the entrance of the tent, as Nikki crawled out. "It's behind our tent."

Kate hitched the sleeping bag up and gazed at her, nonplussed. "Really?"

"Yeah, it's a camping shower with a pouch that you set up in a tree. You fill it with water, and when you open the nozzle, gravity makes it work. Lynn and I already took our showers last night, and we refilled it so there's plenty there. Want to try it?"

"Lead the way." Kate started to throw back the sleeping bag, remembered her state of dishabille, and sank back down against the pillow.

Kim grinned. "I'll wait out here until you're presentable."

Too cheered by the prospect of cleaning up to be embarrassed at Kim's comment, Kate found her T-shirt and panties, pulling them on before she crawled from the sleeping bag. Carrying her clothes, a towel, and some shampoo, she eagerly followed Kim behind their tent where a flimsy box made of canvas and aluminum poles provided a margin of privacy beneath a large red maple tree. Bushes surrounded it, and though it had a moss floor and appeared highly primitive, it also looked quite functional. Feeling grimy as she was, Kate actually thought it was rather clever.

After Kim had disappeared, she undressed and slipped through the zippered opening with her towel and shampoo. She flipped the towel over the canvas wall, twisted the shower nozzle above her as Kim had instructed and water cascaded down.

Her shriek reverberated through the campground and undoubtedly woke whoever had still been sleeping. Sheer shock made her gasp for air, and from the other side of the canvas, she could hear Nikki's accusing tone directed at Kim and Lynn.

"Why didn't you tell her it was going to be cold?"

❖

A few hours later, after the group had said their good-byes and got in their respective cars, Nikki and Kate drove down the short lane to the paved road after them.

When Nikki didn't turn right at the crossroads, but instead went in the opposite direction their friends took, Kate asked, "Where are we going?"

"Thought we could go the long way, take in some scenery."

Nikki knew these back roads well, having grown up in the area, and she wanted to prolong their weekend a little. A cloud of dust kicked up behind the little car as they rattled and shook their way along a narrow band of gravel.

Eventually Nikki found what she was looking for, a small lane half grown over by brush. Kate flung her a sharp look as she made the turn and they began bumping over the ruts of the old logging road.

Nikki smiled. "Ever been parking?"

"You mean…" Kate looked vaguely unsettled. "Here?"

"Nobody around for miles," Nikki found the landing where the trucks had loaded years earlier, and turned the car around so it faced out before turning off the engine. Through the open windows, they could hear nothing but the birds and the breeze rustling the leaves. It was dead silent otherwise, with no sound of intruding engines or urban noise.

They sat quietly for a few moments before Kate remarked in a dry tone, "You take me to such lovely places."

Nikki laughed. "Hey, I'm hoping this will become a very lovely memory."

Kate glanced at her slyly. "You really want to make love in your car?"

"What better way to christen it?" Nikki put her hand on Kate's thigh, caressing it lightly. "Haven't you ever made out in the back seat?"

"Made out, yes," Kate said, laughter lacing her tone. "Actual sex, no. And never in broad daylight."

"Well, there's a first time for everything." Nikki leaned closer and kissed Kate softly, her lips lingering on that wonderful mouth. Moving her hand up slightly, she pressed against the heat between Kate's legs. "Try something new, sweetie."

Kate laughed and, at Nikki's urging, crawled into the back through the opening between the front bucket seats. As she turned and settled against the side of the car, Nikki followed, excitement making her breathe quickly. Slipping her arms around Kate, she pulled her close, delighting in the warmth of her body. Kate returned her kisses eagerly, hunger evident in the way she tugged at Nikki's T-shirt, jerking it loose from her jeans and dragging it up.

Nikki giggled and finished pulling it over her head, then groaned when she felt Kate's hands cover her breasts, teasing the nipples through the thin fabric of her bra. "Here, let me get that off."

As soon as she was free of that encumbrance, Kate immediately replaced her left hand with her mouth, lips closing firmly over the rosy bud. The sensation of her tongue dancing over the sensitive flesh sent a tremor through Nikki's groin, and she reached for Kate, fondling her breast through her T-shirt, making her moan quietly.

The confines of the small backseat made maneuvering tricky, particularly as their passion grew. Kate banged her elbow into the side window as she tried to pull off her top, while Nikki thumped her knee soundly into the back of the console containing the gear shift, but neither of them paused.

"Oh, that's what I want," Nikki murmured as she managed to get Kate's jeans unbuttoned and pulled down to afford her access to the hot flesh. She caught her breath as the silky moisture bathed her fingers, making Kate twitch as she brushed over the firm line of her ridge. "God, you're so wet."

"You make me that way," Kate breathed into her ear. "God, you make me want you so badly."

Nikki exhaled slowly, feeling humbled and elated by the comment as she always did. At times she wondered how Kate could love and need her so much, how she could share the deep emotion that Nikki held for her. So often Nikki felt unworthy of Kate, unable to comprehend what she had done to make her so very fortunate and afraid that she would somehow undo her luck. But then Kate's desire and love for her would show in her face so blatantly that it took Nikki's breath away. Just as it did now.

"I love you so much," she whispered as she fondled Kate, feeling close to tears suddenly.

"I love you, too, my darling," Kate told her as she pushed Nikki's knees apart. "Spread your legs."

Nikki shuddered from the sensation of Kate slipping her hands up her inner thigh and worming her way into the leg of her shorts, disdaining the need to remove them. Kate pushed aside the elastic of her panties and dipped into Nikki's moisture before finding her spot and manipulating her firmly.

"Oh, God, Kate."

"You know, I'm really beginning to like your displays of spontaneity."

Nikki laughed. "I'm just glad I could find this place."

Kate drew back so she could look into her eyes. "You've never been here before?"

"No, but I can always tell how long it's been since a logging road's been used," Nikki told her as she slipped two fingers slowly into her lover, watching as Kate's eyes unfocused with pleasure. "The trees have been replanted and only half grown. It'll be another five years before they're logging here again."

Kate clenched around Nikki's fingers. "As long as we're not interrupted in the next few moments." She quivered slightly. "Or hours."

Nikki bit her earlobe and undulated against the caress between her legs, almost undone by Kate's touch. She used her thumb to flick Kate's ridge lightly. "Does that feel good?"

Kate groaned loudly. "God, you know it does." Her breath was coming quickly now. "Faster, darling. Please."

Nikki increased both the pace and pressure of her thumb on Kate while she began to thrust her fingers in and out of her heat in a perfect counterpoint of rhythm. Kate's attention to Nikki became somewhat haphazard as her pleasure grew, keeping her at a nice level of excitement but not escalating her to a pinnacle. Nikki was fine with that. She wanted to make Kate come first, wanted to see her expression as the sensation overwhelmed her, wanted to hear her throaty moans as she neared and then tumbled over the peak.

Kate uttered short, sharp sounds, not quite grunts, but forceful expulsions of breath as Nikki plunged into her. She was close, Nikki could tell, could feel her shuddering from the sensation. Then abruptly she arched and cried out, half moan and half scream. Avidly, Nikki stared into Kate's face, seeing her lover's expression that was so wanton and so vulnerable and so perfect. Silky walls fluttered around her as she thrust into Kate a final time, thumb pressing tightly on her ridge before slowly easing her touch in slow increments, which corresponded to the relaxing of Kate's body.

"Oh, darling."

Nikki tightened the grip of her other arm around Kate's shoulders, pulling her closer. "I'm here, baby," she whispered. "You're so beautiful."

Kate nuzzled into her neck. "And you are so wonderful. God, what you do to me."

"I love doing it to you," Nikki said, meaning every word reverently.

Kate lifted her head from Nikki's shoulder, drawing back to gaze at her as her lips parted in a sensual smile. She had never lost her intimate hold on Nikki, though it had ceased its intensity as Kate experienced hers. Now, she resumed her interrupted caress, rubbing Nikki gently, but with increasing demand.

"Why don't you lean back a little?"

"Yeah?"

Kate smiled and pushed her back against the side of the car. Nikki found it suddenly difficult to breath as Kate scrunched onto the seat and insinuated herself between Nikki's knees, dipping her head. Her breath was warm on Nikki as she brought her mouth down, and it made

Nikki tremble with anticipation. The actual touch didn't disappoint, and she groaned loudly as Kate began to torment her with skillful lips and tongue.

Looking down, she was overwhelmed by the sight of her lover pleasuring her so freely. Kate's bluish-gray eyes lifted to meet her gaze, a smoldering look of desire and love that penetrated to the bone. Then it all grew too much, and Nikki had to close her eyes as her orgasm crashed over her in a wave. She felt rather than heard the cry in her throat escaping as she surrendered to all the emotion and joy flooding through her.

Slowly, slowly she came back to herself, opening her eyes in time to see Kate sitting up and delicately wiping her mouth with her hand. It was an oddly charming moment, and tears stung Nikki's eyes as she watched.

Kate smiled at her when she became aware of Nikki's gaze. "Good?"

"Tremendous." Nikki abruptly became aware of her awkward position and the crick in her neck. "Ow."

Kate laughed and Nikki gingerly untangled herself. They spent the next few moments pulling on their discarded clothes and straightening up. Then they wrapped their arms around each other and sat embraced in the back seat, exchanging slow kisses and affectionate caresses.

"This was fun," Kate said as she crawled back into her seat.

"Yeah, it was." Nikki slipped back into the driver's seat and started the car, feeling very happy and slightly mussed. "You know, next time we do a road trip, we should stow one of our toys in the glove compartment."

Kate turned to her, a look of absolute surprise widening her eyes. But Nikki saw intrigued interest there as well and smiled placidly as she put her car in gear and eased on down the logging road to the highway.

CHAPTER TWENTY-ONE

K ate luxuriated beneath the warm water of her shower, appreciating it as never before. Privately, she referred to the canoe trip the previous weekend as her "wilderness excursion," and despite the positive front she'd offered Nikki and her friends, she hoped there were no plans for another trip to the great outdoors anytime soon.

Turning the water off, she wrapped a large towel around herself, adding another to bind her wet hair as she stepped out of the bathtub. She strolled into her bedroom and took fresh undergarments from her dresser. Across the bed, a simple but elegant dress was laid out, a deep, royal blue to bring out her eyes, cut low to offer a tantalizing hint of cleavage for Nikki's benefit.

Having declined her grandmother's initial dinner invitation, Kate didn't dare avoid the second request, or further delay the inevitable. Irene was determined to meet Nikki, and Kate could only hope the encounter would not be a complete disaster. Nikki didn't seem overly nervous about meeting the formidable woman and if she displayed the same presence and aplomb as she had at the Historical Society Dinner, it should be more than enough to impress Irene.

Not that Nikki needed to impress Gram, Kate reminded herself sharply as she finished drying off and began to dress. It would just be easier if she did. Contemplating her reflection in the antique mirror as she brushed her hair, Kate wished that Nikki were there to talk to, rather than coming by later to pick her up. Her thoughts drifted to their recent discussion about living together and what it meant to Nikki.

Were they ready to move in together?

She glanced around her small bedroom. She, and perhaps Nikki as well, had been assuming that when the time came, they would move into Kate's apartment above the bookstore. Now Kate wondered if that was entirely fair. Nikki would have to give up her territory to move into someone else's, which could be very difficult.

Then there was Kate who tended to work long hours, a hazard of living right on top of her place of business. How many times during an evening would she pop downstairs to finish a task that could easily have waited for the next workday? She made a point of not doing so when Nikki visited, but was that because she was still a "guest" to a certain extent? If Nikki lived there, would Kate fall back into the habit of spending all her spare moments in the bookstore?

Perhaps they should consider other arrangements altogether, maybe a condo or even a house. Asking Nikki to participate in a mortgage might be a bit much on top of her new car payment, but, on the other hand, Kate couldn't see the contribution exceeding what Nikki already paid for rent.

She took a deep breath. Thoughts of sharing a mortgage, of buying a home together, gave her an uncertain feeling in her stomach and suddenly made clear what Nikki had meant about this being a commitment. Perhaps Kate *had* been regarding the concept more lightly than she should.

She finished doing her hair, frowning as she began to apply her makeup. Was she ready to "marry" Nikki? Simply wanting company around while she dressed for dinner was not sufficient reason to take such a large step. On the other hand, the thought of not having Nikki there in the future was like an ache in Kate's chest, an emptiness that actually frightened her. They needed to discuss it further. Perhaps she would raise the topic after they returned from dinner, since Nikki would surely be spending the night. Kate could no longer imagine a Saturday night without falling asleep next to her lover, or waking up on Sunday morning without being in her arms.

The sound of footsteps ascending the back stairs and the brief tap at the apartment door made Kate realize how much time she had let slip away as she stared blankly at her reflection in the mirror.

"Sorry," she called out as she heard Nikki come in. "I'm running behind."

Nikki assumed a much-put-upon expression when she appeared in the bedroom doorway. "Women! They take forever to get ready." She blinked as Kate froze, staring at her. "It was a joke."

Kate shook herself. "That's not it." Hastily, she finished the last touches to her face and opened her jewelry box, extracting some gold earrings. "You're so beautiful, I actually had to stop to catch my breath."

Nikki blushed a deep red. Dressed in a new outfit that made her look even more attractive than she had the night of the Historical Society Dinner, she slowly pirouetted.

"I hoped you would like it. I bought it yesterday afternoon."

A black silk shirt was tucked neatly into dark trousers that fell gracefully about Nikki's long legs, while a rich wine blazer set off her blond hair and brilliant blue eyes. Nikki had obviously learned her fashion lessons well from Susan during their shopping excursions. She even had on a touch of makeup, her glasses replaced with contacts, her hair brushed neatly into a shining wave of gold about her face. Kate could see she was doing all she could to display her best side for Irene.

"Is it always this formal when you visit with your grandmother?"

"Just on special occasions," Kate explained, slipping on her shoes.

"Meeting me qualifies as special?"

Kate paused, then immediately moved over to her lover and leaned provocatively into her body. "You're very special," she assured her throatily. "In fact, you're the most special thing to ever happen to me."

Nikki leaned down, but didn't quite kiss her, keeping their lips mere millimeters apart. "Lipstick."

"Damn." Time was quickly slipping away and Irene appreciated promptness. Kate didn't want to muss Nikki's makeup either, so she stepped back and picked up her purse. "Shall we take your car or mine?"

"Mine's easier to get in and out of, especially since you're wearing a dress."

"Good point." Downstairs, in the alley behind the store, Kate slipped into the passenger seat of the blue Honda and smiled when she saw that it had been freshly washed, drops of water still beading on the hood. "I really need to buy a practical vehicle like this for myself."

"What would you get?" Nikki asked. "Tiffany Elliot drives a Mustang convertible. Those are really sharp cars."

Kate grimaced. "Let's not discuss the Elliots this evening. Besides, a convertible isn't very good in the winter. I'd like something a little more sedate."

They discussed the merits of various makes and models on the way to Bible Hill, where Kate directed Nikki to the Taylor home located in the Saywood Estates subdivision. She was aware of Nikki's eyes widening as they turned into the paved driveway leading up to the large house on the rise, but all she said when they got out of the car was, "Pretty big for one person."

Kate privately agreed. but her grandmother had her own way of doing things and practicality didn't always figure into it. She took Nikki's arm as they walked up the front steps to the expansive veranda, wanting to reassure her. Kate knew exactly what she was thinking when they rang the bell and Irene's housekeeper answered the door and showed them in, but Nikki managed to confine her reaction to a raised eyebrow.

"Kate, it's so good to see you." Irene Taylor swept across the marble tile of the large foyer to greet them. She was dressed in a green dress that lightened her level gray eyes. Her snowy hair was up, and as she presented a powdered cheek to be kissed, Kate hoped she looked half as good when she reached that age.

"This must be Nikki." Irene looked Nikki up and down with blatant interest. "You didn't tell me she was so stunning, Kate."

"That's just the icing on the cake." Kate hugged Nikki. "It's the inside that makes her so special."

"We can stop now," Nikki mumbled, her face flaming.

"Modest too. I like that. It's very nice to meet you, Nicole."

"Please, call me Nikki." She shifted from foot to foot, obviously still uncomfortable. "You have a very nice home."

"It's far too large for me," Irene admitted as she led the way into the lavishly decorated living room. "But I don't want to give it up."

She invited Kate and Nikki to take the love seat in front of the large fireplace before sitting next to them in a plush armchair. A small blaze crackled in the fireplace; the spring nights were still cool enough to warrant a fire this late in the year.

"Would you care for some champagne?" Irene reached for the bottle that sat in a silver ice bucket on a tray in the center of the coffee table.

Kate waited for Nikki to refuse the offer, but she accepted graciously and sipped the wine when Kate and her grandmother did, indicating nothing of her normal dislike for the liquor. Kate had never seen her drink and wondered how she would react to the alcohol content.

"So tell me, Nikki, where are you from?"

"I grew up outside of town. Beaver Brook."

"Is that on the way to the Annapolis Valley?" Irene responded.

"One way." Nikki's tone was dry, and Kate decided that she probably didn't think much of Irene's lack of geographical knowledge.

"I visited her parents' farm," Kate said. "It's a beautiful property."

"I'd like to meet your parents, Nikki," Irene said.

Nikki looked very uncomfortable.

To spare her a reply, Kate quickly changed the subject, asking Irene, "How is your garden?"

"It's fine." Irene fixed her eyes on Nikki with a look that Kate had learned over the years to be wary of. "Tell me about Stephen's funeral. I wasn't able to return in time to attend."

Nikki brightened. "I didn't go but Kate did."

Irene turned an expectant gaze on her granddaughter, and Kate resisted the urge to sigh "Well?"

"It was a funeral, Gram. Depressing and sad and conscious of a life ended far too prematurely. What did you expect?"

"I would like a little more," Irene pressed. "You knew Stephen, didn't you?"

"Only in high school, and a lot less so once I left for college." Kate sighed. "All right, I can tell you that the entire family was there, including a few I doubt Hannah has seen in decades. It was a little like vultures gathering to see what they could pick up." She waited to see if that rather irreverent statement produced a reaction and was surprised when Irene's expression didn't so much as flicker. Disconcerted, she continued. "Uh, Andrew and Hannah looked pretty upset by the whole thing, though he was obviously putting on a good face...you know, the stiff upper lip of the Man of the House."

Kate allowed herself to dwell for a moment on that gray day when Stephen was laid to rest. She and Susan had stood slightly apart from the other mourners, conscious of being the only ones not related in some way to the family. Andrew had been standing next to Denise, comforting his dead brother's widow, which left Tiffany somewhat on her own. She wasn't isolated, though. Martin had been nearby, and the two had been exchanging glances. Kate hadn't thought much of it at the time, but now in retrospect, as she was thinking about it...

She frowned and made a mental note not to share that with Nikki. Her lover needed no further encouragement to meddle in something that didn't concern her.

"Stephen was a good boy under all that reputation," Irene said somberly. "He liked to have a good time, that's true, but he never meant any harm."

"Did you know him well?" Nikki was staring at her keenly.

"Yes, as a mat—"

"This is wonderful champagne," Kate interrupted. "What year is it?"

The champagne was delicious, and Kate had been thoroughly savoring it. However, it seemed a bit too good for just a family dinner party, and she wondered if the selection perhaps indicated something about Irene's nerves. Was it possible that her grandmother was as unsure about this meeting as Nikki and Kate were?

Irene looked at her oddly. "It's a Jost, '91." Shaking her head slightly, she turned to Nikki with a charming smile. "I hope you're not allergic to scallops."

"No, I like seafood a lot."

"Excellent. As soon as my other guests arrive, we'll serve dinner."

Kate frowned. "Other guests?"

"You know I normally host a dinner party the second Saturday I'm home, Kate. Of course, if we'd had our family dinner as originally planned, I wouldn't have had to combine both events tonight."

Kate didn't like the sound of that. Her grandmother had that look in her eyes, a spark of contrariness that usually boded ill for someone. Nikki didn't seem to be disturbed, but she didn't know Irene. Kate wondered if this was some sort of punishment because their canoe trip had disrupted Irene's plans the previous weekend. On the other hand, having other guests present could cause the dinner to progress more smoothly. It might even keep Nikki from feeling as if she were constantly the center of Irene's attention.

That comforting thought was completely blown apart when the doorbell rang, and the housekeeper escorted Hannah Elliot, her son Andrew, and his wife Tiffany into the living room.

CHAPTER TWENTY-TWO

If Nikki was unpleasantly shocked when Hannah Elliot entered the room, Hannah appeared equally appalled to see who she was about to dine with. Nikki glanced at Irene, detecting a glint of what might have been glee in the light gray eyes as Kate's grandmother observed everyone with keen attention.

You old hag, Nikki thought with a mix of outrage and amusement, *you're enjoying this.*

She decided she wasn't going to let Irene get the better of her. Besides, this situation might actually turn out to her advantage. Certainly, the inquisitive part of her was gleefully rubbing its hands together at the opportunity to find out more about the Elliot family; she was certain one of them must have played a role in Stephen's murder.

She suspected that Irene had devised this evening as a sort of test to see if Nikki could handle the level of society to which Kate was accustomed. If that were the case, then Nikki was determined not to let Kate down, whose eyes, she noticed, were thunder gray, and who was obviously grinding her back teeth.

"Hannah, you know Kate, of course," Irene said, apparently oblivious to Kate's rising ire. "This is Nicole Harris, her…ah, significant other."

Nikki tried not to smile at Irene's brief hesitation as she tried to find a term for her relationship with Kate. She especially tried not to smile at the consternation on Hannah's face. Beyond the Elliot matriarch, Tiffany and Andrew looked on like spectators at a tennis match, eyes shifting rapidly back and forth between all the participants. Nikki thought Andrew looked upset, but Tiffany had a small smile on her generous mouth, as if the whole situation had been arranged for her own private amusement.

"We've met," Hannah managed in a grating voice.

"Ah, so you have," Irene said, as if the matter of the Historical Society Dinner had slipped her mind entirely. "Can I get anyone some wine? It's fabulous."

After distributing glasses to the new arrivals, who were regarding Kate and Nikki warily from their place on the sofa facing the fireplace, Irene smiled placidly. "Hannah was telling me that you were involved in a murder over the winter, Nikki," she said with considerable charm and very little tact.

Kate looked horrified, the Elliots appeared disconcerted, and Nikki had an extremely difficult time not laughing out loud. She was actually starting to like Irene. Perhaps being old granted a sort of social immunity, or perhaps Irene had just decided it did and everyone else was too afraid to challenge her.

"There was a murder. Kate and I discovered who the killer was." She looked with admiration at her lover. "Actually, Kate captured her. I stupidly got bopped over the head and was in the hospital emergency room at the time."

"Rick Johnson made the arrest." Kate was clearly not enjoying the conversation. She glared at her grandmother. "I just happened to be present. Is there a point to this?"

Irene smiled beatifically at her. "Of course there is. Obviously you and Nikki have a knack for this sort of thing."

Kate frowned, not liking that remark either.

"As you may or may not know," Irene continued. "Stephen Elliot was murdered. It's not been in the newspaper yet, but the police have shared that conclusion with Hannah. Perhaps if all of us work together, we can discover who did it since the police are taking such an inordinate amount of time to do their job."

Nikki couldn't decide which was more priceless—the expression on Kate's face or the look on Hannah's. "Are you hiring us?" She could barely suppress the laughter in her voice. A host of favorite fictional detectives filed through her mind, and she immediately quoted the first line that came to mind. "Our fee is five hundred a day plus expenses."

"Nikki!"

"Irene, this is completely inappropriate."

Hannah was louder than Kate, but only marginally. Tiffany didn't say anything, but Andrew frowned mightily and cast a dark look at Nikki that she found intriguing. What did he have to worry about? Her finding out that Martin and Tiffany were having it on behind Andrew's back? She filed the question away as something to pursue later. Irene listened to all the protests with a bemused expression, as if not sure why her perfectly logical suggestion was being met with such disdain. She glanced at her friend.

"Hannah, you were the one who told me all about Kate and Nikki's adventure." Nikki sincerely doubted that Hannah had described the incident in such positive terms. "I'm sure they could help if you'd give them the chance."

"I'm sure you think this is amusing, Irene." Hannah's voice was laced with anger. "But I don't appreciate the joke."

Irene sighed. "It wasn't a joke, merely a suggestion. If you don't want to avail yourself of their talents when they've proven them so aptly, then I'm certainly not going to force you." She smiled brightly and changed the subject. "Shall we have dinner?"

In the dining room, Nikki sat next to Kate, across from Andrew and Tiffany. Hannah took a spot at the opposite end of the table from Irene. Evidently the Elliot matriarch didn't want to give up any more territory, and this was her way of asserting herself. Nikki wondered how close the two women actually were. She hated to think any friend of hers would spring something like this on her.

From that point on the conversation seemed deliberately vague, centering on the weather or the current headlines, avoiding any controversial opinions, and questions about Irene's winter in Florida. Nikki didn't talk much, just listened intently as she ate what was in front of her, most of which she didn't recognize but decided was quite tasty. Kate displayed little appetite, replying with cold politeness to anything directed her way, but not volunteering anything. Nikki suspected she was just waiting until the others had left so she could tear into her grandmother.

Hannah and the rest of her family excused themselves as soon as it was polite to do so. Nikki wasn't sure how that was decided, but in this instance, it was shortly after they had returned to the living room to be served coffee and cake. Hannah pleaded fatigue, and as her grandson helped her on with her coat, Tiffany drifted over to where Nikki was seated on the sofa.

"You know, you don't want to be messing around in this." The brittle blonde spoke in a low voice that only Nikki could hear. "I've seen you watching Martin and me at the tennis courts. Don't go sticking your nose in where you might lose it."

Startled, Nikki looked over her shoulder to see if anyone else had heard the warning—or had it been a threat? Irene was speaking intently to Hannah as Andrew hovered over them, while Kate was near the fireplace, jabbing fretfully at the logs with a thin iron poker. Tiffany hurled another ominous glance at Nikki before she proceeded to the foyer to join the others in offering somewhat chilly farewells.

"Well, that didn't go as well as I had hoped," Irene announced when she returned to the living room. "Hannah can be so short-sighted at times."

"Hannah is short-sighted?" Kate dropped the poker and glared at her grandmother. "What were you thinking? Not only did you misrepresent us as the kind of people that would involve ourselves in such a thing, but did you ever once stop to think how Nikki might feel being around those homophobes?"

Irene lifted a thin eyebrow. "Nikki handled herself admirably. Perhaps you're underestimating her, Kate."

"That isn't the point." Kate's voice became icy. "You know Hannah doesn't like her or approve of our relationship."

"I've taught you the root causes of bigotry," Irene said in a patient tone. "Do you remember?"

"I know. It comes from fear," Kate said. "Fear of the unknown. Ignorance of the truth."

"Exactly. The more Hannah gets to know you, the more she sees both of you in social situations, the less she will fear you, and, correspondingly, the less she will be offended by you."

"I don't give a damn what Hannah thinks."

"Then why are you so upset that she doesn't like Nikki?"

"I'm upset because you placed Nikki and me in an awkward and uncomfortable situation."

Irene gave a nonchalant shrug that frustrated Kate even more. "You're certainly going to have to get over that attitude if you insist on investigating murders."

Kate raised her voice, something Nikki seldom, if ever, heard her do. "We're not investigating any murder!"

"If Hannah doesn't want to hire you, then I will," Irene announced as if there was nothing to discuss. "I want to know who killed Stephen as much as she does."

While Kate was still stuttering the beginnings of a reply, Nikki thought it was time to step in.

"Mrs. Taylor," she said with suitable gravity, "you seem to have the wrong impression. What happened last winter was purely a matter of us being in the wrong place at the wrong time. We didn't set out to track down a killer and we don't choose to get involved in these things intentionally." She paused, floundering as she tried to explain an incident that still confounded her, particularly since it had brought her and Kate together. "I mean, it just sort of happened. Stephen's death is something else altogether. I've been following the case at work. It's really something for the police to handle."

Irene looked disappointed. "But I can afford five hundred a day plus expenses."

"Uh, that was a joke." Nikki said. "I'm not a detective, Mrs. Taylor. I have no idea why Stephen was killed, or who did it. I'm not even sure how they did it. All I know is that somehow he drank, or was injected with, a chemical that they use in the factory. It acted quickly, so it must have been slipped to him at the Historical Society Dinner. Anyone could have done it. A member of his family, a waiter, a cook, or just someone passing by the table."

The catfight between Kate and Hannah had presented the perfect opportunity for a crime to be committed while no one was looking, but Nikki didn't add that.

"You've obviously thought about this a great deal," Irene observed pointedly.

"Yes, and I admit, I find it interesting," Nicky said, earning a frown from Kate. "I would like to know who did it. I would like to know how they did it. Mostly, I'd like to know *why* they did it."

"So would I." Irene placed a frail hand on Nikki's forearm. "I liked Stephen. He was a bit wild as a teenager, but he had a good heart. He deserved better than to die this way. Find out who did it for the both of us."

"Grandmother!"

Both Nikki and Irene turned to look at Kate, who had folded her arms across her chest. Her face was etched with old fear, her voice tight. "You don't know what you're asking. Nikki was almost killed in a fire set by the very person who murdered Sam Madison. I don't want her anywhere near a similar situation."

"If she works at the police station, she's already near it." Irene glanced at Nikki. "You *will* be careful, won't you, dear?"

"I'm always careful," Nikki told her cheerfully.

Kate just threw her hands up and walked away.

❖

Kate didn't look at Nikki as they drove back to her building, aware that she kept glancing at her, but refusing to acknowledge her. She wasn't sure whom she was more upset with, her grandmother for her ridiculous machinations during dinner or Nikki for indulging her. As they pulled into the alley behind her apartment, she got out of the car, barely waiting until it had rolled to a stop. She slammed her door with unnecessary force and headed for the back of her building. Nikki got out of her side and leaned against the roof, the engine still running.

"I suppose this means you don't want me to come in." she called after Kate.

"Does it matter what I want?" Kate ignored the hurt she heard mixed with Nikki's anger. She fumbled with the lock. The key didn't seem to fit properly, or perhaps her hands were shaking too much. "You'll just do whatever you want anyway."

Nikki stared at her in silence, and Kate blinked back frustrated tears as she finally got the door open. Inside, and with none of her natural poise in evidence, she glared back at the car. Nikki was still staring, her face set. Kate's eyes were drawn to hers and she had the strangest feeling that this was one of those moments that could dictate the future. She was balancing on the edge of a choice, considering certain actions and discarding them in a heartbeat, driven by emotions running so hot that she knew they could impact their relationship far beyond this night.

To her great surprise and relief, Nikki seemed to understand exactly what was happening even better than she did, and turned off the car engine.

Walking toward Kate, she said, "Can we talk about this?" Her voice quivered, but she was obviously trying to maintain her composure and not burst into tears.

Kate still hesitated, hurt warring with common sense. She wanted so much to say no and indulge her resentment, but between one breath and the next, she chose not to give into the confused feelings churning her stomach.

"Fine," she said with scant grace. "Let's talk."

They moved inside and sat down in the living room, one on the sofa and the other on the chair, eyeing each other with raw hurt and lingering anger. Eventually Kate decided she had better say something or they would be there all night.

"I don't want you involved in this," she said, as evenly as she could, which wasn't very even at all.

"I know." Nikki's face was pale. "You've made that clear, but I'm already involved."

"You don't need to be."

"It's something I have to do."

"Why?" Kate's cry of uncomprehending dismay came from her heart, and she felt a little more of her carefully wrought composure crumble. "Why do you feel you have to?"

Nikki looked startled at the question, as if she had never really considered her reasons. "I just have to know, Kate. I don't know why, but something about putting all the pieces together in this kind of situation makes me feel alive and useful."

Kate shook her head. "Your job at the hardware store must have been boring, but this one is a lot more interesting, isn't it?" She was trying very hard to understand Nikki and failing miserably. "Why do you need more?"

Nikki frowned. "It's fun, Kate."

"It's dangerous." Kate tried to calm her outrage at what seemed to be a flip response.

"But I'm not really doing anything. I'm just keeping my eyes and ears open." Nikki studied the hands lying limply on her lap, as if she didn't want to look at Kate. "Why are you so afraid for me?"

Kate felt her heart clench. "You don't know what it was like," she said, feeling as if the memory of that night would shatter her, "when I jumped out of Rick's truck in front of the burning cabin, believing you were in there. I don't want to ever feel that way again."

"But I wasn't in the cabin. I had escaped long before you and Rick ever showed up."

"That was pure luck! You could have been in there! You could have *died!*"

"Kate, I'm not going to do anything that will put me in that kind of danger ever again," Nikki said gently. "I've learned my lesson. I'm just going to ask a few questions and see what I can discover, but I'm not going anywhere I'm not supposed to."

"Why can't you just leave it alone?"

Nikki shrugged, somewhat helplessly. "I just need to know, Kate. I can't explain it. I need to know how things like this happen, and what makes them happen in the first place."

"Then become a police officer," Kate retorted, though the concept of Nikki being officially dispatched to dangerous situations didn't seem much better than having her unofficially dispatch herself.

Nikki smiled ruefully. "I'd hate that kind of job, Kate. Do you know what the police in this town *do* most of the time?"

"What you want to do, only they have the training and support to do it properly."

"No, they fill out paperwork and get caught in the middle of domestic disturbances. They write traffic tickets. They track down local drug dealers, but they have to let the Mounties deal with the big ones. They drive around town in the wee hours of the morning and never see anything more exciting than a cat. Sometimes they have reports of stolen property or vandalism, and once in a very brief while, they might get involved in a short car chase. Mostly, they have to clean up after accidents. I don't want to be the one to knock on someone's door and tell him or her that their child is dead because someone was drunk or just plain careless. A case like this is unusual and different, and that's why it interests me. Besides, Kate, I've found myself a part of these murders only because I happen to know the people affected or, rather, because *you* know the people affected." She smiled faintly, as if suddenly struck by the incongruity of her words.

Kate felt an ice dagger pierce her soul. "So it's my fault, is it?"

Nikki held up her hands defensively. "I'm just saying that I happened to be in the vicinity of a really exciting puzzle. Sometimes, you just have to run with the ball you're tossed, Kate."

"Or run away from it."

A serious expression darkened Nikki's eyes. "I don't like running away. I've done it a little too often in my life. I almost did it tonight downstairs, but it wouldn't have solved anything."

Kate inhaled slowly, shaken as they returned to the topic at hand. "No, it wouldn't."

Nikki reached out for Kate's hand. Kate vacillated only briefly before, entwining her fingers in Nikki's in a painfully tight grip neither pulled away from. "I'm sorry if it seems as if I'm taking this too lightly," Nikki's voice was infused with sincerity. "Kate, I swear, whatever I find out, I'll share it with you immediately and let your common sense figure out the next move. And I won't investigate anything on my own without your knowing about it ahead of time." She tilted her head. "We did a pretty good job solving the Madison murder when we worked together. It was only when I went off on my own that things got dangerous. I won't do that anymore."

Kate reluctantly allowed the point. If Nikki had not been in the woods poking around by herself, then perhaps she wouldn't have been accosted by the arsonist, tied up and left to die in the fire that ended up destroying Sam Madison's cabin. On the other hand, if Kate *had* been there, the arsonist might have tied them both up, they both might have been killed, and this whole conversation would be moot.

Kate rubbed her temple with shaking fingers, feeling the beginnings of a headache. She still couldn't believe her grandmother was trying to muscle in on the act, inciting Nikki to take new risks.

"Here, let me." Abruptly, Nikki left her chair and crossed the space between them to sit on the sofa beside Kate, reaching up to massage her temples.

Her fingers were gentle on Kate's skin, making slow circles to draw out the ache and subtly urge her closer. Kate resisted at first, still angry, but she finally relaxed and before she was quite sure what was going on, she was leaning back against her lover, her feet up on the couch as Nikki extended the massage down to her neck and shoulders.

"You don't fight fair," she grumbled.

Nikki sighed. "I was sort of hoping that the fight was over."

"I guess it is." Kate still felt uncertain, but wasn't sure it was worth taking any further. "I'm sorry, darling. I don't like fighting with you."

"I'm sorry, too." Nikki kissed the top of her head. "I know you worry about me, Kate, and sometimes I do things that give you cause, but I'll never allow my curiosity to come between us." She hugged Kate tightly, then paused. "If you really want me to walk away from this, I will."

Kate's heart ached. Because Nikki offered so freely, Kate couldn't accept. Clearly Nikki wanted to pursue this investigation and would only resent Kate if she stopped her. It would create a subtle and insidious breach in their relationship and inevitably drive a wedge between them. Kate still didn't understand *why* it was so important to Nikki, but she had to respect the power of that desire. Despite how much she hated the situation, she had to let Nikki be who she was or risk losing her in the end. Kate shook her head. "No. If you decide not to do this, it has to be for your own reasons not because my fears forced you into it. I just have to trust that you'll think twice and remember why I'm afraid."

Nikki tightened her embrace. "Thank you." Her breath was a warm wash in Kate's ear. "I love you so much."

Moisture stung Kate's eyes. "I love you, too." She found it hard to form the words past the lump in her throat. "That's why this is so hard for me."

"I know." Nikki rested her chin on top of her lover's head. "I won't betray your trust, Kate. I'll stay safe."

"I'm going to hold you to that."

Nikki hugged her again, and they settled back against the sofa, taking respite in one another. Resting her head beneath Nikki's chin, Kate prayed they wouldn't have any disagreement worse than this, though she suspected there would be other battles in their future. They needed to always choose as they had this night, to stay and face their problems rather than go off in separate directions to nurse hurt feelings and wounded pride that could only escalate the rift. If they could always get past that initial flare of outrage and talk to each other, Kate thought they stood a good chance of surviving as a couple.

She just wished it wasn't so difficult to make that choice.

CHAPTER TWENTY-THREE

Nikki woke with a start, thinking she had only dozed off for a few moments, but it was 4:15 the next morning. She could feel the nearness of her lover still asleep beside her. Kate's quiet presence soothed Nikki's soul and tempered her discord. She wasn't sure what had disturbed her. Perhaps her dreams, formless and unremembered, had left her unhappy in their aftermath.

They hadn't made love upon going to bed, their feelings still a bit raw and tender, and Nikki wondered if that had caused her restlessness. Sighing, she rolled over and slipped her arm over Kate, drawing close to her warmth and nuzzling into the soft hair at the nape of her neck. Closing her eyes, she tried to get back to sleep, but it stubbornly eluded her. Her mind continued to race, replaying the argument from the previous evening.

She didn't blame Kate for not understanding why investigating the Elliot family was so important. She didn't really understand it herself. Partly it was the seductive nature of dabbling in forbidden things, but did it go deeper than that?

She remembered her youth when she felt so different from the rest of those people around her, particularly her older siblings. Jeff and Julia were outgoing, popular in school and throughout their rural community, involved in many of the local activities. Although Nikki had been fairly athletic and participated in a few of the intramural sports, she remained shy and reserved overall, with very few close friends. Then Jaime had died and everything had changed.

Nikki's mind shied abruptly away from that dark path as it always did, automatic in its avoidance.

She became a complete loner after that, losing herself in television and books, searching out the latter in the library and at flea markets and yard sales. Mysteries were her particular favorite. The main characters always seemed to do whatever they wanted, and she wanted to be so clever and intuitive that she could dig out the truth where others couldn't. Perhaps if she *had* been as perceptive as those detectives, she could have seen beyond the surface at a critical time and prevented what should never have happened.

Kate stirred in her arms, as if she were trying to escape her own dark dreams. Nikki brushed her lips over her lover's smooth forehead, and Kate made a small sound in the back of her throat, her breathing smoothing over to settle into a regular rhythm, asleep once more.

Is this worth the pain and confusion it's causing her?

Nikki wished she could just walk away; things would be so much simpler without this compulsion to look beyond her everyday life to discover what motivated and affected others. Yet the thought of letting it go in favor of a Bed, Bath & Beyond mindset depressed her.

Besides, she wouldn't have many opportunities to play detective. This was Truro, after all. Although there had been three murders since the beginning of the year, that was so out of the ordinary that the small town was probably being listed as the current murder capital of the Maritimes, perhaps even all of Eastern Canada. Deaths such as those of Sam Madison and Katherine Rushton, and the new events involving the Elliot family, would probably never happen again in Nikki's lifetime.

She exhaled slowly and settled closer to her lover, feeling drowsiness start to drag her down. On some level, Nikki realized that if she gave in to Kate's fears, it would redefine their relationship, and not necessarily in a good way. It would take away a certain amount of her independence and inquisitiveness. Ironic, since she knew those were the traits that first attracted Kate and initially brought them together. Nikki's insight was fleeting, skating along the surface of her mind in that subconscious haze before sleep took over. She wasn't even sure if she would remember any of this when she awoke later.

❖

The sun pouring through the window heralded a bright Sunday morning, and, faintly, Nikki could hear church bells chiming. The curtains wafted in a spring breeze that brought with it a tinge of green and new growth. Kate had apparently decided to start things without waking her, and Nikki couldn't conceive of a better way to be drawn out of sleep than by the fingertips that traced searing patterns over her skin. Kate sought out her lips, kissing her deeply as she melted into her. Still pleasantly fogged from sleep, Nikki responded instinctively, seeking out those special places in her lover, never fully conscious until the instant of complete surrender, arching helplessly as she cried out Kate's name.

Afterward, she blew away a strand of her own sweat-soaked hair and gazed up at Kate who hovered above her, her warm eyes shaded to a soft blue.

"Good morning," Kate said." Good morning yourself." Nikki wiggled happily, still feeling the tremors ripple through her. "It's so hard to believe that you've never been with a woman before me. You're such a natural."

Kate looked smugly pleased and embarrassed at the same time. Nikki found it adorable. "I'm glad we made up."

"I am, too." Kate began a second, lazier exploration of Nikki's body. "Whatever shall we do today?"

Nikki couldn't assemble a logical thought. "Hmm, I think you're already doing it."

Another intensely pleasant interlude passed before they finally rose and, dressed in robes and little else, enjoyed a light brunch that they ate at Kate's formal dining table. As Kate perused the business section of the Sunday newspaper, Nikki skimmed the sports, comics, and entertainment sections before turning to what else was going on in the province. Truro was too small to publish a paper seven days a week so this publication originated in the city, granting more extensive coverage than the small town's paper usually did. A small item caught Nikki's attention.

"Listen to this. There was a car accident in the city last night."

"So?"

"Pat Spencer suffered minor injuries in a two-car collision early Saturday evening. He was treated for minor injuries and later released. Police are asking for any information leading to the identification of the second vehicle, which fled the scene." Nikki frowned, puzzled. "I wonder if someone was trying to shut him up."

Kate looked displeased. "It was an accident. Besides, Pat Spencer is a fairly common name. There's no reason to believe it's the man you're thinking of."

"No reason to think it isn't, either. I can get the particulars when I go into work Tuesday." Nikki evaluated the expression on her lover's face and decided that she should let the topic go, at least for the rest of the day. They only had Sundays to spend together, and allowing external things to occupy their attention would disrupt what little time they had. "Have you ever played tennis?"

Kate appeared startled at the comment, or perhaps it was the abrupt shift in conversation, but shook her head. "Once, I think, but it was just trying to hit the ball. I've never actually played a match."

"Would you like to go down to the courts and hit a few?"

"I have a better idea. Let me get my clubs out of the closet, and we can go down to the driving range for the rest of the morning."

"You mean…golf?"

Nikki tried not to look as dismayed as she felt. She knew that a lot of people placed the two sports into similar categories, but for her there was no comparison. Tennis demanded a great deal of physical effort, stamina, quickness, and eye/hand coordination. Not only did players have to contend with their own game, but the competitor across the net. On the other hand, a person could play golf alone, and walking from the cart to the ball was the only exercise it provided. Old men played it, for crying out loud, meandering over the extensively manicured courses like cattle grazing in a particularly lush field.

Still, Nikki reminded herself, she had aggravated Kate enough this weekend. Would it really kill her to spend the afternoon hitting a few of the silly little golf balls?

Quickly forcing a bright smile onto her face, she put down the paper. "Hey, I guess I have to learn sometime. Do I need to rent some clubs?"

Kate beamed at her, obviously pleased to be sharing her favorite pastime. "I have an extra driver and putter. But when we play a round, you should either rent or buy your own set."

"I'll do that," Nikki lied, keeping the smile carefully in place.

❖

The wind was stiff at the driving range, coming in over the marsh stretching out behind the town's biggest mall. Nikki was glad she had worn a thick sweatshirt over her T-shirt and jeans. This land could not be built on because of the danger of flooding every year, so Nikki supposed a driving range was one way to use it. She could also see some people flying model airplanes and kites nearby, exulting in the flat, open space devoid of power lines or trees, a rarity in the area made up primarily of forests and rolling hills.

Waiting as Kate rented the balls, Nikki stood on a strip of artificial turf, uneasily holding two drivers and gazing at the line of golfing aficionados stretching out on either side of her. She was pleasantly surprised to recognize Andrew Elliot hitting balls only two slots down. His back was to her, but she easily identified his profile as he lifted his head sideways before taking his shot. He didn't seem to be doing very well, many of the balls barely ten feet off the ground as they foundered through the air, but he doggedly kept at it, shanking one after another.

Nikki meant to keep half an eye on him as she and Kate played, but she found the game harder than she'd expected, and forgot about him as she tried to absorb Kate's lessons on technique. To her astonishment, her non-athletic lover seemed to find this sport easy, forcing Nikki to reevaluate a few preconceived notions she had been cherishing.

When Kate hit the ball, it invariably took off as if launched from a cannon, whistling through the air so quickly that Nikki had difficulty tracking it until it finally landed a significant yardage away. This continued until her last ball, at which point Kate said a few encouraging words to Nikki, presumably to console her for flubbing the ball a few times and generally embarrassing herself.

"Would you put the clubs back in the car please, darling?" Kate asked, picking up the buckets herself.

Nikki had done really well, she thought. But newcomers often seemed to take to the sport naturally, then the tightness would start, and suddenly the ball would refuse to go where they wanted. She gazed over at Nikki, who was standing at the back of the SUV, watching another car some distance away. Kate focused in on the vehicle and recognized Andrew Elliot sitting in the driver's seat, speaking to Pat Spencer, who was leaning through the window.

Andrew appeared upset, his face an ugly red. The conversation grew more heated, and Kate kept watching as she walked toward Nikki. Pat strode away from the car, and Andrew spun out of the parking lot and sped down the street until he turned the corner by the mall and was lost to view.

"Hear anything interesting?" Kate asked in a deliberately foreboding tone.

Nikki didn't take notice of Kate's pique, accepting the question at face value. "No." She clearly regretted that fact. "I was too far away, and they were talking too low. But whatever it was, it really made Andrew mad. I wonder who he was talking to."

"Pat Spencer. Stephen's friend." The words were out before Kate could stop them, much to her chagrin. Why couldn't she have kept her mouth shut?

"That was Pat Spencer?" Nikki's eyes were alight.

Kate didn't sigh, but she did get into her vehicle with a certain resignation. They had settled this issue the night before, she reminded herself as she started the truck. Nikki was going to pursue whatever lead dropped into her lap, and Kate was just going to have to accept that fact. She didn't even know how much of it was honest concern over Nikki, and how much of it was her own sense of impropriety about poking around in someone else's business. If Nikki wasn't discreet in her investigations, both Nikki and she could be humiliated, and Kate really did not like scenes of any sort, particularly public ones of the kind Hannah and she had indulged in at the Historical Society Dinner.

It was all so uncouth.

"So," she said, wanting to think about something else as they pulled out of the parking lot, "Can I interest you in a round of golf sometime?"

"Sure. You know, I didn't realize how good you are. You can really smack it a long way. Further than most of those guys."

Kate shrugged, though she was pleased by the compliment. "My father taught me. He and I used to play together a lot, particularly when I was a teenager." She smiled in remembrance. "He was always so proud of me. Other men wouldn't have wanted an adolescent girl around when they were playing golf, but Dad liked showing off how far I could hit to all his friends."

"That's cool." Nikki hesitated. "Do you miss them? Still, I mean. As much?"

Kate thought of the couple that had been killed on an icy highway between the Annapolis Valley and Halifax, after a visit to her at the university. She had been only twenty-two, and for a time, it seemed she wouldn't survive the aftermath despite the support of her grandmother and friends like Susan and David. She blamed herself for the accident, not the drunk driver who had collided with them. Even now, it made her angry. Her parents had been such loving and kind people, while so many of their peers, lacking their innate goodness, seemed to live forever. It was just so bloody unfair.

"All the time." Her voice was suddenly husky. "You would have liked them. And I know they would have adored you."

Nikki looked away, blushing. "I'm glad you think so."

Kate turned right at the stop sign. "Hungry? We didn't eat much before we left."

Nikki brightened. "Let's go to the Mayflower. It's open on Sundays, and I'm not really in the mood for fast food."

Unlike most provinces in Canada, Nova Scotia forced most retail businesses to close on Sundays, leaving only a few places like the corner convenience stores and drug stores open. Some people liked it. Other people thought it was a ridiculously archaic law. Kate, as a businesswoman, was personally split on the issue that inevitably came up for public discussion every few years.

She readily understood the additional money that could be made by staying open the extra day, as well as the convenience provided for those customers who had a limited amount of time to shop. On the other hand, an inescapable sense of peacefulness descended upon the province on that one day of the week. Less traffic clogged the streets, and more people strolled down the sidewalks. People visited relatives and friends, or spent time at home with their families. Everything just seemed more relaxed, and Kate also enjoyed not having to open her bookstore all seven days in order to compete with the chain outlet in the mall.

For that reason alone, she appreciated it. During the past several years, Sunday had been her only day off. If another referendum took place, Kate would vote to keep it the way it was, just for the small business people like her who desperately needed that guaranteed day of rest.

Crossing Queen Street at the lights, Kate took Lorne Street to Prince and turned left, which was all she could do since the town's main thoroughfare was one-way, where she drove for a couple of blocks until she reached Ingles Place, yet another one-way street. She was pleased to see a parking spot in front of the diner. Of course, it was a little late for lunch and too early for dinner, so probably plenty of tables were available.

Inside, Addy greeted Nikki cheerfully and Kate in a more subdued tone. Kate thought the buxom waitress was a little intimidated by her, although she had always tried to be friendly the few times she had patronized the diner. Of course, this was Nikki's hangout, along with her friends. Kate ate at the Emporium Tearoom up the block whenever she chose to go out for lunch. As she slipped into the vinyl booth, she felt as if she were back in her college days in a similar diner located in Wolfville, not far from Acadia University. She wondered if it still existed, and if the students still hung out there between classes.

Addy dropped the menus off. Kate was pleasantly surprised to see a list of low fat alternatives beside the traditional hamburgers, fries, sandwiches and what she heard was probably the best fish and chips in town. She decided on a green salad and something called a chicken wrap. Nikki followed suit, and after Addy took their order and retrieved the menus, they sat staring at each other for so long that they both started to smile.

"I'm sorry. I just like looking at you sometimes."

"I like looking at you, too." Kate touched Nikki's hand fleetingly. She wanted to hold it and would have, but the diner was still a public place, and neither the town nor Nikki was quite ready to defy certain conventions. "Sometimes when we're in bed and you're asleep, I watch you. It fills my heart. I could do it all night." She lowered her voice. "I love you so much. I want to shout it to the world."

I want to marry you, she almost added, but managed to catch herself before saying it out loud. At the last instant, she realized she wanted to convey such an important revelation in far better surroundings than a downtown diner. She wanted roses and candles and champagne and even a diamond ring if that was required. Nikki was right. Living together was only the first step on a much longer road, and when the time came, Kate intended to do it properly.

To keep from displaying anything prematurely, Kate dug into her jacket packet and pulled out a small package. She had retrieved it from the console of the SUV before coming into the diner, and now she slid it across the table.

"This is for you. I was going to save it for your birthday, but all things considered, maybe you should have it now."

After Nikki accepted the present and stripped away the wrapping paper, she looked blank as she uncovered the box. "A cell phone?"

Kate folded her hands on the table. "The first three months are paid for. I just...I want you to be able to call me or someone else if anything happens. Just in case, you know?"

Nikki hesitated, then finally smiled. "A cellular might come in handy now and again. It's a really thoughtful gift."

"Do you know how to use it?"

"I'll figure it out." She unfolded the sheet of instructions and scanned it intently.

Kate was fascinated. She had never met anyone who actually read the instructions to something electronic before poking and prodding first.

Nikki caught her eye. "Thank you for this," she said, this time with more enthusiasm. "It means a lot to me."

"You're very welcome."

Kate would have said more, but their meals arrived and it was too difficult to talk and eat while pieces of grilled chicken breast, peppers, onions, tomatoes, and lettuce kept spilling from the pita wrap. Both she and Nikki became occupied with the challenge, laughing occasionally as they caught each other's eye while trying not to lose most of their meal onto their laps.

Kate knew without a doubt that she wanted to spend all her future Sundays just like this one.

CHAPTER TWENTY-FOUR

Nikki frowned at the small phone lying on the table by the door and shrugged as she picked it up and shoved it into her inside jacket pocket. She had never found much use for the pesky little electronic devices that seemed to sprout from everyone's ear like some insidious technological growth, but she suspected it had been as much a gift for Kate as from her. A part of Nikki resisted the idea of Kate wanting to keep tabs on her via the cell phone, but on the other hand, considering what all their recent arguments had been about, it seemed fairly reasonable to go along with it for Kate's peace of mind.

That Nikki was only going over to the grocery store a block away didn't dissuade her from taking it along. She should probably start carrying it with her everywhere. Otherwise, she might forget it at some crucial time, thus making it useless and angering Kate.

Inside the large grocery superstore, Nikki retrieved a basket, glad she had Mondays off to do all her chores. This was the best time to shop, with few lines at the checkouts and plenty of discount bargains on the perishables left over from the weekend. Nikki didn't stop long at each section where she had to pick up something, from the mushrooms in the produce section to the frozen blueberries at the other end of the store. She lingered at the magazine rack, checking out the books that were twenty-five percent off, though she preferred to buy them at full price at Novel Companions. She started abruptly when she felt a nudge behind her, a sinking sensation developing in the pit of her stomach as she turned to see her sister. She hadn't seen Julie face-to-face for over a year, thanks mostly to good luck and a little planning. She certainly hadn't expected to see her today.

Julie shared Nikki's light hair, but not her blue eyes, possessing brown ones instead, set beneath dark brows. Her face was plump but not pleasant, mostly because of the way she set her mouth, as if she constantly tasted something sour. She had become increasingly more portly since her marriage, and she was obviously eyeing Nikki's sleek form with disapproval and a touch of jealousy. Perched in the grocery cart, Julie's youngest stared at Nikki with wide eyes, undoubtedly seeing only a stranger rather than his aunt, chocolate smearing his face from the cookie clutched in his hand.

"I hear you and your girlfriend dropped by Mom and Dad's a few weeks ago."

Nikki couldn't quite tell if Julie's tone was spiteful or humdrum.

"That's right. We took the canoe back after the camping trip, and Mom invited us in for supper." Nikki was still recovering from that encounter. Her parents had been completely charmed by Kate, the three of them getting along like gangbusters as she watched in absolute amazement. Nikki wasn't sure what this portended, but it was a vast improvement over how she'd imagined their introduction might go.

"How can you parade your perverted lifestyle in front of them like that?"

So it *had* been spiteful on Julie's part. Nikki was somewhat relieved. She would have hated to think that her sister had mellowed significantly during the previous year, and she had missed the cause of it.

"Mom and Dad didn't seem to mind. In fact, they invited us back for a barbeque on Canada Day. They seemed to like Kate a lot."

She knew that one would really stick in her sister's craw since their parents barely tolerated Julie's husband. The very first time Julie had brought him home, Roderick, a local lawyer with aspirations for politics, had displayed a sort of condescending disdain for farm life that had immediately put him on Lorne's bad side. Relations hadn't improved much from there.

"Don't be ridiculous," Julie insisted. "They were just being polite because she was a stranger."

"Polite is all they are with Rod. If it's good enough for you, it's more than good enough for me." Nikki paused, not only had they been far more than just polite to Kate, they had made Nikki feel accepted in a totally new way, even though it was Kate to whom they were so warm. "What do you care anyway, Julie? We're not off to visit you in the near future."

"You wouldn't be invited," Julie said coldly.

Nikki thought that Julie might change her mind, particularly if Roderick realized how much influence Kate held in the town. Nikki was surprised she wasn't as upset by Julie as usual. Had time distanced her so much from this sibling viciousness that it no longer affected her? Or had something else changed? Was she grown up enough to look at her sister and realize where the spite was coming from? Come to think of it, hadn't Kate told her that people only acted like that because they were miserable and wanted to spread the misery around?

Nikki scrutinized her sister more closely and saw a remarkably unhappy individual. Was it her marriage? The four kids? What had really etched that discomfort around her narrowed eyes and pinched the lines around her mouth, or had those always been there?

"You have a nice day, Julie," Nikki said dryly, deciding their conversation wasn't worth pursuing. "I have to finish my shopping and go home before Kate gets off work. We're having dinner together."

The shock and displeasure in Julie's eyes was more satisfying to Nikki than it probably should have been, yet at the same time, seeing her sister again saddened her. As she stood in the checkout line, she found herself reexamining her life. Once she and Julie had gotten along. At least, Nikki thought they had, even if she didn't remember it clearly. She acknowledged that being the oldest in the family probably held its own stresses, though it hadn't prevented Julie from lording it over Jeffery and Nikki. She probably would have tried to bully Jaime as well, if he hadn't totally ignored her most of the time.

Or had he?

Nikki caught her breath at the thought of her younger brother, the one the family rarely spoke of. For a moment, she faltered in her stride, the memories affecting her in a way Julie no longer seemed able to. Was that the real reason she and Julie had avoided seeing each other? To avoid thinking of the sibling that wasn't there? She wondered how different her life would have been had Jaime had lived or, better yet, if he had only decided that life had been worth living.

She wanted to blame Julie and Jeff, just as Julie had blamed her after the funeral, but it was futile. No one really knew why he had done it. Most of the time, Nikki kept the memories buried, but lately, they seemed to pop into her mind more and more. Swallowing the lump in her throat, she was surprised that she had somehow returned home without remembering much of the walk, unlocking the door automatically, and carrying her groceries into the kitchen where she dropped them on the counter.

❖

By the time Kate arrived from the bookstore, Nikki had a casserole baking in the oven and the table set in the tiny dining area between the kitchen and the living room. Predictably, Kate had brought a bottle of wine to go with dinner because she knew she was unlikely to find any at Nikki's. Dinner was delicious, but Nikki couldn't find much to say. Relaxing in the living room in front of the television after doing the dishes, Kate snuggled against Nikki and drew her face to her with a finger beneath her chin.

"What's wrong?" she asked softly.

Nikki shook her head. "Nothing."

"I don't believe you."

Nikki hesitated, before bending her head in a sort of surrender. "I ran into my sister today at the grocery store."

Kate knew Nikki didn't get along with her siblings, but wasn't aware of the details. She probably thought it was because Nikki was gay, and while that was part of the reason, Nikki had never told her the rest. She had never wanted to. It was far too painful, and she wasn't sure what sharing it would accomplish other than upset Kate as well. "Was she very unpleasant to you?"

"She was her usual charming self." Nikki closed her eyes and rested her cheek against Kate's soft mat of auburn hair. "I don't really want to talk about her. She was awful when I was kid, and I don't want her to affect me now that I'm an adult."

Kate hugged her lightly. "Was she really that bad, or are you blowing it out of proportion from a kid's point of view?"

Nikki sighed. Obviously, Kate wasn't going to let it go as easily as she had hoped. "When Julie was nine, she yanked me out of the stroller, threw me on the floor, and then tried to run me over with it. It's one of the favorite family stories that Mom and Dad pass on. I'm surprised they didn't share it with you."

Startled, Kate let out a sound, half laughter, half in shock.

"I'm serious." Nikki smiled faintly despite her feelings. It *was* funny in an absurd, tragic way. "For whatever reason, she really resented me. Mom wouldn't dare leave me alone with her, and, later, Julie only babysat us if Jeff was there, too."

Kate caught it immediately, of course.

"Us?" She drew back from the embrace so she could look at Nikki. "I thought it was only you, Julie, and Jeff."

"Yeah, well…I guess I never told you about Jaime, did I?"

Kate frowned. "No. Who is…he? She?"

"He." Nikki paused. "He was my younger brother."

"'Was'?" Kate's voice was very gentle.

Nikki swallowed hard. "He…died when I was fifteen. He'd just turned fourteen."

Kate was silent for a moment, absorbing Nikki's words as she stared at her. "I'm sorry. How…" she began delicately, and then stopped.

Nikki hesitated, finding it difficult to form the words. "He hanged himself in the barn."

Kate immediately swept her up in an embrace, holding her tightly. "Oh, God, I'm so sorry, darling," she said, her voice ragged. "I didn't know."

Nikki accepted the embrace, clinging to Kate tightly. "We don't talk about it much. It's been over ten years now." She managed a weak shrug. "It's okay."

"I don't think it is." Kate brushed her lips over Nikki's ear. "Otherwise, you probably would have told me about it before now."

Nikki pulled away. Not abruptly but enough to grant some distance between her and her lover, suddenly feeling smothered, as if the air had become too thick to breathe. "Can we talk about something else?" She didn't like the edge in her tone, but was unable to suppress it entirely.

"Of course. If that's what you want."

"It is." Nikki grabbed the remote off the coffee table and started flipping through the channels, hoping to find something on which to focus her attention. Beside her, Kate stayed silent, either waiting for Nikki to settle on something or considering what she would say next.

"Nikki?"

"Yeah?"

"Why does your name start with an 'N' when all the rest start with 'J'?"

Nikki was surprised by the question. Whatever she thought Kate might have wanted to ask, that certainly wasn't it. "Nicole is actually my middle name. When I was five, I demanded that everyone call me by it rather than my first name, just to be different." She rolled her eyes briefly. "That just sort of sums up me and my family. I was always apart from them, in more ways than one."

"I never knew that." Kate put her hand on Nikki's forearm. "May I ask what it is?"

Nikki didn't want to answer but decided that it was probably time to share that as well. "Jessica. I've never liked it."

Kate didn't seem to agree, but she nodded.

"Don't you ever call me that" Nikki eyed her sternly.

"I promise."

Nikki was silent a moment. "What's yours?"

"I'm Kathryn Marie. Dad always called me Katie, then it was shortened to Kate, and, well, here I am."

"Here you are." Nikki glanced at her. "I'm really glad you are."

"I am too." Kate leaned over and kissed Nikki lightly. "I'll be here forever, my darling. I'll never let you go."

For the moment, because she needed to, Nikki let herself believe Kate's words without reservation.

CHAPTER TWENTY-FIVE

Kate adjusted her glasses as she looked up from a psychology book about teenage suicide and its effects on surviving family members. She hoped that she could learn something if she just kept at it. Books usually helped her figure out what she was experiencing, as well as how to deal with what others were going through. Nikki's revelation had jolted her, and what she had read so far frightened her. She grieved for Nikki and for her brother whom Kate would never have a chance to know.

So much goes on behind the masks people wear, she thought. So much that can't be detected until too late.

The tinkle of the bell over the door prevented her from resuming her research, and she hastily shut the book, slipping it beneath the counter. She glanced up expectantly at her new customer, except she doubted that Denise Elliot was here searching for the latest bestseller, and she tried not to frown. Moving around the counter, she greeted the woman who stood uncomfortably next to the magazine rack. Dressed in a modest blue dress and black blazer, she had deep stress lines around her dark eyes. Her brunette hair fell lank to her shoulders, as if she found time to wash and brush it, but not do anything else with it.

"Denise? Can I help you?"

"I don't know. I was talking to Irene—"

"Say no more." Kate held up her hand, tasting something sour in her throat. "Did she tell you to talk to me?"

"Actually, she thought perhaps you could offer some advice."

Kate was seriously annoyed with her grandmother, but she motioned to the spare stool behind the counter. "Coffee?" She moved over to the pot. She needed it even if Denise didn't.

"Please. Double cream and two sugars."

Kate winced at the desecration of a perfectly good cup of black coffee, but added the requested items and took the steaming mug over to Denise, who sipped it immediately.

"What's going on?" Kate noticed that Denise's fingers were trembling slightly as she wrapped them around the mug.

"I think I've found something, but no one wants to hear about it."

"What?"

Denise pulled a letter from her purse. Kate recognized the government letterhead of Revenue Canada. Never a good sign for a business, she thought as she unfolded the rest of it and began to read, but it simply requested verification on social insurance numbers for some employees concerning their T-4 slips. Granted, it was a second request and a little more forceful than the initial letter, but sometimes that happened. Certainly, for a company the size of Elliot Manufacturing, somebody had taken a little too long to track down all the numbers before the government computer issued a follow-up. Puzzled, Kate glanced up at Denise.

"I'm not sure what's wrong. This is just a request for verification. It's pretty standard during tax season. What are you doing with it?" She knew Denise stopped working after marrying Stephen, which was no big surprise. Before that, she had been his secretary.

"I found it locked in his desk at home when I cleaned it out last week." Denise's face was troubled. "Kate, Stephen didn't handle payroll. He was the president, not the accountant."

Kate tilted her head, still not seeing where this was going. "And?"

"He was really disturbed by something just before his death. There are a couple of names checked. I think he was having a problem with those employees."

"What kind of problem?"

"I don't know. The day of the Historical Society Dinner, when we were getting ready, I asked him what had been worrying him. He mentioned there was some problem with the IT payroll at work. We were running a little behind schedule so I decided we could talk about it later." Her breath caught, her face altering in a reminder of how there was no "later," and Kate covered her hand comfortingly.

"Have you told the police?"

Denise nodded, looking vaguely helpless. "I don't know if they ever checked it out."

"Have you asked them?"

"Not really." Denise leaned forward. "Kate, I can't explain it any better than this. Stephen was far more upset than he should have been over a part of the company he has little to do with. I know in my heart he just wasn't telling me something." She paused, looking uneasy. "That's why I made a photocopy of the letter before I gave it to the police."

Kate wasn't sure how accurate Denise's assessment of the situation was. Possibly Stephen's wife, in her grief, was clutching at straws to explain such a tragic event, and the police were assuming that's what she was doing. "How many other people know about this letter?"

"I tried talking to Hannah about it, but she said I was being foolish." When a certain dislike colored Denise's dark eyes, Kate was not surprised. Hannah had always been disdainful of her in-laws. "Maybe that's why I went to Irene. She's always been…well, very kind to Stephen and me. She thought that since you have your own business and were able to handle that mess with Sam Madison in February, you would have a better idea about what I should do."

"Grandmother is very kind." Kate ignored the part of her that wanted to scream about a meddling old lady who couldn't stay out of things.

"No one else wants to hear what I'm saying, Kate. Maybe they have reason. Maybe I *am* blowing this all out of proportion." Denise glanced away, her face crumbling slightly. "But Irene thought that maybe you would listen."

Kate squeezed her hand. "I am," she said with as much sincerity as she could manage. "Can I keep the letter? I'll see what I can find out."

It would do no harm, she thought, and perhaps just the knowledge that someone was taking her seriously would ease Denise's mind. She didn't have to know that Kate totally agreed with the police and Hannah Elliot. The letter was merely another bit of typical government bureaucratic paperwork, nothing sinister, despite what Denise might want to believe.

"Thank you, Kate." Denise pulled out a tissue to dab her eyes. "It's been very difficult."

"I can see that."

"I miss him," Denise said simply.

"That's understandable." Kate offered a few more platitudes as she escorted Denise to the door, once more promising that she would see what she could find out. As soon as she returned to the counter, she grabbed the phone and punched in Irene Taylor's number.

"I just spoke to Denise Elliot," she spat out angrily as soon as the receiver was lifted. "What are you playing at, Grandmother?"

"There's no need to take that tone with me, young lady. Are you telling me that you can't help her?"

"There's nothing to help her with." Kate had the uncomfortable feeling that she was going to lose this one before she even started. "It's a request for verification, Gram. The government sends these things all the time. Sometimes numbers get transposed on the T-4s, or the computer just isn't finding it. It's nothing."

"Then why was Stephen upset about it?"

Kate sighed, exasperated. "I don't know that he was, Gram. I only have Denise's opinion, and, frankly, at a time like this, that's not the most reliable testimony."

"Will you check on it?"

Irene's tone was one that was not to be argued with. Kate closed her eyes, frustrated. "Will that be the end of it if I do? If Nikki and I check this out and it turns out to be nothing, will you leave it alone?"

A brief pause, then a small sigh of resignation. "Yes, I will."

"Gram, why was Denise talking to you about this, anyway?"

"Sometimes the Elliot grandchildren find it easier to confide in me. Hannah has never been the easiest person to get along with."

"Indeed," Kate said, as if this was news to her.

"Spare me your sarcasm, darling. Honestly, I've always been there for them, especially when they were young. I'll never forget that night Stephen called me from jail just after his car accident."

"What car accident?"

"He and Martin and Pat Spencer were in a crash on Robie Street." Irene sounded surprised that Kate didn't know about it. "They ran into the light pole by the cemetery. There was alcohol involved, of course. You know how wild the boys were when they were teenagers, Kate, and apparently, everyone agreed that Pat was the driver. He was the most severely injured. That's why he walks with a slight limp today."

"What do you mean 'everyone agreed that Pat was the driver'?"

Irene lowered her voice. "Between you and me, Kate, I've always believed Stephen was behind the wheel that night, but if he was, nothing more was ever said about it. Pat ended up in court and was sentenced to three years of community service."

"My God." Kate was appalled. "How were you involved? Did you bail the little bastards out of jail?"

"Of course not. They had to accept the consequences of their actions. I merely broke the news to Hannah and arranged for my lawyer to represent them."

"I still don't understand why they look to you."

"I've always lived next door to their family, Kate. They inevitably made their way to my place. Honestly, don't you understand about being neighborly?"

Kate, who rather hoped her neighbors would mind their own damned business when it came to her, didn't respond. Instead, she rolled her eyes and picked up the mug Denise had been drinking from. A smudge of lipstick on the rim required more than a quick rinse, and she put it aside to take upstairs later. "Gram, I really don't want you to encourage Nikki to involve herself in things she shouldn't."

"What are you, Kate, her mother?" Irene's barb snagged deeply. "You just worry about that letter. Nikki can look after herself." Irene paused, as if distracted by something. "I have to go, Kate. Someone's on the other line."

"Fine. Good-bye, then."

She put down the phone, a little more gently than normal because what she really wanted to do was slam it into the cradle so hard the plastic would shatter. She didn't remember her grandmother being this hard to get along with. Or did she just feel like that because in previous years, she had simply gone along with whatever Irene wanted, whereas now she was digging in her heels? She couldn't afford not to, she thought darkly. Nikki was involved, and the need to protect her was almost impossible for Kate to ignore.

Yet, Nikki had made it quite clear that she wasn't going to tolerate this kind of attitude from Kate, particularly when it implied she was in charge of her on any level. Kate would have to loosen up if she didn't want to cause a permanent rift between them, though she wondered where this protectiveness was coming from. She honestly didn't think she considered Nikki to be a child. If she did, this was a very unhealthy relationship. On the other hand, it was commonly accepted that men were often protective of their women, though some men were more possessive than caring.

Disturbed by questions for which she didn't really have the answers, Kate pulled out the book she had been reading before Denise interrupted her. She wondered if there was a book out there that dealt with the various struggles of lesbian courtship. If so, she needed to read it as soon as possible.

CHAPTER TWENTY-SIX

When Nikki saw the letter Kate dropped on the table in front of her, she noticed it was from Revenue Canada before she realized it was addressed to Elliot Manufacturing, Inc. Intrigued, she read it and then looked up at Kate in confusion.

"What's this?"

"Apparently it came across Stephen's desk and upset him." Kate poked at her food, and Nikki wondered at the tone in her voice. She couldn't quite identify it, and she considered it as she read the letter a second time.

"Why was he upset?"

"I don't know. This type of letter routinely comes to businesses around April and May, particularly to large companies. It's just to verify names, addresses, and social insurance numbers."

"Do you get them?"

"I have on a couple of occasions." Kate sipped from her mug of coffee and shrugged lightly. "A student would accidentally give me an incorrect SIN, and I either had to track it down or send a note back to Revenue Canada saying that was the one I was given and had no reason to alter it."

"What happens then?"

"Sometimes they send a second notice like this one because something really *is* wrong with the number, or because I didn't get back to them quickly enough. They won't process the income tax claim of the person until the employer responds. Sometimes, it's just a computer error that they didn't catch before sending out the second request. Sometimes they determine that the original number on their computers was incorrect and change it to the information the employer gives them."

"So it's not really important?" Nikki was clearly disappointed. "How did you get it?"

"Denise Elliot gave it to me." Kate took a bite of toast, chewing deliberately. "Grandmother wants us to see if it's significant or if Denise is simply overwrought. Since you find this sort of thing interesting, I'm giving it to you."

"You don't really believe it's anything, do you?" Nikki eyed her suspiciously.

"It's evidence of a sort. You're not going to see much paperwork that crosses the desk of Stephen Elliot. Don't forget how crucial the paper trail was in solving the Madison murder."

"That's true." Nikki glanced at it again. "Would Stephen normally deal with these letters?"

Kate hesitated, and Nikki leaned forward, suddenly expectant, though of what, she wasn't sure. "No, from what I'm told, payroll usually handles those things without the CEO ever seeing them. Furthermore, Denise told me that Stephen believed there was some problem with the executive payroll."

"What does that mean?"

"I don't know, and neither does she." Kate sighed. "I won't lie to you, Nikki. I'm really not enthusiastic about this, but if you absolutely have to pursue this, this is information you should have."

Nikki considered Kate's words, on all its levels. "Thank you."

"You're welcome." Kate returned to the newspaper.

Nikki leaned back in her chair, regarding her carefully. Obviously Kate was humoring her a bit, which she wasn't sure she liked. On the other hand, Kate could have tossed the letter in the trash, or waited a while and returned it to her grandmother with a report that it was nothing. Instead, she'd given it to Nikki. That was good enough. Picking it up, she stared at the names, wondering what Stephen would have detected, especially considering that normally he would never see such a letter. Who was in charge of payroll?

Andrew Elliot, of course, Nikki realized with a certain chill of anticipation. The man was currently being hassled by Pat Spencer over something that didn't make either of them happy. Did it relate in some way to this? Had Stephen confided in his good friend about what was worrying him? Nikki wished she knew either Pat or Monica Henderson so she could ask them. Granted, that never stopped the detective characters on television, but Nikki had to live in this town. There was a fine line between being nosy and being flat-out intrusive. Get a reputation for the latter and no one would talk to her about anything.

"What are you thinking?"

Kate was scrutinizing her and Nikki grinned. "How I can get to talk with Pat Spencer. You know him, don't you?"

"You want me to call him?" Kate looked resigned if unenthusiastic.

Nikki offered her most appealing smile. "It would really help."

Kate glowered a bit, but with a sigh, she reached for the phone book on the counter behind her, retrieved the portable phone, and started looking for the number. Nikki had no illusions about how aggravated she was and how creatively she would need to make it up to her. She only hoped Pat would be home and agree to talk.

Kate spoke for only a few moments, while Nikki, able to follow half the one-sided conversation, had a puzzled expression when she finally hung up.

"That was odd."

"Yes?"

"I spoke to a woman—"

"Monica Henderson," Nikki stated with authority.

"Maybe. She didn't give a name. She said she hadn't seen Pat for a few days, nor had he been to work. Furthermore, she let it slip that the police are very anxious to speak with him."

"He hasn't been seen for awhile? That means he would have disappeared around the same time we saw him talking with Andrew at the driving range. I wonder if the cops know about that."

"I'm sure they do. We weren't the only ones who saw them talking there."

"They might know about it, but not with you giving me clues that they're overlooking." She looked back at the paper. "I bet Lynn could figure out something about these names. She's an accountant."

"I sincerely doubt she would even if she could." Kate said. "She's not an accountant for the company and would have no business being involved with it. You'd only get her in trouble. After all, it's not as if you should have that letter either."

"What would you do if you were me? And don't say 'wash your hands of the whole thing.'"

Kate smiled, as if amused at how well Nikki knew her, certainly well enough to predict what she would say in certain circumstances. "I would find out as much as I could about the people listed in the letter. See if you can figure out why Stephen checked two of the names."

Nikki knew Kate thought such mundane fact finding would keep her out of trouble, and she tried not to grimace at this silent agenda. But she also agreed that it might be a good idea. As long as she had the social insurance numbers, she could find out practically anything she needed to know about the people involved. It wasn't entirely ethical to use them in that manner, of course, but they gave her a great advantage when it came to digging out details. That was why citizens were advised so strongly to be careful about giving them out.

She folded the letter and slipped it into the pocket of her robe, intending to stick it in her wallet later. Draining her orange juice, she felt drowsy. She had dropped by Kate's after her evening shift, passionately needing to see her lover. Kate had been surprised, but equally as happy to see her, despite being roused so early in the morning.

They'd made love, and Nikki had joined her for breakfast, but she planned to crawl back into bed as soon as Kate went downstairs to open the store. Fortunately, she had clothes tucked away for such occasions and didn't need to make a special trip back to her apartment. Powder had enough food and water out that he shouldn't notice if she didn't return for a day or so.

"Heavens, look how late it is." Kate closed the paper. She had showered and dressed while Nikki made breakfast and was now eyeing the clock.

"I'll clean up," Nikki offered. "You go ahead."

"Thank you, darling." Kate paused long enough on her way out to kiss Nikki thoroughly, and Nikki gathered up the dishes and popped them in the dishwasher before moving into the bedroom.

Sometimes she found it hard to drift off during the day, even with the dark blinds pulled down over the windows. Traffic was much heavier, and the large trucks passing by on Prince Street sometimes shook the hundred-year-old building. Her own apartment wasn't much better since it was just as old, and Queen Street just as heavily trafficked.

She wondered if they should consider finding a totally new apartment in a quieter neighborhood, or perhaps even out in the country. If they did move in together, they would most likely choose Kate's apartment, but she wasn't sure she would be entirely comfortable here. It was lushly decorated, the decor so elegant and refined that sometimes Nikki was scared to relax. She certainly wouldn't prop her feet up on the heavy oak coffee table the way she did on her own scarred, cheaply manufactured pressboard one. She probably wouldn't be able to keep any of her furniture, either. Kate's was so much nicer, but Nikki had lived with her things for a long time, and, frankly, they were all she had. She wasn't particularly attached to her possessions, but on the other hand, she didn't want to always have to use Kate's things.

But she did love this bed. She rolled over luxuriously, burying her face in the plump pillows and delighting in the firm support of the thick mattress. Kate's fragrance still lingered on the fine linen sheets. The queen-sized space allowed Nikki to sprawl in a way that her narrower double bed didn't, and the expensive comforter was wonderfully fluffy, light, and efficient.

Yes, she definitely wouldn't mind giving up her old bed to be able to sleep in this one every night. Its charming sleeping companion was purely a bonus. Powder would adore it as well, if Kate would allow the cat in the bedroom. As easy-going as Kate was, that would still be asking a lot from her.

Of course, demanding that Powder give up his natural inclination to be lord of all he surveyed would be asking a lot from *him*.

❖

"I'm not bothering you, am I?" Nikki's mother Adele stood in front of the counter in jeans and a western type shirt, her boots scarred and dull from mud.

Startled, and guilty that she had just been fantasizing about the young woman currently tucked into the big bed upstairs, Kate said, "Of course not." She gestured to the extra stool behind the counter. "Please, have a seat. Would you like some tea or coffee?"

She could detect the faint but distinct odor of horses and wondered what had brought Adele Harris into town.

"Tea would be lovely, thank you." Adele perched gingerly on the high wooden stool while Kate set the kettle to boil. "I've never been in here. This is a very nice store, Kate."

"Thank you." Kate located a few herbal tea bags and allowed

Adele to select her preference. "So," she said, once she'd poured boiling water into both their cups, "what brings you by?"

"I was at the Bargain Shop across the street, and when I saw your store, I realized I'd never been inside. I thought you wouldn't mind my stopping by. I'd visit Nikki but she's always sleeping at this time of day."

Kate was tempted to mention that Nikki was, in fact, sleeping directly upstairs, but she restrained herself. Lorne and Adele were trying very hard to be comfortable with her and Nikki, but they were still a bit shaky with the whole concept of two women being together. She didn't need to be blatant about Nikki being in her bed, any more than if Nikki were the Harris's' son and currently asleep in Kate's bed. Of course, the Harris's would probably be a great deal more upset if it *had* been their twenty-six-year-old son.

"I don't mind at all." Kate gestured, taking in their surroundings. "The building is old, but I like it. It makes the store distinctive in a way that a newer structure probably wouldn't." She knew she was prattling, but it didn't seem the time or place to get into anything heavier with the woman, such as the death of Nikki's younger brother, for example, though she was extremely curious about that tragedy. It clearly still affected Nikki on a profound level.

"I remember when this was a hardware supply depot. I used to come in with my father. It was always so dark and dingy looking." Adele glanced around. "Who knew there was such a lovely building under all that grease?"

"You wouldn't believe the things I had to clean out when I started the renovations." Kate said. "Honestly, there were things on the top floors that had been there since the 1800s."

The two of them were silent for a moment, and Kate wasn't quite sure what to say next. She doubted Adele's visit was as innocent as she claimed. "I really enjoyed dinner…"

"I'm so glad you came by…"

They stopped in confusion, looking at each other, and then Adele touched Kate's arm fleetingly. "Lorne and I…well, we like you, Kate."

Kate was tremendously flattered. "Thank you. I like you, too."

"It hasn't always been easy." Adele gazed down at her teacup. "We never really understood why Nikki is…well, the way she is."

"She's a remarkable young woman."

Adele looked vaguely startled, a touch of color rising in her cheeks. "I suspect you're quite a remarkable woman, too." She took an urgent sip of her tea as if her throat was dry. "Kate, we might not understand it, but we do want Nikki to be happy. From what we can tell, you make her very happy."

Kate felt a slight stinging at the back of her eyes. "Nikki makes me very happy as well."

"I'm glad. Lorne and I both want you to know that you're always welcome in our home."

These honest words of acceptance surprised and gratified Kate. She put her hand on Adele's. "Nikki will appreciate it, as well. She's told me many times that she deeply regrets the distance between you."

"We regret it, too." Moisture glinted in Adele's eyes. "We want her to know we love her." She bent her head. "We haven't always shown it as well as we should."

"That's in the past. Let it go and start fresh. I'm sure Nikki will be willing to do the same. She misses you both."

As Adele dabbed her eyes with her sleeve, Kate promptly grabbed for the box of tissues and offered her one. "Look at us," Adele fussed as she accepted it, seeming embarrassed.

"It's important that families maintain their ties. Sometimes you have to work hard to mend a frayed strand, but the effort is worth it in the long run."

Adele took a restorative sip from her tea and looked anxiously at Kate. "May I ask you a question? It's rather personal, but I don't think I can ask Nikki—"

"Go ahead." Kate hoped she wouldn't regret her willingness to listen.

"What makes you…" Adele trailed off, flustered. "Why did you choose Nikki, and not…well…"

"A man? It just worked out that way." Kate sipped her tea, realizing why Adele was asking. "No one has the real answer why someone is the way they are. It doesn't have anything to do with how someone is raised or what he or she is exposed to. Otherwise we'd all be heterosexual, since that's the cultural environment we experience from the time we're born. It might be a genetic thing, but what makes one child out of several gay when all his or her siblings brought up in the same manner are heterosexual? Ultimately, we are as God made us, and to deny that would be to deny Him."

Adele looked uncomfortable. "A lot of people would say this is against God and His will," she said, not argumentatively, but as if honestly trying to comprehend some new and strange reality.

"There would be. But we both know that people who hate will always find a reason, whether by taking a quote from the Bible out of context for promoting their agenda, or using the Koran, a book of peace, to justify ramming a plane into a skyscraper. It can't be wrong to love, Adele. If it is, I'd still rather be wrong than allow hatred and ignorance to dictate my actions."

Adele was silent for a long moment, studying her cup before she raised her head to meet Kate's eyes. "Thank you for speaking to me about this. I really do want to understand."

"I know," Kate said kindly. "We all do. Adele, I was married to a wonderful man and had everything a woman was supposed to want, but no matter how hard I tried, it wasn't right for me. It took a great deal of self-examination to discover why, and it wasn't easy, but I'm very grateful I accomplished it. It's all right to want to talk. In fact, if more people talked about the things that trouble them, this world would be a much better place."

"I think you're right." The chime of the bell over the door interrupted what she would have said next, and Kate rose as a customer entered. Adele also stood up, placing her cup carefully on the counter. "I should go. I've wasted enough of your time, and I still have to drop by the co-op and pick up some feed. Will you come by for dinner Sunday?"

Kate smiled widely. "I'll speak with Nikki and find out if we're free," she promised. "I'll call you Friday."

"We'd love to see you there." Adele gathered up her purse and left the store. As Kate went to help the customer peering uncertainly at the nonfiction section, clearly looking for something in particular, she wondered if parents ever really understood their children. Or if children ever understood their parents.

CHAPTER TWENTY-SEVEN

So what have you found out so far?" Irene Taylor handed Nikki a ginger ale.

Her summons was the first call Nikki had received on her new cell phone from anyone other than Kate, and since it was Friday afternoon and Kate would be working most of the day, she had accepted the invitation.

"I've spent most of the past week checking out the names on the letter that Kate gave me," she said, happy to have someone with whom to share her thoughts. Unlike Kate, Irene relished criminal details like Nikki did.

"The one Denise found?" Irene sat down and poured herself a cup of tea.

"Yes. Three of the names check out. I looked up their phone numbers and called them." Faintly embarrassed, Nikki felt her cheeks warm. "I pretended to be someone with Revenue Canada checking on SIN numbers. Everyone I spoke with seemed legit. They just had a digit transposed or were off by one, you know, '123' rather than '124'. Plus, they were all new employees hired this year so this was the government's first chance to detect any mistakes in their T-4 forms."

"What of the other two? Were they the names Stephen checked?"

"I don't know yet. The problem is, the names don't have street addresses listed, only P.O. boxes. I don't know where they live, and I can't find a phone number for them. They're not listed in the book. I asked a few people I know who work for Elliot Manufacturing, and they don't have a clue as to who they are or which part of the plant they work in. I'm hoping if I watch the post office, I'll be able to catch them when they pick up their mail and ask them a couple of questions."

"Would the post office give you any information about who rents the boxes?"

"I doubt it," Nikki said. She had been pressing her luck with the phone calls as it was. "They probably couldn't anyway, under the Privacy Act." She sipped her ginger ale, enjoying the bubbles. "No, I think I'm going to have to do a good old-fashioned stakeout."

Irene's eyes widened perceptibly. "A stakeout? When will you be doing this?"

"Later this afternoon, around four. It's the time of the month the bills come in, not to mention next week's flyers. Assuming they work the day shift, then they'll probably be by after work to pick up their mail."

"What if their wives or girlfriends have already picked it up?"

Nikki shrugged. "Then I'll have wasted my afternoon."

"Are you going to lurk in the bushes in the back?"

Nikki swallowed back a laugh. "No, I'm going to sit on the bench in front of the Catholic church. It's right across from the post office, and I'll be able to watch the boxes through the plate glass window." She glanced outside. "Fortunately, it's a nice day. I'd hate to have to do it in the rain."

"I want to come along."

"Excuse me?"

"I want to come with you on your stakeout," Irene insisted. "What will we do if we spot them picking up their mail?"

"I'm not sure." Nikki wondered if this was such a good idea. "I guess we can follow them and find out where they live. Once I have a street address, I can get the phone number and call them about their social insurance number."

"Yes, let's do that," Irene said with enthusiasm. She stood up. "Let's go now. I know it's only three thirty, but if we get there ahead of time, then we might catch the wife or girlfriend."

Nikki hesitated before surrendering to the inevitable and followed Irene outside. The Honda was parked in front of the large house, angled to one side of the circular driveway near the front steps.

"What a cute little car!" Irene exclaimed as Nikki tucked her into the passenger side.

Nikki was amused. "I'm glad you like it." She slipped behind the wheel and started the vehicle. On the way back to Truro, she stopped at the drive-through at one of the many donut shops dotting the area and had to wait behind a large pickup truck. "What would you like?"

"I'm not really hungry."

"It's not for eating, it's for camouflage," Nikki explained. "No one looks twice at people sitting on a bench enjoying a donut. They might look twice at two people just sitting and staring at the post office."

Irene's face lit up. "That's so clever." The truck left and it was their turn at the window. "I like chocolate…and a glass of milk. You can't have a donut without milk, you know."

Well, I know Kate can't, Nikki thought idly as she turned to the young woman serving at the window. *Now I know where she gets it.*

After they'd collected their order, she drove to the lot behind the Catholic church and parked. They carried the distinctive brown and gold donut bag past the flowerbeds, to the nook located in front of the tan brick building and sat on a cast-iron bench shaded by a large elm.

Built during the seventies, the Catholic church reflected the architecture of the time: a one-story Art Deco structure, all angled corners and sharp edges, looking more like an art gallery than a place of worship. It was distinctly out of place with the other churches that lined this street, most of which were the tallest structures in town, boasting heavy stonework, soaring steeples, and the architecture of the late 1800s. They looked more traditional and, well, far more churchlike to Nikki, though she had never ventured inside any of them.

From this angle, they had a clear view of the interior of the post office where boxes lined the wall to the left of the sun-drenched entrance. A slight breeze rustled the new leaves of the elm as Nikki opened the bag of donuts. She handed the chocolate glazed to Irene, along with a paper napkin.

"How will we know if the person we're looking for shows up?" Irene peered across the street. "I can't see any numbers from here. I can barely see the boxes."

Nikki opened her windbreaker slightly to reveal small, but powerful field glasses hanging around her neck. They were very compact, the type normally used for sporting events and bird watching. "I checked out the location of the box numbers earlier in the week. The first one, 501, is on the upper row at the far right. The second is on the bottom row to the left. We were lucky. It would be more difficult to see someone access them if they were in the middle of the wall. If anyone goes close to either of them, I'll use the glasses to see if that's the box being opened."

"That's very clever. Really, the more I get to know you, Nikki, the more impressed I am with you."

Nikki felt the blood warm her cheeks. "Thank you, Mrs. Taylor."

"Please, call me Irene." She put her hand on Nikki's forearm, a mannerism Nikki recognized as she looked down at the hand, noting that it trembled slightly. It was elegant, with long fingers, one of which bore Irene's wedding rings, both encrusted with diamonds. Age had wrinkled the skin and dusted it lightly with spots. "I think we're going to become good friends, Nikki."

"I'd like that a lot, Irene."

Irene patted her arm once before returning to her donut and milk. She took a bite, chewing as she looked across the street. "So what do you really think is going on, Nikki?"

"I honestly don't know. Maybe it would be easier if I were more familiar with the players…" She trailed off uncertainly.

"What do you need to know?" Irene said immediately.

Surprised, Nikki glanced at her. "Well, Pat Spencer, for one. He seems to be the one in the middle, but I can't figure out how he fits in. I know he and Stephen were friends."

"*Best* friends," Irene said. "Pat and Stephen were like two peas in a pod since grade school. A lot of people didn't understand it, but I did."

Nikki chewed her Boston Cream slowly. "Why didn't people understand it? Because Stephen was rich and Pat…uh, wasn't."

"Pat and Stephen both came from the same type of stressful home life. Both had fathers that were most…" She paused, clearly searching for the word. "Unkind to them while growing up."

"Abusive, you mean?"

Irene sighed. "I suppose that's what it was, in different ways. Hannah's son was very much like her, the apple not falling far from the tree. She raised him hard, and he raised both his sons the same way, with cold indifference and little to no approval. Andrew responded by working harder, by trying to do everything the 'right' way. Stephen just rebelled in every way he could."

"So Andrew was the 'good' son while Stephen was the 'bad'?"

"Exactly. Though Stephen's approach seemed to be more successful. Neither seemed to impact their father, but while Andrew's sterling character was ignored, Hannah doted on Stephen. She spoiled him unmercifully."

"What about Pat?"

Irene's lips tightened. "His father was a little more direct in his disapproval of him. That *was* abuse, both physical and mental." Her voice lowered. "He drank, you see."

"Ah." Nikki absorbed the information. "Did they live in the Court Street Trailer Park?"

Irene frowned and looked at her, astonishment in her eyes. "How did you know that?"

"Just that for a wealthy family, the Elliots seem to have a lot of ties to that place. I hear Tiffany's from there, and so's Martin."

"Well, Hannah did not come from money." Irene said with a touch of primness. "That doesn't mean you should think any less of her."

Nikki bit the inside of her cheek. "I couldn't possibly think any less of her," she said sincerely.

Her irony seemed lost on Irene. "In any event, Pat introduced Tiffany to Stephen, and they began dating. Hannah was appalled, of course, but everyone was surprised, including Stephen, I think, when she dropped him for Andrew. At the same time, Denise came along, a very nice, acceptable girl that even Hannah could approve of, and finally Stephen seemed to settle down and become the man he should be in the family."

Nikki liked gossip as much as the next person, and this was truly glorious stuff. "Was that why Andrew was passed over for CEO, his unfortunate choice of wife?"

"I'm not sure, but certainly some people think so." Irene lifted her paper cup and drained the last of her milk, dabbing delicately at the white moustache on her upper lip with a lace handkerchief. "You know, I want to thank you for bringing me along. I find this very exciting."

Nikki chuckled. "Well, I don't know how exciting it'll be, but it's certainly a lot more fun to share it with someone. Plus, I don't think two people having a conversation are as suspicious as one person sitting by herself."

"Does Kate enjoy this?"

"We've never done a stakeout together. We did case someone's house once, looking for clues. We found them too." Nikki sobered slightly. "Kate was a little more willing to go along with me back then. Now, she just worries about me. I really can't blame her, I guess. That fire scared her. It scared me, too."

"But not enough to give this up."

"No." Nikki shook her head. "I just wish Kate liked this the way I do."

"Does she really need to?" Irene eyed her curiously.

"It's easier when two people share the same likes and dislikes."

"I'm sure it is, but I suspect it's also very boring to be so much alike."

"You don't think shared interests are important? Sometimes I worry that Kate and I have so little in common."

"Like what?"

"Lots of things," Nikki floundered. "She likes golf, I like tennis. She likes classical music while I like rock. She's town and I'm country. She's so refined, and I still have straw stuck in my hair. We're just different in so many ways." She wasn't sure why she was telling Irene this, but it seemed impossible to stop once she began. The concerns she had nourished for some time poured out with little restraint.

"Believe it or not, Nikki, those things are quite minor." Irene said. "I was married to my husband for over fifty years, quite happily for the most part. We did share a few interests, but overall, we were very different kinds of people, and we celebrated that difference. Kate's parents were the same way. Thomas had his fishing, his business, and his golf. Winifred had her books, her charities, and her flowers, yet I don't doubt that they would have been together for as long as James and I were."

"But differences can tear relationships apart." Nikki felt anxiety tighten her throat.

"No, trying to change those differences is what tears a relationship apart. Of course, there's nothing wrong with moderating one's behavior to accommodate the other. Instead of you playing tennis or her playing golf every spare moment, only play once or twice, and spend the rest of your free time doing something together that you both like. That's the key to a successful relationship, Nikki. Respect both yourself and your partner. Don't try to change her to fit what you want, and don't let her try to change you."

Nikki was silent, astounded by the advice, not only that she was being offered it, but how profound it was, but she barely had time to think about it when Irene nudged her sharply. "My dear, isn't that—"

Startled, Nikki watched Tiffany Elliot get out of her black Mustang in front of the post office. Surreptitiously she lifted the field glasses. Tiffany was at the upper box, retrieving the mail. To Nikki's increasing surprise, she went to the second one, unlocked it, and withdrew its contents as well.

"This doesn't make any sense." She lowered the glasses. "Why would she be picking up somebody else's mail? Unless... what if they're really her boxes?"

"Why would she have post office boxes in Truro?" Irene seemed just as bemused. "She and Andrew live at Shortt's Lake. They would have their mail delivered directly to their house."

"The real question is why would she put the boxes in someone else's names?" As Tiffany came out of the post office, Nikki turned her head away in an effort not to be recognized. Her gaze settled on a dark sedan parked unobtrusively in front of an office building a half a block up. When Tiffany pulled away from the curb in her Mustang, the vehicle quietly followed her down Prince Street. Nikki didn't recognize the driver, or his passenger, but she did recognize the attitude radiating from both the car and the two men in it. It was a very similar attitude to the one she encountered every day at work.

"I think the Mounties are watching her," she told Irene.

Irene looked very concerned. "What does this mean?"

"I'm not sure. Let's stop by the police station before we go home. I finally have some of the right questions to ask, even if I don't have any of the answers yet."

CHAPTER TWENTY-EIGHT

Ican't believe you, Gram," Kate said through clenched teeth. "Are you telling me that you were *stalking* Tiffany Elliot?"

"We weren't stalking her," Nikki protested from where she sprawled over the sofa. She and Irene had dropped by the bookstore after their afternoon together, and Kate had immediately taken them upstairs, leaving the store in the hands of Todd and Beth. "We were staking out the post office, trying to see who owned the boxes. Who knew she'd be the one to show up?"

An ache radiated from Kate's temples. How could she have kidded herself that researching that damned letter would keep Nikki out of trouble? Now her grandmother was involved, and despite the fact that Irene looked serene and quite pleased with herself as she perched in her chair, sipping tea, Kate now had two people to worry about.

"How do you know they're hers? Maybe she was doing her husband's employees a favor." Even as Kate said it, she knew how lame the suggestion was. Irene gave her a pitying look, and Nikki put a hand over her mouth to hide her smile. "Fine." Kate stopped her pacing and glared at them. "What do *you* think is going on?"

"I think Stephen checked off those names because he knew they didn't work for Elliot Manufacturing."

"What?"

"You should have seen her, Kathryn." Irene was obviously still thrilled by what she perceived as a great adventure. "We stopped by the police station, and Nikki had an officer check to see if either person had renewed his driver's license in the past five years."

"They just told you?" Kate was appalled.

"I said I thought I saw a fender bender." Nikki shrugged. "Besides, Della knows me."

Despite herself, Kate asked, "What did she tell you?"

"Neither name has ever been issued a driver's license in Nova Scotia, or applied for a motor vehicle registration. Neither has ever had a ticket or a court summons for absolutely anything." Nikki looked very proud of herself.

"So they don't drive and they obey the law. What's so exciting?"

"C'mon, Kate, neither of these men drives, neither owns a car, they don't pick up their own mail, they don't have a street address, they don't have a listed or unlisted telephone number, no one seems to know who they are or which part of the plant they work in, and for whatever reason, their social insurance numbers are suddenly throwing up a flag with Revenue Canada." Nikki ticked off each point on her fingers. "It isn't what I found out about the people behind those names, Kate. It's what I didn't. Truro is too small for me not to get something on these guys. But if they don't really exist as anything but a name and number on that letter, and, presumably, on the Elliot payroll, then there's nothing for me to find."

Sinking down on the love seat across from Nikki, Kate let the information wash over her. Irene leaned forward, putting her cup on the coffee table. "Kathryn, you're the business woman. What do you think this means...assuming Nikki is correct in believing that these people really don't exist outside of the Elliot payroll?"

"Perhaps someone has set up phony employee records. They could list a work history, then take the checks issued to those names and cash them at the local grocery store or even have a direct deposit in a bank if the account had been set up properly. The checks would never bounce since they're coming from the Elliot payroll, and no one would complain that they're stolen. The extra money could easily be pocketed every pay day with no one being the wiser." She shook her head. "It doesn't make sense, though. Even if this person was embezzling a few extra paychecks from the company, we're only talking about two or three hundred dollars a week, maybe an extra twenty or thirty thousand a year at most, after deductions. The risk involved if they're caught just isn't worth that kind of money."

"Depends on how poor the person is," Nikki said.

"Then we're not talking about the Elliots," Kate countered smartly.

"Well, who says it's only minimum wage positions we're talking about here? Maybe these names are listed in a much higher tax bracket."

"That would explain how Stephen picked up on the names, Kate," Irene said. "He wouldn't necessarily recognize every employee on the plant floor, but if he discovered these names on an executive payroll, then he would certainly know if he had ever worked with them."

Nikki nodded enthusiastically. "That's right. If these are employees making large salaries, say, forty or fifty thousand a year, then that's an extra hundred thousand that goes into Andrew and Tiffany's pocket. For that kind of money, people will take all kinds of risks."

"Hold on." Kate put her fingers to her temples, feeling ganged up on and wanting to halt the stampede of wild guesses. "You still need valid social insurance numbers to create an employee record. Even if the numbers were created out of thin air, any accountant would know they'd be flagged come tax time. They'd only be able to draw those paychecks for a year. I doubt someone like Andrew Elliot would consider a hundred thousand dollars worth losing everything for."

"But as chief accounting officer, he'd be the only one who could set it up without being caught," Nikki argued. "If it was anyone else in accounting, a supervisor would have picked up on it and reported it to the higher ups, namely him."

Irene, after looking sharply at Kate, sighed. "No, Kate is right, Nikki. It wouldn't be worth it. Andrew makes hundreds of thousands every year as a stockholder of the company. Why risk his share of that for a much smaller amount, particularly if he knew he could be caught after only a year?"

Nikki jumped to her feet, taking her turn at pacing around the living room. "You're assuming this has only been going on for a year, or that these are the only phony employees receiving a pay check." Her face brightened visibly. "Or that the numbers aren't valid to begin with. Kate, maybe these two SINs were flagged because the original owners of the numbers died or something."

"What do you mean?" Kate asked, although it was starting to become clear.

"Identity theft is big business," Nikki said. "You can buy social insurance numbers illegally if you know the right people. There's a big market in fake IDs. Sometimes the SINs come from prostitutes or runaways or drug addicts, people living on the streets where no one keeps track of them and have reason to give authorities false names when they do run into trouble. Andrew could have bought a list of four or five numbers from a dealer and put them all on the payroll. Then you're talking about a half a million extra dollars going into his pocket every year with little fear of being caught. All it requires is a little bit of extra paperwork, and we all know that accountants love paperwork."

Kate's mind was already running ahead. "So he sets up the P.O. boxes as addresses so an income tax return could be filed every year for each employee, thus preventing an audit. If the addresses were scattered around to different post offices in the towns and villages that feed into Truro, then no one would notice who was picking up the mail, particularly if there isn't much mail to pick up. They wouldn't be receiving regular bills or letters from anyone. It would just be junk mail and flyers."

"And the occasional income tax return," Nikki added. "Not to mention the HST rebates. Man, they're hauling it in from anyone. I'm surprised they didn't give these guys phony kids so they could claim a child tax credit as well."

"They'd need birth certificates."

"Easily bought from the same dealer that could always be used to apply for more SINs." Nikki shook her head at the possible scope of it, though she doubted the swindlers had become that complicated. "Of course, if the real people belonging to the numbers ever turn up, either dead or working at another job somewhere else, then the SIN would be registered with Revenue Canada as a duplicate. It's probably what happened here, and it was just bad luck that two of them were flagged in the same year. That's the sort of thing that makes an auditor take a second look. Even then, it would probably be assumed that anyone with an illicit background was using the fake SIN, not the law-abiding citizens working for Elliot Manufacturing and dutifully paying taxes in Nova Scotia every year."

"The higher pension, tax, and employment insurance contributions that the company has to pay would be noticed," Kate pointed out.

"Would it in a company that size, Kate?" Nikki regarded her seriously. "Who, other than the person doing it, would be in the position to notice, unless someone came across it purely by accident?" She paused, raising an eyebrow. "Of course, having a letter from Revenue Canada show up on your desk when it's normally supposed to go to payroll might make someone wonder what was going on."

"So…" Kate mused aloud, trying to envision this scenario, working out the various angles. "Do you think that when Stephen saw this second request from Revenue Canada, he got curious and checked it out with payroll? That maybe he caught on that the people named on the letter don't actually work for Elliot Manufacturing."

Nikki looked excited. "Andrew discovers that Stephen is snooping around the books, or maybe Stephen even confronted him and told him to clean up his act before he called the cops. This is family, after all. He'd probably give him the chance to fix it first. Instead, Andrew kills him at the Historical Society Dinner before he could tell anyone else about it."

"Hold on a minute." Kate had lost herself momentarily in the possibilities, but it was time to put on the brakes and apply a little common sense. "We're just making things up now. We don't have any proof. Theories aren't enough to take to the police. I don't even think Rick would listen to us."

"I think the police already know." Nikki glanced at Irene. "At least part of it, anyway. They might not have enough to tie anyone directly to the murder, but I'm pretty sure I saw some Mounties following Tiffany. If Revenue Canada is about to come down on Andrew, then it won't take too much to connect him to Stephen's death."

"Assuming Andrew killed Stephen. What about Tiffany? She must be involved if she's picking up the mail. How does this connect with your theory about her having an affair with Martin? What of Pat Spencer? He's Stephen's best friend and was very upset by his death, but apparently, he's also involved with Martin and Tiffany."

Nikki looked stymied. "Could it be blackmail?" she suggested after a minute, but her voice was more hopeful than certain.

Kate eyed her. "How do you mean?"

"Okay, think about this. Martin and Tiffany are in on it with Andrew. Pat Spencer discovers they killed Stephen, but rather than go to the police, he wants them to cut him in on the action. He sets up a meet at the motel for the first payment. Once they start paying, he intends to bleed them dry."

"But now he's disappeared," Kate murmured.

"Yes, and he could be dead," Nikki said. "Maybe it's not just one murder we're looking at here."

Irene suddenly clapped her hands in applause. "Bravo." Her voice was warm with approval. "You two work together like a well-oiled machine, Kate. I can see how you were able to solve the Madison murder so easily when the police had yet to make an arrest." She looked back and forth between them. "What's our next move?"

"Oh no." Kate rose to her feet. "There's no next move." She glanced at Nikki. "Be happy you discovered this much. Share it all with Rick. Let him and the rest of the police department handle it from here."

Nikki looked momentarily rebellious, then lowered her eyes. "Fine, I'll talk to Rick."

But she didn't say she'd let it go, and Kate felt a sinking sensation in the pit of her stomach. What was Nikki really planning to do next? And how could Kate prevent it?

❖

"Don't go," Kate whispered, wrapped around Nikki like a warm blanket.

They were sprawled together on the sofa, enjoying another lazy Sunday in Kate's apartment as rain pattered down steadily outside. When Nikki made an abortive attempt to leave, Kate pulled her back down, holding her not only with her arms, but her legs as well.

Nikki relaxed in the embrace. "It's getting late. If I want to go home tonight—"

"Do you really want to?"

"You know I don't." Nikki nuzzled her ear. "But it's almost nine. You have to work tomorrow, and I need to feed Powder and clean out his litter box and do my laundry and the shopping and everything else that needs tending after the weekend. If I stay I won't get enough sleep for that." She lowered her voice to a husky growl and slipped her hand under Kate's T-shirt, stroking her back lightly. "Neither will you. I'll start touching you and you'll start touching me, and the next thing you know, it's three o'clock in the morning and we're just coming up for air."

Kate sighed. "You're right," she said, squirming slightly at Nikki's playful caresses. "It's just...I hate not waking up next to you. It's such a cold way to begin the day."

"One day you won't have to," Nikki said. "Neither of us will."

Kate hesitated and then buried her face into Nikki's neck, hugging her tightly. Nikki knew what she wanted to say. She wanted to say it herself. It just wasn't the right time.

"All right, so you can't stay. Give me something to keep me warm until I see you again."

Nikki laughed and slipped Kate's T-shirt over her head, her lover helping out enthusiastically. Nikki's T-shirt followed, then their jeans and undergarments. They briefly attempted to move toward the bedroom, but their desire got the better of them and they arranged themselves on the sofa instead. Nikki thought it was just as well. In that big, comfortable bed, she'd never leave in the drowsy aftermath.

Kate's skin was warm, almost fevered, and Nikki delighted in it, groaning as she pressed her body into her lover's. Silken skin slid over skin, fingertips tracing delicate patterns of sensation along sides and breasts, teasing nipples that hardened and ached with need. Kate's breath was a rush in Nikki's ear, a warm panting that heightened her own pleasure as she dipped her fingers in the wellspring of her lover's never ending moisture. She so loved the soft sounds Kate made—the brief catches at the back of her throat, the quiet moan of pleasure, the quivering keen as she neared her peak. Nikki lost herself in the rhythm of her caress, responding to Kate's hands on her, seeking out her mouth to capture it in a searing kiss as they raced together for the summit.

For an instant, they shuddered as one, the sensation almost overpowering, holding them back briefly before they joyously surged together on the wave of bliss. Nikki groaned loudly, aware that Kate shared her pleasure in that moment of passion, before slowly she grew conscious of descent, of returning to the here and now. Prosaic concerns suddenly reigned. Nikki had a cramp in her left leg, the muscles in her back and sides were vibrating with the strain of remaining on the sofa without falling off, and she tasted the salt-sweet flavor of sweat and mutual stickiness painting their skin. Beneath her, Kate chuckled and shifted, freeing her arm to shake it out, undoubtedly to ease the pins and needles sparking along it.

It definitely would have been more comfortable in the bed, Nikki thought, but perhaps not as much fun. She slid over until she was lying beside Kate and reached up to the back of the sofa for the blanket folded there. With Kate's help, she managed to drape it over them, snuggling with her in the warm aftermath.

"That was lovely," Kate murmured.

"Very nice." Nikki glanced toward the television, the background drone to their lovemaking. A rerun of a police procedure show was just beginning its opening sequence, and she settled closer to Kate as she recognized the episode. "Ooh, I like this one."

Kate laughed. "Well, I guess that means I'll have you for at least another hour."

Nikki bent closer and kissed her on the nose. "You know I want to stay. I hate leaving you."

Kate made a small sound of assent in the back of her throat. "I know, but you're right. You have things to do tomorrow and so do I."

Nikki kissed her again, then turned her attention to the television. Kate was not a big fan of these types of shows, but she had made an effort to share Nikki's enjoyment of them.

Nikki remembered what Irene had said about a couple respecting each other's differences, and she brushed her lips over Kate's ear. "You don't have to watch this if you don't want. We can watch something else, or spend the next hour talking or something."

Kate's response surprised her completely. "Do you still think Pat Spencer is dead?"

"Well, something has made him disappear." Nikki happily leapt on the subject. "I'm wondering if Stephen told him what was going on. Or maybe he's just doing what we're doing, trying to figure it out as he goes along, and that's why he's harassing the rest of the Elliots."

"It's possible. He and Stephen have been friends for a long time. Pat even took the fall for him when Stephen was in a drunk-driving accident."

"What? When did this happen?"

Nikki listened intently as Kate filled her in on what her grandmother had told her. "You know, that's a hell of a thing to have over someone. No wonder Pat ended up as a shift foreman at the plant."

"It's not an executive position. Just sort of middle management."

"I guess Stephen wasn't as grateful as he should have been."

"Or perhaps Grandmother is making assumptions where she shouldn't, and Pat was actually the driver after all." Kate squeezed

Nikki, snuggling closer. "Are you going to speak to Rick about what you discovered?"

"Do you really think I have enough to take to him?"

"Are you trying to renege?"

Nikki smiled with a touch of resignation. "Rick's on the day shift this week. I'll drop by the police station tomorrow and fill him in on everything."

"That would make me feel a great deal better."

"I definitely like it when you feel better," she muttered playfully, her hands straying to places she had so recently explored on her lover's body.

"Don't start anything you won't finish." A particularly grotesque sequence on the television screen suddenly caught Kate's attention, and she made a face. "Oh. Oh, dear. What is *that*?"

"Um, how the bullet shattered in his liver, I think."

"Is that why you like this show?"

Nikki laughed. "One of the reasons."

CHAPTER TWENTY-NINE

Powder greeted Nikki loudly as she entered her apartment, explaining at length how little he appreciated her recent absences, how horrid she was for neglecting him so often, and, worst of all, that his water dish was low and just what the hell was she going to do about that! He meowed and muttered and twined around her ankles so much that Nikki nearly dislocated her shoulder as she refilled his water and food dispenser, slamming into the fridge in an attempt not to compound her crimes by inadvertently stepping on his tail. Fortunately, Powder appeared to have forgiven certain of her sins by the time she crawled into the bed and laid her head wearily on the pillow, if his leaping up beside her and curling up on the other side of the bed was any indication. Nikki fell asleep to the steady rumble of his purring.

The next morning flew by as she took care of all of her chores. After returning from the store and putting away her groceries, she didn't feel like making anything for lunch. Instead, she hopped into her car and drove to the Mayflower Diner for a chicken wrap, then walked down the street to the police station, conscious of her promise to Kate. She did nurture the faint hope that Rick wouldn't be in so that she could claim she had at least tried, but, unfortunately, he was, and she spent his lunch hour filling him in on everything she had discovered over the past few weeks.

At the end of the confession, Nikki stomped down the station's cement stairs and strode angrily to her car.

"Well, that didn't accomplish a whole lot of anything," she muttered out loud as she slipped behind the wheel and glared out the window in frustration. Rick had been less than enthusiastic about the information that she had discovered and reiterated in unflattering terms that she *had* to keep her nose out of things that didn't concern her. It was rapidly becoming his mantra, Nikki decided, and she was sorry she had wasted any part of her day off trying to convince him her theories had some validity.

She wondered what she should do next. Kate was busy in the bookstore, of course, while the rest of her friends were at work. She didn't know anyone who might be available for a tennis match. She decided that she might as well head home and take a nap before staying up as late as possible. She could adapt more easily to the night shift at the police station if she started adjusting her body's clock on Monday rather than trying to do it on Tuesday.

Besides, she really had been neglecting Powder dreadfully the past few weeks and needed to spend some time with him. Cats were far more independent than dogs, of course, but they still needed personal attention every so often. Maybe she'd dig out the harness and take him for a rare but entertaining walk outside.

She pulled out of the police station parking lot and turned left down Forester Street before turning right onto Prince. She followed the traffic impatiently until she reached the lights at Walker Street, glancing at the brand-new Sobey's store that had been built on the corner during the winter, significantly altering the landscape of the street. She missed the old, familiar buildings that had contained a paint store and a dairy for as long as she could remember.

She was glad to reach Queen Street, where traffic was lighter and she could relax a little as she drove up the street. The light ahead was turning yellow, and it was such a nice day that she slowed rather than try to beat it. As she idled at the red, she noticed that the car turning right off the side street was none other than Andrew Elliot's blue sedan. Wondering why he would be leaving work in the middle of the day, she lifted her head like a hunter catching a scent and drove up the street after him as soon as the light changed.

Cruising past her apartment building without a second thought, she followed him down Elm Street onto Willow. He was probably heading home, taking the old Halifax highway out to Shortt's Lake rather than the 102, but Nikki decided to follow him anyway. At the railway crossing just outside of town, the red lights began to flash, indicating an oncoming train, and Nikki slowed, glancing down the tracks to see a large freight train approaching. To her surprise and disgust, Andrew had accelerated instead, his large car leaping forward as he tried to beat the train, barely managing to clear the crossing before the barriers dropped down.

Trapped, Nikki could only watch and fume impotently as the freight train that seemed to stretch on forever rumbled past.

❖

This is insane, Kate thought as Denise withdrew the key from the lock of the large house overlooking Shortt's Lake and held the door open for her. She entered the foyer uneasily, wondering what on earth had prompted her to go along with the woman's suggestion.

When Denise had called earlier in the morning offering to let her into her brother-in-law's house, Kate had been hesitant, but intrigued. After all, this was technically breaking and entering, even if the sister-in-law had provided tacit permission by providing a key. But if Kate found some hard evidence, the type that would put Andrew and Tiffany away once and for all, then the case would be over and Nikki would have to let it go.

It wasn't the best reason for doing this, but events had conspired to lure her here. Shortly after Kate had opened the bookstore, Todd had shown up unexpectedly, asking if she needed any help since he had nothing better to do now that exams were over. Not five minutes after his arrival, Denise had called. The timing was serendipitous, the sort that Kate just couldn't ignore.

Leaving the store in Todd's hands, she drove over to Bible Hill, picked up Denise, and headed out to the lake. She pulled into the driveway only after making sure no other vehicles were in the yard, that Andrew was indeed at work, and Tiffany was in the city doing her weekly shopping.

"I still can't believe it," Denise said bitterly as she led the way to Andrew's study, winding through the expansive living room and hallway. "I *knew* that letter meant something. Thank God Irene convinced me to talk to you."

"Yes, thank God," Kate said dryly, wishing not for the first time that her grandmother had stayed in Florida just a little while longer. Or, at least, had restrained herself from calling Denise and filling her in on everything Kate and Nikki had discussed in front of her. "You know,

Denise, this is all circumstantial and it's entirely possible we're wrong. It's mostly guesswork at this point."

"Isn't that why we're here? To find some real proof that will put them behind bars, where they belong?" Tears were bright in Denise's eyes. "Damn Andrew. How could he kill his own brother?"

"We're not sure he did."

"Now Pat's disappeared," Denise went on as if she hadn't heard a word. "I suppose he's dead as well. He and Stephen were such good friends. He probably found out what was going on."

"Then he should have gone to the police." *Just like we should be doing,* Kate added silently and somewhat guiltily as they stepped into Andrew's study.

Andrew was more than just an ordinary sports fan. He was a fanatic. The room was more like a museum than a study. The walls were covered in memorabilia, and, in a large glass cabinet in the corner, three footballs were proudly displayed like rare sculptures. A hockey stick autographed by Canada's foremost hockey player, apparently Andrew's pride and joy, was stretched prominently across the wall above this glass shrine. In a photograph hanging under the stick, the Great One stood next to Andrew at what appeared to be a sports celebrity function, perhaps an auction. The athlete had undoubtedly forgotten about this moment captured in time the second it was over, but Andrew wanted to remember it for the rest of his life.

Kate could imagine how much Nikki, also being a sports fanatic, would have enjoyed looking around this shrine.

"Here are some papers." Denise opened a desk drawer and plopped several folders onto the desk. "I don't know if they'll tell us anything. What are we looking for, exactly?"

"Anything tied to the company itself." Kate observed the pile of paperwork uneasily, not wanting to touch it and compound her guilt. She had no right to be here. She should really apologize to Denise and get them both the hell out of there before they were caught. Instead, she picked up a folder from the top of the stack and flipped through it quickly. "A ledger recording any transactions or payments from the names on the letter would be particularly useful."

"We might find something in here." Denise reached up behind a painting of a baseball player hitting a home run to reveal a wall safe. "Tiffany showed it to me one day. She thought it was silly, like something one would see on television. She said if someone really wanted to conceal a safe, they should build it in the laundry room behind the dirty clothes hamper. No one ever wants to go in there."

"She has a point," Kate said. "I don't suppose you—"

"Have the combination? You bet I do." Denise looked oddly triumphant in a shamed sort of way, like a little girl who knew she wasn't supposed to be acting this way, but having an inordinate amount of fun doing so. Nikki would have had exactly the same sort of expression on her face had she been there instead of Denise. Acting illicitly provided a great thrill. "Tiffany was really mad because Andrew wouldn't give it to her, and he used to tease her about it by saying it was the most important date in history. She could never figure it out, but I did. It's 9 right, 28 left, 19 right, and 72 left."

"September 28, 1972?" Kate translated, puzzled. "What happened on that date?"

Denise offered her a wry look. "Paul Henderson scored the winning goal in the Soviet Summit series."

Kate rolled her eyes. "Of course he did."

Ironically, she understood its importance to Andrew. It had been a significant period in Canadian history, as a matter of fact. She had been in junior high at the time, and classes were let out so that students and faculty could watch the history-making hockey game. She still remembered the cheers and the astonishing sight of her teachers hugging each other, as well as how excited her parents had been when she returned home. Her father hadn't even gone to work that day, something that had shocked her profoundly, yet also underscored the importance of what was going on.

The moment had affected Canadians, even those who weren't hockey fans, in a way that perhaps people from any other country wouldn't easily understand. America's identity was, at that time, tied up mostly with the Vietnam War. Canada's meanwhile was entwined with Paul Henderson's goal and a marijuana-smoking Prime Minister's wife. It summed up the basic difference between the two countries in a way that nothing else did.

Kate suddenly thought about Nikki, who hadn't even been born when Henderson scored the goal and the entire country celebrated. She had absolutely no awareness of that period and regarded it as nothing more than a footnote in sports history, as opposed to the cultural statement it had signified to Kate and her parents. She felt old.

Dismissing this musing with difficulty, she watched Denise twirl the dial and yank on the handle, twisting it down. The heavy door swung open, and Kate could see what appeared to be a ledger inside. She held her breath as Denise pulled it out and flipped through it before handing it to her.

"Is this what you mean?"

Kate skimmed through it, realizing it was a handwritten payroll book rather than the computerized reports normally used in large companies. It was dated from fifteen years earlier, and as she skimmed the list of ten names, she recognized two of them immediately.

This has been going on for fifteen years? She was dumbfounded. Checking the figures at the bottom, she felt light-headed. Assuming it had started then and continued until this year, whoever had set this up had embezzled millions from the company. Since they had found it in Andrew's safe, she had a pretty good idea who the chief suspect was. Nikki had been right.

"This is all the evidence anyone needs, I think," she said quietly. "My God, they had these individuals 'working' for fifty hours a week at the highest wage the company could offer." She shook her head. "Stephen must have come across this and confronted Andrew with it."

Denise, who was leaning over Kate's shoulder, abruptly made a small sound at the back of her throat and put her hand to her mouth.

"Oh, Denise, I'm sorry." Kate cursed her insensitivity. "I shouldn't have reminded you of his death."

"No, that's not it." Denise's face was pale.

Confused, Kate stared at her. "What is it?"

"That's not Andrew's handwriting. It's Stephen's."

Stunned, Kate looked down at the book. "But, if this is Stephen's handwriting, that means he had to have known about it fifteen years ago."

Denise stumbled from the room, and Kate was torn between going after her and searching for more evidence in the safe. For the moment, curiosity and an odd sense of urgency dictated her actions. Denise needed a moment to herself anyway, just to adjust to what must surely be a profound shock. At least, that's what Kate told herself as she put the book on the desk and reached into the safe to retrieve several envelopes. She flipped through them, realizing they were copies of income tax forms for the names on the list for the previous five years. The individuals should have these copies. Finding them in the possession of the company's accountant helped prove that these names were without substance.

Kate had to take all this to the police, even if she were in trouble for retrieving them from Andrew's home. But if she could keep Nikki from falling into something that she couldn't handle...something really dangerous...however, would Denise go along with Kate's desire to hand these papers over to the police, considering that her husband had been involved in what was obviously a conspiracy?

The brothers must have had a falling out. Stephen had ended up on the losing side, and now things were unraveling rapidly. She shouldn't be surprised it had turned out to be fratricide. One was more apt to be killed by a member of the family than by a stranger.

She heard a sound from another part of the house, a muffle, and incoherent noise, as if someone had been about to say something and was stopped. Kate frowned. "Denise?" She heard a few more thumps, almost as if something had been dropped, but the woman didn't respond.

Kate was about to call again when the door to the study swung open, and as she recognized the man in the doorway, she realized that everything she had assumed was completely wrong.

CHAPTER THIRTY

Nikki usually enjoyed the sound of the train's wheels clacking over the rails, but today it held a jeering note, as if the train delighted somehow in stymieing her progress. Frustrated, Nikki glanced to her left and behind her, seeing if she could make a U-turn and drive back to the street leading to the highway. That would get her to Shortt's Lake ahead of Andrew, assuming he was headed to his home. But he might be headed somewhere else, and she couldn't follow him.

She drummed her fingers on the steering wheel, resisting the urge to slam her fist into it. As she did, she realized how upset she was and that she was acting impulsively, the very thing she had promised Kate she wouldn't do.

Not being able to find out why Andrew had decided to leave work in the middle of the day, she told herself sternly, wasn't the end of the world. Her relationship with Kate was far more important.

Thoughts of her lover prompted a smile, and she reached down for the cell phone lying on the console beside her. The train had slowed considerably, undoubtedly requiring some kind of track change farther up the line; she could be sitting here for another twenty minutes or so. She put her car into park and shut off the engine, as many behind her were also doing, and dialed the number for Novel Companions. A male voice answered the phone rather than that of her beloved.

"Todd? What are you doing there?"

"Hey, Nikki. We've finished exams, and I don't have to go back until the middle of June. I dropped by to see if Mrs. Shannon needed any help today."

"Good for you." Nikki was pleased. She could talk with Kate and not worry about taking her away from her customers. "Is she handy?"

"Actually, she's not here."

"Will she be back soon?"

"I don't know. She and Mrs. Elliot went out to Shortt's Lake to visit Mrs. Elliot's brother-in-law."

"What!" Nikki sat bolt upright, gripping the steering wheel. "What did you say?"

In a bemused tone, Todd said it again.

"Why did she and…who, Mrs. Elliot? Which Mrs. Elliot? Hannah?"

"Um, I'm not sure. She's Mrs. Shannon's age, with brown hair. She's sort of pretty for an older woman."

"Sort of pretty" didn't describe Tiffany, who was a bombshell at any age, and it definitely did not describe Hannah. It had to be Denise. Why the hell were they going out to Andrew's? Nikki found it hard to catch her breath. Was that why Andrew was suddenly on his way home?

"Damn it. When did she leave?"

"Earlier this morning. Mrs. Elliot called not long after I got here. Mrs. Shannon went over to Bible Hill to pick her up. I don't know if they've gone out to the lake yet." Todd paused. "Do want me to tell her anything?"

"No, I'll take care of it. Thanks, Todd." She grimaced and threw the phone down on the seat. To her great relief, she could see the end of the train in the distance and she started the car, leaning forward as if she could somehow hurry things along. Finally the caboose passed and the lights stopped flashing.

Nikki barely waited for the barrier to clear her roof before she floored it, pulling away with a screech of tires and a bit of blue smoke in her wake that she noted in the rearview mirror. She didn't know how fast her new car could go, but she was determined to find out. It only took fifteen to twenty minutes to get to the lake via this road. Andrew was probably already there, and her heart pounded as she sped out of town and flew through the communities between Truro and Brookfield. The road normally posted 70 to 80 km/h speed limits, and as she kept the needle hovering around the 120-km/h mark, she prayed a Mountie wouldn't be lying in wait. She would have gone even faster if she were more familiar with the twists and turns on the road.

As she came to the crossroads that made up the small village of Brookfield, she noticed the blue sedan parked at a drugstore on the corner. She pulled into the parking lot behind the car, blocking it. As she sat there, catching her breath, Andrew exited the store, a bag and a newspaper tucked under his arm.

Nikki leaped out of the car to confront him. She wasn't sure what she was going to say, but it would be far better to do it here in a parking lot than have him surprise Kate in his home. Besides, this was a public place, and he probably wouldn't try anything with so many people passing by. Even if he did, someone would call the police, and right now, letting them deal with this situation sounded like a really good idea, despite her earlier reluctance to involve them.

Andrew frowned. "Would you mind moving your car?" He took a second look, finally recognizing her. "Hey, what are you doing?"

Nikki clenched her fists. She was in pretty good shape, but he was a big man, over six feet and bulky. She wished she had thought to get the tire iron out of the hatchback. "I know what's going on. I know all about the phony employee records."

He stared at her blankly. "What?"

"I know you killed Stephen." Her voice shook. "He found out about you cooking the books, didn't he?"

Andrew stared at her, obviously torn between surprise and outrage. A little fear shadowed his eyes. "Are you crazy?"

Nikki dug into the back pocket of her jeans, pulling out the letter from Revenue Canada and brandishing it at him like a weapon. "I'm talking about this," she snarled. "These two people don't exist as anything but an SIN and a post office box number on the Elliot payroll. How long have you been lining your pocket with their paychecks, Andrew? And how many others do you have on that executive payroll?"

Andrew snatched at the letter, staring at the two names that had been checked and that Nikki had circled for good measure. "These two? They're in the IT department."

"The what?" Nikki responded blankly. "IT?"

"They're computer specialists," Andrew repeated with more patience than a great many other people would have displayed after being accosted in a parking lot. "They keep the plants operating smoothly, both here and in Windsor."

Nikki stared at him, scarcely able to believe that he was coming up with such lame answers. "Have you ever met them? What do they look like?"

Andrew paused, uncertainty coloring his eyes. "I'm sure I have, at the company picnic or one of the Christmas parties." Obviously he was having a problem putting a face to the names.

"Oh, yeah? Did you ask them how hard it is to be traveling between Truro and New Glasgow when they don't own a car, or have a valid driver's license for Nova Scotia?"

"What?"

"These two men don't own their own vehicles, they have no street address, no one else in the plant has ever met them, they have your wife picking up their mail, and, best of all, they don't need their paychecks because they don't really exist."

She waited for him to say something, but he looked dazed, so she threw some more facts at him.

"Why the hell do you think Revenue Canada is flagging those SIN numbers? Why do you think the Mounties have your wife under surveillance?"

Nikki wasn't entirely certain of the last part, of course, but she thought she'd toss that in just for good measure. She was on a roll, feeling quite powerful as she stepped closer to him, momentarily forgetting the situation, only aware of a wild sense of exhilaration at confronting the man.

"What happened, Andrew? Did Stephen figure out what you were up to? Did he realize you had set up the executive payroll to pay people he had never actually met and demand you stop?"

"I don't administer the IT payroll," he finally responded, his face a dark mix of anger and confusion. "Stephen does...I mean, he did."

That stopped Nikki cold. "What?"

"He always took care of the IT payroll. That was his department before Father's death." His mouth twisted bitterly. "Even after he became president, he stuck with it. Every two weeks, accounting received the hours and expense accounts from him so we could make up the paychecks, but he was the one who handed them out. It was always a major pain every January. I actually had to fight with him to get all the necessary paperwork so we could make up the year end."

"But Stephen didn't handle payroll."

"Who told you that?"

"His wife did. Denise said that when he found this letter, he got upset."

"I guess he never told her what he did, and frankly, he *should* be upset by that letter," Andrew blustered self-righteously. "It was the second notice from Revenue Canada. I gave him the first and told him that he needed to find out why there was suddenly a problem with social insurance numbers that had been perfectly fine for fifteen years. He didn't seem to want to listen to me. I had to put the second notice right on his desk."

"Is this the first time you've ever gotten this kind of notice for the IT payroll?"

"Yes."

Nikki looked down at the letter, seeing it in a new light. "Did you kill your brother?"

He didn't seem to notice she didn't have any kind of authority to be asking these sorts of questions. "No." His tone grew ragged. "We had our problems, I'll be the first to admit that, but…I loved Stephen. I would never hurt him." He paused, regaining his composure. "What do you mean, these people don't exist? They've worked for us for fifteen years."

"No, Andrew, they haven't." Nikki stared at him. "Do you love your wife?"

"What the hell kind of question is that?"

"Are you aware that she's having an affair with your cousin, Martin?"

His face darkened. "Who the hell do you think you are?" he demanded, looming over her, and suddenly she realized how big he was. She danced backward a few steps.

"You're telling me you didn't have anything to do with this scam? Why are you going home in the middle of the day?"

"My wife is ill." He appeared too angry to realize he really didn't owe her any answers. "She called me to come home, and I stopped by here to pick up the prescription she needed."

"Why didn't she have it delivered? Why'd she need you? You don't have any help at that big house of yours?" As she said it, she remembered that Kate was supposedly at that house, lured there by yet another Elliot spouse. "Damn it, where do you live? My girlfriend is there with Stephen's wife. If what you're saying is true and Stephen is behind this, then maybe Denise is involved too. Maybe she's already taken care of Tiffany, and that's why she's ill. Didn't Stephen's death look like a heart attack at first?"

Not much of this was particularly coherent, but the fear that came over Andrew's face was very real. Without speaking, he gestured angrily for her to get out of his way. Suddenly terrified beyond reason for her own loved one, Nikki promptly jumped into her car and backed away from his sedan. Andrew maneuvered out of the parking lot, pulling quickly onto the street leading out of the village as Nikki followed him.

He raced out of Brookfield, past the highway overpass and down the Pleasant Valley Road to the turnoff leading to the lakeside community. She kept close on his tail as he sped through the twisty road bordered by woods and large houses on one side and the sparkling waters of the huge lake on the other.

As he pulled into a paved driveway leading to his home, Nikki's heart jumped into her throat as she identified the familiar black SUV. Then she realized that the situation was even worse than she had anticipated. The battered green car she had seen at the Tideview Motel belonging to Monica Henderson was parked right behind Kate's truck.

Chapter Thirty-One

W hat the hell are you doing here?" Martin Elliot demanded before yelling over his shoulder. "There's another one in here, Pat."

Kate was not only deeply humiliated at being caught snooping, but a sense of imminent danger crawled up the back of her spine. She didn't know what Martin was doing here, or the other man who was undoubtedly the missing Pat Spencer, but she had a feeling they weren't supposed to be in the house any more than she was.

"Where's Denise?" Her tongue felt twisted, her throat full as she focused on the bottle he was carrying. It was full of a clear liquid, probably the same chemical compound that had killed Stephen.

"What are we going to do?" The voice was Pat's. He sounded panicked, as if things were not going according to plan.

Kate couldn't see anything beyond Martin, suddenly large and threatening, even though he had yet to make a move. Why wasn't Denise saying anything?

Chilled, Kate drifted behind the desk, trying to keep it between her and Martin. She also tried very hard to avoid making any sudden moves, as if confronted by a dangerous animal.

"Shut up," Martin shouted over his shoulder at his unseen companion. "Let me think." He stared at Kate from beneath lowered eyebrows. "This might work in our favor, but we have to set things up before Andrew gets home. Tiffany would have called him by now."

"What's going on?" Kate looked around frantically for something, anything, to help her out of what was turning into a very disturbing situation. She cautiously reached behind her and grasped the shaft of a golf club poking out of an umbrella stand.

"I don't know what the hell you're doing snooping around here, but you're going to be very sorry." Martin stepped closer, and Kate tightened her grip convulsively on the club. He wasn't aware of her weapon. He was glaring at the payroll book and income tax returns lying on the desk.

"What are you doing with those?"

"They're payroll books from the Elliot Manufacturing IT department." She tried to edge back a few steps.

"I know that. I arranged to have them put in the house." He jerked his head. "Where did *you* get them?"

"From the safe behind me."

"Put it all back where you found it."

She hesitated, then, as he raised a fist, she quickly picked them up, turning to push them back in the safe. She kept an eye on him as she did so, but he didn't come any closer. He was wearing gloves, something a person didn't do this time of year…not unless they were intended for something other than warmth. He obviously didn't want to leave any fingerprints. Meanwhile, she was leaving hers all over the place. Her hands shook as she picked up the file folders and replaced them in the drawer that Denise had left open.

"How did you manage to plant this evidence?" She kept her tone conversational, as if they were just passing time in her bookstore, though she had never been so terrified. She scanned the study, looking for a way to escape.

Martin glanced at his watch. Obviously he was on some kind of timetable. "Tiffany is more creative than people think. She always pretended she didn't know the combination, but she did. Andrew's such an asshole."

"What have you done with Denise?"

"The same thing we're going to do to you," He smiled unpleasantly. "We just have to arrange it properly. Andrew will catch you snooping around in his study, kill you both, then kill himself out of remorse. The cops will find all the evidence right here, including the bottle of poison that killed Stephen. End of story."

"They know you're sleeping with Andrew's wife." Kate found the club once more as she kept her body angled to conceal her right hand.

"That's my alibi." He grinned. "Right now, Tiffany is in Halifax at a hotel after making a big show of checking in under her own name. No matter what else happens, she'll swear I was with her, even if she has to admit she was having an affair."

"The police will figure it out."

"No, they won't." Martin shrugged. "They'll have a nice, neat solution to a crime that's giving them headaches. They won't look a gift horse in the mouth."

"Nikki will know." She wished she could snatch the words back even as they left her mouth.

"Then that's a complication Pat and I will have to take care of before too long." He reached out, and Kate yanked the club from the stand.

She swung wildly, smashing it across his forearm. With a yelp, he yanked it out of her hands and threw it aside.

Kate didn't wait for him to regain his balance, but plunged past him into the hallway. She tried for the foyer, but faltered when she saw Pat standing between her and the doorway. Denise was sprawled on the carpet at his feet, blood staining her temple. Kate dashed the other way, hoping to find another exit, with Martin only a step behind. He was so close that she could feel a rush of air as he neared, and she dodged instinctively as he swiped at her, leaping for the stairs that led to the second floor.

Her breath came hard as she dashed up the steps, running down the hall and flinging herself into the first bedroom she saw, slamming the door behind her. She fumbled at the lock, twisting it a scant second before Martin thudded into the door, making it shudder in the frame. She ran over to the dresser in the corner, pushing it against the door as a further barricade. It was surprisingly light, and she realized it had to be empty, making this a guest bedroom. She probably wouldn't have been able to move it otherwise, and she doubted it would delay her pursuer long.

Blood rushing through her veins like thunder in her ears, she ran over to the window, throwing it open in hopes of finding a quick escape. Unfortunately, the landscape sloped dramatically away from this side of the house, dropping more than two meters to the graveled shore of the lake. If she tried to jump from the second story, she'd essentially be doing Martin's job for him.

Martin was slamming himself repeatedly at the door, uttering a strange little laugh every so often that chilled her far more than his curses. Martin was apparently enjoying this pursuit, deriving a sort of twisted pleasure in the hunt. She tried not to let the dark thought of what would happen when he caught her overwhelm her. She needed to think clearly, keep moving, stay one step ahead of him.

Across the room she discovered two doors. The first fronted a closet devoid of any possible weapons. The second led to a small bathroom, and she plunged inside, slamming the door behind her and locking it, providing another miniscule measure of safety, though she knew it wouldn't hold long. Another door here let her into a second guest bedroom.

Heart in her throat, she tiptoed to the door of the second bedroom and opened it very quietly. Through the crack, she could see Martin still battering away at the door down the hall. Clearly he wasn't any more familiar with the layout of the house than Kate was, and though she found that odd, she was grateful.

As the other door gave way and he forced his way inside the first bedroom, she slipped out of the second bedroom and dashed light-footed down the hall toward the stairs. As she passed the first door, then rushed down the stairs, she could hear him kicking the bathroom door, screaming curses at her.

She had forgotten about Pat, who yelled at her sudden appearance. "You idiot, she's down here!"

She cursed silently as footsteps pounded across the ceiling, then ran down another hallway, confused as she turned the corner, expecting to find a kitchen and discovering a dining room instead. She slammed through a third door to find herself back in the hallway by the study. In her panic, she had somehow become turned around and ended up back at the north end of the house. She ran back into the study. At least she could find things there to help defend herself. Flinging open a display case containing Andrew's baseball collection, she scooped up several of the balls from the top shelf.

"She's back in the study." Pat directed Martin from the living room. He sounded very annoyed at his companion, and scared. "Hurry it up, you stupid son of a bitch. Andrew could come home any minute. You don't want to be chasing her around when he shows up."

"Shut up," Martin shouted. "Get the other one out to the black SUV. We'll put them in the back and drive it into the lake. That'll confuse things for a while."

Kate caught her breath and set herself, her arm cocked, ready for her hunter to appear. Time slowed, and she wondered what he was waiting for. Was he just outside the door, out of sight, waiting for her to let her guard down so he could pounce?

As he suddenly appeared in the doorway, she almost dropped the ball in her hand. He grinned, huffing, his face flushed as he stepped deliberately toward her. She knew now that he was enjoying this chase hugely, in a way that sickened and terrified her.

Angry, she drilled the first baseball at him with all her strength. She had always been the last one picked by the kids on the softball diamond when she was growing up, and she now regretted that physical liability profoundly. She wished she had grabbed another golf club. She could hit golf balls with a deadly velocity and skill that she lacked with baseballs, assuming he gave her time to set up her swing.

Martin ducked and cursed, but the projectiles barely slowed him as he charged her. Frantically she grabbed for the baseball bat at the bottom of the case and threw it as well, the wood impacting his chest with a dull thud that made him cry out. Backpedaling desperately, she dodged around the desk at the same time he lunged for her. Hopefully she could use it as another brief barrier, but he didn't come around the desk after her, offering her an escape route on the other side. Instead, he leaped over it in one huge rush, grabbing her and slamming her against the wall.

She struggled with him frenziedly, trying to wiggle free, and they stumbled around as he grappled with her. She managed to duck through his arms and sprinted for the door. She had only taken a few steps before he lunged after her, grabbing her by the hair and yanking her back. The small of her back impacted with the desk, the pain shooting through her to drain what little strength she had left.

As she fell back onto the surface, he was suddenly on top of her, his greater weight immobilizing her. She tried to scream, but his hands closed around her throat, and all she could do was beat weakly at his forearms as they shut off her air.

Darkness crowded the edges of Kate's vision as he tightened his grip, and all she could think of was how very angry Nikki was going to be at her for dying in such a foolish place, at such a foolish time, in such a foolish way.

CHAPTER THIRTY-TWO

W here's Tiffany's car?" Andrew demanded as he leaped out of his sedan, glaring at Nikki as if she knew.

"Who knows? Did she really call you from here? Or did she just want to get you out here?"

He took an abortive step toward her before someone came out the front door and caught both their attention. Nikki immediately recognized Pat Spencer from the driving range, astounded to see him carrying Denise Elliot over his shoulder. She appeared to be unconscious if not dead, her arms dangling boneless and limp. Crimson dripped from a wound on the side of her head.

"Hey!" Andrew shouted. The sight of a woman being carried helplessly from his house undoubtedly aroused all of his natural protective and territorial instincts, even if he didn't know what was going on. He rushed across the yard aggressively, fists clenched.

Denise's body kept Pat from running back into the house before Andrew reached the front steps. Clumsily, he dumped the woman on the front porch and turned to meet Andrew, the pair colliding like two rival bears during mating season.

Pat's momentum and the fact that he was on a higher level gave him a slight edge, and they careened down the stairs, tangled like a misshapen spider creature. Landing on the ground at the base of the steps, they began to pound on each other, fists flailing wildly, grunts issuing as the blows landed. Neither of them appeared to be particularly adept at this form of combat.

Andrew was larger than Pat, but some of it was fat while Pat was lean and wiry. But he was hampered by his leg and had trouble finding leverage as they rolled around in the dirt. Andrew was obviously fighting for what he believed was the sanctity of his home and family, which lent him a ferocious strength. Pat merely looked as if he wanted to escape, his eyes wide with fear and panic.

Nikki circled frantically, trying to get past them onto the front porch. When the men locked each other in some kind of hold, she took full advantage. Vaulting over them, she dashed up the steps to where Denise lay crumpled on the porch and immediately felt for a pulse. Relieved to feel a faint throb beneath her fingertips, she stood up again trying to control her panic. Where was Kate?

She could hear some kind of a commotion inside the house, though it was difficult to detect its cause since the cursing from the fight in the front yard was so loud. Wishing she had a gun, and wishing she had called the police as soon as she saw Pat, she moved quickly but quietly inside. Fear for Kate rose thick in her chest and she wanted to run through the house screaming her name but didn't dare. She needed a better idea of what was happening and who else might be inside. She doubted Pat was working alone.

Looking to her right, she noticed a large living room decorated in lush ivories and greens. There was blood on the carpet. Was this where Denise had been attacked? The clatter seemed to be coming from the rear of the house, and she moved steadily toward it, alert for one of Pat Spencer's associates. Why had Tiffany called her husband home, particularly since he seemed completely oblivious of all that was going on, including her extramarital affair? Was he really that stupid? Or had things been going on that he just didn't want to see until they were shoved in his face?

The thought of her cell phone sitting uselessly on the seat in her car made her want to shout noisy curses, but keeping low and silent, she peeked carefully around each corner before moving past it. The turmoil became louder and she heard several crashes, as if someone was throwing things. Looking down a hallway she saw a baseball sail through a doorway, hit the wall, rebound to the right, and roll down the carpet toward her.

She took another step, wondering if someone was trashing the house to make it appear a robbery had happened. Or, hell, maybe it *was* a robbery. At this point, she wasn't sure of anything anymore. Wishing yet again that she carried a weapon, she crept along the passageway, finally reaching the open door.

She heard thumps and thuds, as if someone was fighting, and as she peered around the corner of the doorframe, she could see a man's back. He was bent over something on the desk—a woman, kicking frantically as he choked the life out of her. Nikki froze, horror briefly overcoming her as she recognized the shoes and the tailored pants. Then a white-hot rage blasted through her.

She stepped inside, her eyes raking the study, desperately seeking something—anything—that she could use as a weapon. A tiny bit of common sense screamed at her that Martin Elliot was a great deal larger and more powerful than she was, that he could easily knock her aside and go back to hurting Kate with only a momentary pause unless she brought something effective to the fray.

Sidestepping the balls rolling about on the floor, she spotted the display on the wall to her right. Like a great many children in the Maritimes, both male and female, Nikki learned to skate and play hockey at a young age. Without a second thought, she wrenched the autographed stick from the wall and brought the heel of the blade down across Martin's arm in as vicious a slash as she had ever used on an opponent in the hockey rink. A bone snapped like kindling, and Martin screamed in a high voice, staggering back from Kate and cringing away from the attack. With the same smooth motion, Nikki turned the stick and used the tip of it to butt-end him in the solar plexus, knocking him into the wall.

As he sagged on unsteady knees, Nikki slammed the stick across his back, cross-checking him with the same intensity she had used to clear the front of her team's net during a scrum. Martin crashed to the floor and was still writhing when she leaped on him, driving her knees into his ribs. Feeling the jolt all the way to her spine, she realized too late that this tactic didn't work nearly as well without the proper kneepads.

Swiftly, she smashed Martin as hard as she could across his head and the battered stick splintered in her hands as his skull slammed into the carpet. Finally, he slumped, limp and unconscious beneath her. She hit him again for good measure with what was left of the stick before tossing aside the shattered pieces. Her knees stiff and aching, she hobbled to her feet.

An odd silence descended upon the room, and Nikki felt a cold chill of shock. Almost afraid to look, she turned to the desk, seeking out her lover, not knowing how badly she was hurt. To her relief, Kate had somehow managed to stand up, a hand gingerly touching the ugly, purplish marks on her neck. Staring at Nikki, she leaned weakly against the desk and coughed, her breath a coarse rasp that penetrated to Nikki's bones.

"Oh, God, are you all right?" Nikki whispered, feeling light-headed. She reached out a trembling hand, feeling oddly frozen, unable to take a step toward her. Her heart was hammering so hard in her chest, it felt as if it would explode.

Kate uttered an inarticulate cry and threw herself at Nikki, who was barely able to get her other arm up in time to catch her. Holding her tightly, Nikki turned them so that she could keep an eye on Martin over Kate's shoulder, needing to be sure that he wouldn't get up unexpectedly. Feeling suddenly tired and weak, she had to dig deep inside herself for self-control as she tried to comfort Kate.

"It's okay," she crooned, her face in the thick auburn hair. "Katie, it's all right now. I'm here."

After a few moments, during which both of them shook like leaves in a windstorm, Kate gradually stopped crying, her sobs slowing to soft gasps of breath, gentle hitches in the back of her throat. Nikki managed to retain some semblance of her own composure, but only because she desperately wanted to be strong for her lover, who needed her so badly.

"They surprised us," Kate said in a voice still harsh and low from the damage to her throat. Her cheek was pressed against Nikki's chest, her head tucked up under her chin as she clung to her. "Pat must have killed or knocked Denise out...she was lying on the floor so still. I tried to fight, but Martin was too strong. I never considered that anyone would be out here. Denise said that Andrew was at work and Tiffany was shopping, but she was really helping create a setup to kill Andrew and frame him for the entire thing."

"Denise?"

"No, Tiffany." Kate gulped. "She's in Halifax right now, arranging an alibi for her and Martin."

"What about Pat's alibi?"

"I don't know." A pause, then a bitter laugh. "Martin didn't mention that part. He was too busy trying to kill me."

The words almost made Nikki's heart explode. "Damn it, why didn't you call me?" She grasped Kate's arms and shook her, absolutely furious.

Kate looked profoundly embarrassed. "I didn't think…" she apologized weakly. "I'm sorry..."

Nikki pulled her close again, hugging her desperately. How much danger Kate had truly been in was beginning to sink in, and she felt sick in the pit of her stomach.

"Don't you ever do this again," she whispered fiercely. "Don't you ever go off on your own and leave me behind again."

"I'm sorry," Kate repeated, her voice muffled from where her face was pressed into Nikki's chest. "I'm so sorry, Nikki. I was so worried about your safety that I completely forgot about my own."

"No kidding!"

Nikki wasn't very happy with Kate at the moment and knew they would have to discuss this further, but right now, she couldn't stop hugging her. *Never again,* she swore silently. *I'm never going to leave you again.*

She didn't release the embrace until the big man lying on the floor groaned. Kate drew away shakily and moved around the desk, picking up the phone to dial 911 as Nikki retrieved a golf club from the bag leaning in the corner.

"C'mon," she warned Martin as he blinked fuzzily at her. He didn't try to rise to his feet, but she nudged him with the club anyway, making him yelp as she jarred the broken bone in his arm. "Just give me an excuse to knock the crap out of you again."

Andrew and Denise suddenly appeared in the doorway. His eyes were wild, his hair disarrayed, his suit torn, but he wore a triumphant expression. Clearly, he had subdued Pat, which gave him a cocky strut. He had his arm around Denise, who still looked woozy, supporting her as he held a towel to her head, trying to staunch the bleeding.

"I got him," he announced to Nikki. "I knocked the son of a bitch out like a light and tied him up with his belt. Now, does somebody want to tell me just what the hell is going on here…"

He trailed off, and his eyes widened as he spotted Martin sprawled amid the splintered pieces of the hockey stick.

"You son of a bitch, I can't believe this," he howled, looking very much as if he wanted to weep in that moment of horrified comprehension. "Wayne Gretzky personally gave me that stick!"

CHAPTER THIRTY-THREE

The police knew from the beginning that one of the Elliots had murdered Stephen." Nikki poked her fork into the piece of chicken.

Beneath the table, Kate could feel their knees touching, all the connection they could manage in these surroundings, but a comfort they both required. Neither of them seemed to be able to stop touching the other, as if needing constant reassurance that they were both there and whole.

"They didn't have enough evidence to link a particular member of the family to the death," Kate finished Nikki's thought, "but they were methodically building a case to convict Martin and Tiffany, working with Revenue Canada and the RCMP to tie it all together."

"That's normally how these things operate." Lorne Harris eyed Nikki sternly. Her latest adventure had obviously terrified him because he had called every day to make sure that both she and Kate were all right. "They should have been the ones to handle it all along."

"On the other hand, jumping in with both feet and stirring things up can also get the job done," Irene Taylor interjected smoothly from her place at the head of the table. She had made all the arrangements for this gathering to celebrate not only Kate and Nikki's solving of the case, but their new living arrangements as well. "It's obviously a very successful investigation technique."

"It's a thing of the past, Grandmother," Kate said fervently, taking a sip of her wine. "This is the last time we'll ever be involved with anything like this."

Nikki glanced at her from the corner of her eyes, smiled briefly, and returned to her dinner. If she didn't agree with Kate, at least she wasn't about to voice that opposition publicly.

"The Elliots lost so much." Adele had appeared slightly intimidated upon entering Irene's grand house, but after her hostess had applied considerable charm and warmth, she had relaxed considerably as dinner progressed. "I know I shouldn't feel sorry for them after all they've put you through, but it's still hard to believe. It's frightening to see how quickly a family can turn on each other. All that money and success and they still weren't satisfied."

"That's because they never understood what was truly important." Kate paused. "I take that back. Andrew seems to. He went rushing out to the house just because Tiffany told him she was sick and needed him. He really loved her, and it's just about destroyed him to know how she was using him."

"He was blinded by the boobs," Nikki said disdainfully, earning a snicker from Irene and a stern look from her parents. "So was Martin. He and Pat were the ones who coerced Stephen into setting the whole thing up way back when Stephen was the head of the IT department. They'd always held the drunk-driving thing over him, along with a few other past indiscretions. He was already responsible for the six people working in the IT department, and adding four more to the books didn't seem like a big deal, particularly if it kept Martin and Pat off his back. He wouldn't consider the extra money worth it, but for Martin and Pat, fifty thousand a year was more than sufficient to keep their mouths shut. Tiffany didn't come into it until near the end."

"When Martin and Tiffany got involved in an affair, he let it slip what was going on," Kate explained. "She immediately wanted to 'help,' maybe because of the illicitness. I guess the boys were just glad to have someone look after the mailboxes."

After a week or so of steady interrogations and interviews, the police had figured out who exactly had done what to whom and why, but, finally, the whole story had come out. Of course Rick Johnson and the chief of police had extensively lectured Kate and Nikki regarding their interference. Only the fact that they had prevented Andrew's imminent demise had kept the scolding from being much worse. Even Nikki was conscious of how lucky they'd been.

"But who killed Stephen, and why?" Irene's eyes were keen, glancing back and forth between Kate and Nikki. That she was fully enjoying the whole situation was readily apparent, and Kate stifled a smile. She was getting to know a completely different side to her grandmother.

Nikki made a small sound of what might have been disgust. "When the SINs were flagged, Stephen realized the scam had gone on for too long. He wanted to shut it down immediately, confess everything, and take his lumps. Hannah might have been upset, but she probably wouldn't have pressed embezzlement charges against him, or taken away his job, especially if he claimed he was being blackmailed, but Martin and Pat probably would have gone to jail."

"They all let it go on for far too long," Kate put in. "They had become comfortable with the situation...until the SINs were flagged."

"Tiffany convinced Martin that she could keep Andrew handling the IT payroll account without becoming any the wiser. She doesn't regard his abilities very highly, but neither she nor Martin is really a businessperson. They really didn't know what Stephen had to do to keep this scheme going for fifteen years."

"Pat got the chemicals they needed from work." Kate sipped her wine. "That was their first mistake. They thought the chemical compound they came up with would make it look like a heart attack and that would be the end of it, but Hannah requested an autopsy. They thought she would be prostrate with grief, never expecting that she would demand to know why he died. When the toxicology report clearly showed an abnormality in his system, everyone, including the police, knew it was murder."

"Martin slipped the compound into Stephen's wine while he was distracted at the Historical Society Dinner." Kate regretted her contribution to the distraction. Perhaps if they hadn't attended, none of the recent events would have happened, including nearly being throttled. One good thing *had* come of it; Nikki finally understood her deeply imbedded fear in the wake of the cabin fire. She now possessed the same type of fear for Kate, and while it might fade after a time, for now, it still dictated certain of their actions, particularly toward each other.

"Things just went downhill from there," Nikki concluded. "Kate and I started snooping around, but, more importantly, Hannah and Andrew were doing their best to help the police by giving them access to the company's books. Meanwhile, Denise was doing some investigating on her own, which brought us into it."

"Martin and Tiffany decided to solve two problems at once, not only by making it appear that the murderer and embezzler was Andrew, but by killing him at the same time, freeing Tiffany from the marriage without losing any of his estate. She and Martin were planning on an early retirement to someplace warm. I think Pat just wanted to be shed of the whole thing."

"What happened to all the money?" Lorne asked, pouring cream into his coffee. "Did they spend it?"

"Martin lived off his." Nikki smiled shyly at her father, obviously proud to be showing off her hard-won knowledge. Kate was just happy that her grandmother had invited the Harrises over for dinner and even happier that Nikki's parents had accepted. "He didn't have any income of his own, but because he was an Elliot, people, including his own grandmother, didn't really notice that he always had money with no way to account for it."

"What about Pat Spencer?" Irene looked faintly distressed about the boy she remembered, not having witnessed the man carrying Denise out of Andrew's house with every intention of dumping her into the lake.

Kate sighed. "He received a lot of money on top of his regular paycheck, but, unfortunately, he has an expensive hobby that his girlfriend doesn't know about. He likes to gamble." That was why Pat had been in Halifax the night he had his accident. It was his biweekly visit to the casinos where he went through his extra paychecks like water through a sieve. "He just wasn't part of the family and was always conscious of it."

"No one goes through money like a gambler." Irene looked unusually somber. "I feel sorry for Hannah. Her whole family has been shattered."

"Hopefully, we've learned a lesson from this terrible time." Lorne raised his glass in Nikki and Kate's direction. He looked slightly self-conscious as he said, "Families need to stick together."

"Amen," Adele said as they all drank to the sentiment. She glanced at Nikki. "Are you all moved into Kate's?"

Nikki shook her head. "I have a couple of months left on my lease. That gives me a place to store my stuff while we figure out where everything is going to go."

Holding onto each other amid the shattered remains of Andrew's sports memorabilia, they had silently come to a mutual agreement. They couldn't continue to live apart. Life was too precious to waste time living alone. Once Kate was released from the hospital, where it was determined there were no lasting effects from Martin's assault beyond sore muscles and a stiff neck, Nikki stopped by Queen Street, retrieved her cat and her clothes, and drove everything over to Kate's apartment.

While Kate had been tucked away on the sofa with a heating pad and a hot mug of tea, Nikki recruited Todd to help her bring down a dresser from the collection of furniture Kate stored on the upper two floors. He had even proved handy enough to put a cat flap in the apartment door that granted Powder the run of the entire building. The cat didn't lavish undying affection on Kate, but he had shown a little more tolerance toward her over the past week. Once in a while, he even hopped up onto the counter in the bookstore while Kate worked, though he failed to purr when she patted him gingerly.

Kate could accept the arrangement. So could Nikki. Perhaps it wasn't the "marriage" Nikki had expected, but it was the next step on the path toward permanent commitment. The rest, Kate suspected, would happen in its own time and place, just as everything else had in their relationship.

"Our tastes in décor aren't entirely compatible," she said with a smile at Nikki. "But I'm sure we'll figure out which pieces need to be stored on the upper floor and which ones will blend."

"My furniture doesn't blend easily." Nikki laughed. "Your old couch is probably going to end up back in the barn, Mom."

"It's been through every one of my children's apartments," Adele said placidly. "I expect it's served its time. Set it free, Nikki."

"I guess that means we can throw it out," Nikki translated for Kate.

Kate smiled and didn't say anything. She just enjoyed watching her lover laugh and talk with her parents, displaying an ease and happiness that had been missing for so long. There were still wounds to be mended in Nikki's family, but this was a promising start.

She caught Irene's eye, and her grandmother raised her glass in a silent toast. Kate smiled and returned her tribute, now very glad that she had returned from Florida early this year so that they could share this adventure.

And as she held up her glass, Kate could feel the tie binding her heart to Nikki's so strongly that she knew nothing would ever sunder it.

About the Author

Gina lives in the Maritimes and is single but working on it. In the meantime, she lives with two cats named Max and Nyetcha. She likes tennis and hiking in the spring, summer and fall, and stays inside in the wintertime, rarely venturing out unless convinced she has to. That's when she does most of her writing.

Books Available From Bold Strokes Books

Fresh Tracks by Georgia Beers. Seven women, seven days. A lot can happen when old friends, lovers, and a new girl in town get together in the mountains. (1-933110-63-5)

Empress and the Acolyte by Jane Fletcher. Jemeryl and Tevi fight to protect the very fabric of their world: time. Lyremouth Chronicles Book Three (1-933110-60-0)

First Instinct by JLee Meyer. When high-stakes security fraud leads to murder, one woman flees for her life while another risks her heart to protect her. (1-933110-59-7)

Erotic Interludes 4: Extreme Passions. Thirty of today's hottest erotica writers set the pages aflame with love, lust, and steamy liaisons. (1-933110-58-9)

Storms of Change by Radclyffe. In the continuing saga of the Provincetown Tales, duty and love are at odds as Reese and Tory face their greatest challenge. (1-933110-57-0)

Unexpected Ties by Gina L. Dartt. With death before dessert, Kate Shannon and Nikki Harris are swept up in another tale of danger and romance. (1-933110-56-2)

Sleep of Reason by Rose Beecham. While Detective Jude Devine searches for a lost boy, her rocky relationship with Dr. Mercy Westmoreland gets a lot harder. (1-933110-53-8)

Passion's Bright Fury by Radclyffe. Passion strikes without warning when a trauma surgeon and a filmmaker become reluctant allies. (1-933110-54-6)

Broken Wings by L-J Baker. When Rye Woods meets beautiful dryad Flora Withe, her libido, as hidden as her wings, reawakens along with her heart. (1-933110-55-4)

Combust the Sun by Andrews & Austin. A Richfield and Rivers mystery set in L.A. Murder among the stars. (1-933110-52-X)

Of Drag Kings and the Wheel of Fate by Susan Smith. A blind date in a drag club leads to an unlikely romance. (1-933110-51-1)

Tristaine Rises by Cate Culpepper. Brenna, Jesstin, and the Amazons of Tristaine face their greatest challenge for survival. (1-933110-50-3)

Too Close to Touch by Georgia Beers. Kylie O'Brien believes in true love and is willing to wait for it, even though Gretchen, her new boss, is off-limits. (1-933110-47-3)

100ᵗʰ Generation by Justine Saracen. Ancient curses, modern-day villains, and an intriguing woman lead archeologist Valerie Foret on the adventure of her life. (1-933110-48-1)

Battle for Tristaine by Cate Culpepper. While Brenna struggles to find her place in the clan, Tristaine is threatened with destruction. Second in the Tristaine series. (1-933110-49-X)

The Traitor and the Chalice by Jane Fletcher. Tevi and Jemeryl risk all in the race to uncover a traitor. The Lyremouth Chronicles Book Two. (1-933110-43-0)

Promising Hearts by Radclyffe. Dr. Vance Phelps arrives in New Hope, Montana, with no hope of happiness—until she meets Mae. (1-933110-44-9)

Carly's Sound by Ali Vali. Poppy Valente and Julia Johnson form a bond of friendship that becomes something far more. A poignant romance about love and renewal. (1-933110-45-7)

Unexpected Sparks by Gina L. Dartt. Kate Shannon's attraction to much younger Nikki Harris is complication enough without a fatal fire that Kate can't ignore. (1-933110-46-5)

Whitewater Rendezvous by Kim Baldwin. Two women on a wilderness kayak adventure discover that true love may be nothing at all like they imagined. (1-933110-38-4)

Erotic Interludes 3: Lessons in Love ed. by Radclyffe and Stacia Seaman. Sign on for a class in love…the best lesbian erotica writers take us to "school." (1-9331100-39-2)

Punk Like Me by JD Glass. Twenty-one-year-old Nina has a way with the girls, and she doesn't always play by the rules. (1-933110-40-6)

Coffee Sonata by Gun Brooke. Four women whose lives unexpectedly intersect in a small town by the sea share one thing in common—they all have secrets. (1-933110-41-4)

The Clinic: Tristaine Book One by Cate Culpepper. Brenna, a prison medic, finds herself drawn to Jesstin, a warrior reputed to be descended from ancient Amazons. (1-933110-42-2)

Forever Found by JLee Meyer. Can time, tragedy, and shattered trust destroy a love that seemed destined? Chance reunites childhood friends separated by tragedy. (1-933110-37-6)

Sword of the Guardian by Merry Shannon. Princess Shasta's bold new bodyguard has a secret that could change both of their lives: *He* is actually a *she*. (1-933110-36-8)

Wild Abandon by Ronica Black. Dr. Chandler Brogan and Officer Sarah Monroe are drawn together by their common obsessions—sex, speed, and danger. (1-933110-35-X)

Turn Back Time by Radclyffe. Pearce Rifkin and Wynter Thompson have nothing in common but a shared passion for surgery—and unexpected attraction. (1-933110-34-1)

Chance by Grace Lennox. A sexy, funny, touching story of two women who, in finding themselves, also find one another. (1-933110-31-7)

The Exile and the Sorcerer by Jane Fletcher. First in the Lyremouth Chronicles. Tevi and a shy young sorcerer face monsters, magic, and the challenge of loving. (1-933110-32-5)

A Matter of Trust by Radclyffe. When what should be just business turns into much more, two women struggle to trust the unexpected. (1-933110-33-3)

Sweet Creek by Lee Lynch. A celebration of the enduring nature of love, friendship, and community in the heart-warming lesbian community of Waterfall Falls. (1-933110-29-5)

The Devil Inside by Ali Vali. The head of a New Orleans crime organization falls for a woman who turns her world upside down. (1-933110-30-9)

Grave Silence by Rose Beecham. Detective Jude Devine's investigation of ritual murders is complicated by her torrid affair with pathologist Dr. Mercy Westmoreland. (1-933110-25-2)

Honor Reclaimed by Radclyffe. Secret Service Agent Cameron Roberts and Blair Powell close ranks to find the would-be assassins who nearly claimed Blair's life. (1-933110-18-X)

Honor Bound by Radclyffe. Secret Service Agent Cameron Roberts and Blair Powell face political intrigue, a clandestine threat to Blair's safety, and the seemingly irreconcilable differences that force them ever farther apart. (1-933110-20-1)

Innocent Hearts by Radclyffe. In a wild and unforgiving land, two women learn about love, passion, and the wonders of the heart. (1-933110-21-X)

The Temple at Landfall by Jane Fletcher. An imprinter, one of Celaeno's most revered servants of the Goddess, is also a prisoner to the faith—until a Ranger frees her by claiming her heart. The Celaeno series. (1-933110-27-9)

Protector of the Realm: Supreme Constellations Book One by Gun Brooke. A space adventure filled with suspense and a daring intergalactic romance. (1-933110-26-0)

Force of Nature by Kim Baldwin. From tornados to forest fires, the forces of nature conspire to bring Gable McCoy and Erin Richards close to danger, and closer to each other. (1-933110-23-6)

In Too Deep by Ronica Black. Undercover homicide cop Erin McKenzie tracks a femme fatale who just might be a real killer…with love and danger hot on her heels. (1-933110-17-1)

Stolen Moments: Erotic Interludes 2 by Stacia Seaman and Radclyffe, eds. Love on the run, in the office, in the shadows…Fast, furious, and almost too hot to handle. (1-933110-16-3)

Course of Action by Gun Brooke. Actress Carolyn Black desperately wants the starring role in an upcoming film produced by Annelie Peterson. Just how far will she go for the dream part of a lifetime? (1-933110-22-8)

Rangers at Roadsend by Jane Fletcher. Sergeant Chip Coppelli has learned to spot trouble coming, and that is exactly what she sees in her new recruit, Katryn Nagata. The Celaeno series. (1-933110-28-7)

Justice Served by Radclyffe. Lieutenant Rebecca Frye and her lover, Dr. Catherine Rawlings, embark on a deadly game of hide-and-seek with an underworld kingpin who traffics in human souls. (1-933110-15-5)

Distant Shores, Silent Thunder by Radclyffe. Dr. Tory King—along with the women who love her—is forced to examine the boundaries of love, friendship, and the ties that transcend time. (1-933110-08-2)

Hunter's Pursuit by Kim Baldwin. A raging blizzard, a mountain hideaway, and a killer-for-hire set a scene for disaster—or desire—when Katarzyna Demetrious rescues a beautiful stranger. (1-933110-09-0)

The Walls of Westernfort by Jane Fletcher. All Temple Guard Natasha Ionadis wants is to serve the Goddess—until she falls in love with one of the rebels she is sworn to destroy. The Celaeno series. (1-933110-24-4)

Change Of Pace: *Erotic Interludes* by Radclyffe. Twenty-five hot-wired encounters guaranteed to spark more than just your imagination. Erotica as you've always dreamed of it. (1-933110-07-4)

Honor Guards by Radclyffe. In a wild flight for their lives, the president's daughter and those who are sworn to protect her wage a desperate struggle for survival. (1-933110-01-5)

Fated Love by Radclyffe. Amidst the chaos and drama of a busy emergency room, two women must contend not only with the fragile nature of life, but also with the irresistible forces of fate. (1-933110-05-8)

Justice in the Shadows by Radclyffe. In a shadow world of secrets and lies, Detective Sergeant Rebecca Frye and her lover, Dr. Catherine Rawlings, join forces in the elusive search for justice. (1-933110-03-1)

shadowland by Radclyffe. In a world on the far edge of desire, two women are drawn together by power, passion, and dark pleasures. An erotic romance. (1-933110-11-2)

Love's Masquerade by Radclyffe. Plunged into the indistinguishable realms of fiction, fantasy, and hidden desires, Auden Frost is forced to question all she believes about the nature of love. (1-933110-14-7)

Love & Honor by Radclyffe. The president's daughter and her lover are faced with difficult choices as they battle a tangled web of Washington intrigue for...love and honor. (1-933110-10-4)

Beyond the Breakwater by Radclyffe. One Provincetown summer, three women learn the true meaning of love, friendship, and family. (1-933110-06-6)

Tomorrow's Promise by Radclyffe. One timeless summer, two very different women discover the power of passion to heal and the promise of hope that only love can bestow. (1-933110-12-0)

Love's Tender Warriors by Radclyffe. Two women who have accepted loneliness as a way of life learn that love is worth fighting for and a battle they cannot afford to lose. (1-933110-02-3)

Love's Melody Lost by Radclyffe. A secretive artist with a haunted past and a young woman escaping a life that has proved to be a lie find their destinies entwined. (1-933110-00-7)

Safe Harbor by Radclyffe. A mysterious newcomer, a reclusive doctor, and a troubled gay teenager learn about love, friendship, and trust during one tumultuous summer in Provincetown. (1-933110-13-9)

Above All, Honor by Radclyffe. Secret Service Agent Cameron Roberts fights her desire for the one woman she can't have—Blair Powell, the daughter of the president of the United States. (1-933110-04-X)